NO
BOUNDS

NO BOUNDS

TORIE SENSENY

atmosphere press

To moja ciocia za nieustanną pomoc w prowadzeniu mnie
przez labirynt mojego osobistego hotelu Overlook.
jesteś moją skałą i bardzo cię kocham

CHAPTER ONE

Every night for the past six years, I have endured the infernal clanging of a crowbar against the grated window above my bed, making it nearly impossible to focus on anything else. This evening, the noise was attempting to interrupt the book I was enjoying. It was a bit redundant and dramatic, if you ask me. Plus, reading was the only vice the King Cobra's oh-so graciously allowed me to have. Not that the majority of the gang members cared about what I thought in this horrid place, anyway.

My "bedroom," if you can even call it that, is hidden in the farthest corner of the basement. It reeks immensely of mildew and the air is always extremely heavy, even in the winter. And from the small, barred window in my room, there used to be a train looming above the building at night—but it stopped about three years ago. Noisy as the train was, keeping me up at night during my first few weeks, it was my only reminder that life existed outside these cement walls. Now, all I hear at night are the noises of fighting up in The Pit and the choir of drunken idiots.

And though the bedroom is large enough to house my books, dresser, mattress and lamp, it's not spacious enough for me to fully shift comfortably, especially with a wingspan as wide as mine. Not that I would know how to use my wings anyway. Ross has threatened many times that he would either cut or shoot them off if I even tried to teach myself how to fly. As much as I hate being a freak, if they were removed, it would be like burning all of my books or stealing a piece of my soul.

WHACK! Thunk! WHACK!

Geez, Louise! The large goon was **really** not going to allow me to finish reading this page. It wasn't like I wasn't already dressed or anything. All right, yes, I hadn't fully wrapped my hands yet, but it wouldn't take more than a couple of minutes to do so.

"You better be ready when I get downstairs, freak!"

Unfortunately, I could recognize that voice anywhere. Not that I hadn't already identified him with how hard he'd banged the crowbar against the ceiling's grated window. They had sent Gregory, Ross's eldest son, the two-hundred-pound dark-skinned brute, same age as me. He was now standing on the other side of the door. We may both be eighteen, but I'd like to stress that the commonalities stop there—I'd be incredibly surprised if this moron even knew how to read. I mean, how? Really, how did he manage to be a senior in high school without repeating a grade or all of them at least twice? His brain cells had, without a doubt, all been replaced by sheer muscle.

Which, I suppose works to his advantage as a running fullback for the Julewood Bulldogs varsity team, an insignificant piece of information that he loves to tell me every chance he gets as if that makes him superior to me. And for as long as I've known him, he has never once called me by my name. Not that it matters in this place because I'm seen as something less than human anyway. A "tourist attraction," "a sideshow," and a way to swindle more money out of gamblers.

Ross Templeton, leader of the King Cobras, ran his gang more like the mafia, what with his scare tactics and shady dealings. He owns a series of other businesses—laundromats, gyms, and one grocery store run by Ross's wife, Susan—and they make the bulk of their money through bare-knuckle fighting. It is held in their headquarters, a warehouse in the middle of nowhere in Northeast Philadelphia. Although, if my memory serves me correctly, it resembles more of a barn than a warehouse, with its large sliding front door and old cement dividing walls. Warehouse, barn, or whatever you want to call it, it had also served as my training grounds as Ross endeavored to transform his newly acquired freak into a fighter with a single-minded live-or-die philosophy in the ring.

Yet, being profitable for the King Cobras means I don't have to look at the wrong end of Ross's gun again. It took three weeks for the gunshot wound to my shoulder to heal, after I severely injured Gregory's face with my claws two years ago. Most of the major injuries I have accrued have healed in spans ranging from a few days to a couple of weeks. Though strangely, there are still a few I don't think ever will, but what am I supposed to do about it with how low on the totem pole I am?

Held here against my will for the last six grueling years, I have hardly ever left the small space of my decrepit bedroom, unless it was on nights they had me fighting... or to use the bathroom. How kind of them, right? But what can I do? This has become my normal. And I know my current situation is my fault. I deserve it too, because who would want a freak for a child unless they could profit from it?

See, one of the main reasons I came to be imprisoned in this hellhole is that I started to shape-shift into some rejected mythological-winged-feline-humanoid at the ripe age of twelve, while I was playing dodgeball in gym class. Although, my life was pretty close to hell at that time anyway. When you're a lanky girl with naturally white curly hair, grey eyes, and a low self-esteem, you're already an easy target for bullies. Yes, my skin was quite fair, but it didn't warrant them calling me "Albino Girl." And yet, that's what I got saddled with. It wasn't the cleverest of nicknames, but what more can you expect from a group of twelve-year-old bullies? But something in me snapped that day. I hardly remember the few minutes before or after it happened. What I *do* know is that the kids who were trying to pick on me during that class are still dealing with what I "allegedly" did to them. Two of them are on life support, one is confined to a wheelchair, and the rest deal with permanent reminders on their skin and psyche.

My parents were so disgusted and repulsed by my "true form" that they sold me to the King Cobras, a gang that ran more like the mafia, what with their scare tactics and shady dealings. And after six years, I really couldn't tell you much about my parents, not that I could blame them for what they did, even if I wanted to. Yes, it still hurts to think of how easy it was for them to sell me when they were the two people who are supposed to love me unconditionally. But I wouldn't want me either.

I could have run away, but to where? Especially with no money in my pockets and no one to turn to. Not that those things had stopped me from trying anyways. I must have broken down at least three wooden doors and made it as far as five blocks before Ross's men found and dragged me back to the warehouse. They then installed the current thick metal door to prevent any other escape attempts. But even that didn't stop me from trying to destroy the metal door. There would have been more efforts if I hadn't broken both of my shoulders and arms, and if Ross hadn't threatened to leave me without food or water for a week. However, the dents I made are still visible to this day.

Then, for extra assurance that his prized possession wouldn't somehow find a way to elude the imposing metal barricade without him noticing, Ross had a tracking device implanted into my neck. That said, and as far as I know, I'm the only one of my kind—whatever my kind is. Also, as far as I know, there is no such thing as vampires, werewolves, or any of the other monsters one reads about in books or sees in movies. So, how I got lucky enough to be born like this when other supernatural creatures don't exist, God only knows—if *He* even exists. I'd like to think so, but after so many years of this hell—I'm not so sure.

But, returning to the moron most likely making his way

downstairs... Gregory seemed to take an inordinate amount of pleasure handcuffing and injecting me with two serums before each of my fights. These serums were designed for the "safety" of the King Cobras while still providing a good show for their criminal clientele.

The first is used to force a partial shift because how else is the crowd supposed to know I'm a freak of nature? And yet, how the King Cobras obtain both serums, I'm not exactly sure. But it wasn't done legally; I know that much. And as painful as it is to shift into my "true form" because I rarely do so, this partial shift is pure agony. My body tries to fight against the serum so it may fully shift and defeat it, but in the end, it fails.

The second is a form of sedative with an ounce of alcohol to dull my senses enough to decrease my agility and hamper my ability to use my full strength. They started using the second serum three years ago, after I accidentally killed five of their best fighters. I was as surprised as everyone else that it took Ross that long to have his "underlings" inject this particular serum on me *before* fights instead of continuing to waste all their tranquilizer darts. Kind of humorous in a dark and sick sort of way.

WHACK! WHACK!

"Get your butt over here, freak! Don't make me come in there," Gregory shouted from the other side of the door.

I rolled my eyes before placing my book face-down on the bed and rising from the creaky old mattress propped up by three plastic pallets, the large flat rectangular structures used to carry shipments. What kind of shipments? I didn't want to know because it was most likely illegal. And as I stood on one of the other four pallets lining the floor of this mold-encrusted space I called my bedroom, my weight seemed to sink into a corner of the pallet I was on.

Muddy water gushed under my feet, which could only mean two things—the first being last night's rain must have flooded the basement again, and the other being Gregory must have placed the wood boards outside of my door to prevent the water from draining into the grated hole in the hallway. Either way, I wasn't going to give him the satisfaction of hearing me complain; he'd already be pleased to witness the aftermath of these natural and manmade disasters in my room. I decided instead to continue to get ready.

After tying my thick white hair in a ponytail with a rubber band that had most likely been peed on or rolled in the grimy soil from the city streets, I walked over to the thick metal door and turned around, clasping my hands behind me. The door is yet another thing designed for the "safety" of all the King Cobras members. It has four small sliding windows that can only be opened from the outside.

As the first window slid open, I waited for the familiar ice-cold metal of the handcuffs to slide around my wrists and click shut; however, there was an unusual pause to this set of procedures.

"Goddamn it, Gregory," shouted a voice belonging to a King Cobras member named Ash. "You screwed in the boards so that Vivila's room would be flooded!"

I might not have been able to see Gregory's face, but I knew him well enough to guess that he would answer Ash's frustration with an eye roll and a smirk. I remained in position as I heard footsteps trailing away, only to return about five minutes later and followed by the whirling sound of a drill. When the next two windows opened, two heavily tattooed hands took a firm grasp around my biceps, slamming my back against the metal door and momentarily knocking the wind out of me. I took a few deep breaths so I wouldn't groan at the stinging pain radiating up and down my spine. I knew the arms to be Ash's, and he was only being forceful because Gregory was present. The King Cobras' leader's son wasn't above ratting people out. But oh, how the handcuffs dug into my skin as there was little space between me and the thick metal door, and my back continued to throb to no end. And though the pain wasn't anything I hadn't experienced before or couldn't handle, it still took an inordinate amount of willpower not to yelp and give Gregory the satisfaction he desired.

Lastly, the final window in the door slammed open with such vigor that the door vibrated for a couple of seconds. Gregory wasted no time injecting the first serum into my neck. I felt the stinging warmth as my ears grew into sharp points. My pupils elongated into slits. Then, the excruciating pain of both my upper and lower canines extended. Unfortunately, neither my wings nor tail are able to tear through my skin, but it doesn't stop either from constantly trying. The fur that usually grows around my mouth and other areas is nearly nonexistent. My claws barely protrude either, so overall, I look like I'm wearing some semi-elaborate costume done by a professional makeup artist.

When the second serum was slammed into my neck shortly thereafter, I immediately knew that something about it was off. Everything in front of me blurred into a strange Jackson Pollock-impressionistic blob, causing me to feel extremely dizzy. I stumbled to the closest stack of books to prevent myself from falling to my knees. Neighboring stacks collided against one another before scattering into a huge mess on the floor and causing the preexisting mold and dust particles to fly into a nearly invisible cloud. My sneeze was large enough to make me lose my balance and my already-throbbing back bombarded against the large pile of books.

Get up, get up, Vivila! And whatever you do, don't cry. Not in front of Gregory. Not in front of the imbecile, I thought as I tried to shake off whatever was happening to me; whatever was in that second serum. *Something is terribly wrong, terribly wrong, terribly—God, I won't be able to give Ross a good fight tonight. And if I don't give him a good fight, he will whip me so hard after everyone leaves that I'll feel the lashes from six months ago.*

I knew that wasn't possible, but I knew he'd find a way to

make it possible; he always does. And to top it all off, my anxiety made my breathing shallow and my hands tingle, so out of control that they started to curl into themselves. It didn't help that I was losing circulation in my wrists from the handcuffs, somehow feeling like they were tightening even more. Despite my efforts, I felt my claws begin to pierce my palms. *Not here, not here, not here. Ross will kill me and then revive me to torture me for bleeding before the fight even started.* I know that statement to be false and irrational because of how much money I make him, but in my anxiety-stricken state, it seemed very true.

"Back away from the door, freak! And if the muddy water from your room soils my shoes, I'll make sure Dad gives you fifty lashes!" Gregory aggressively announced, followed by a short chuckle, failing to hide his amusement toward my struggles.

Ignoring the numbness spreading up my arms and surprised the huge moron knew how to use such a word as "soil," I used as much strength as I could without slipping further into the chaotic mound of books. I rocked until I had gained enough momentum to get myself onto my knees before a wave of dizziness washed over me. I wanted to cry, especially as Gregory's snickering turned into a burst of laughter. But I won't cry. I won't, I won't, I won't. If only I could lie on my mattress and wait for the serums to wear off, but I knew that wasn't going to happen anytime soon. After a few trials and errors, I managed to stand on my feet.

I heard locks shift and the heavy deadbolts clang open. I could only guess that Ash was trying to get an answer from Gregory as to why he was laughing. It wasn't a surprise when Gregory kept laughing in reply to Ash's inquiries. As much as I wanted to cry, I wanted to be angry at Gregory even more. It was pretty obvious that he was the reason the dosage of the second serum felt terribly off. I wanted to be angry, but the need to fight off the sudden hit of nausea won over. *But I can't let the nausea win... I won't let it win. Why? Because I need to give Ross a good fight. No! I* will *give Ross a good fight tonight. I will, I will, I will!*

"You better give the boss a good show tonight, V. There's a lot of money riding on this fight, and we have a special guest the boss wants to impress," Ash said, the volume of his voice and the moaning of the door growing, indicating he was entering the room.

I didn't dare speak, fearful of giving away how much the second serum was affecting me, so I simply nodded. However, I must have put too much force in the movement of my head, because I stumbled over to the metal door to stabilize myself, causing it to slam shut. I heard Ash's shoes rushing over to me, his strong hands supporting my waist. While I couldn't see Ash's light-skinned face nor his black dreads that were always tied up in a ponytail, I could feel his one green eye and one brown glower towards Gregory.

"What the heck did you do?" Ash asked.

"I doubled the dosage, so what?" Gregory replied matter-of-factly.

"Are you frickin' kidding me? The boss is going to have our asses for this!"

"I'm not losing to her tonight. And like you said, it's an important night for my dad."

Ash cursed under his breath about something to do with the endless lengths Gregory was willing to go through to win before walking over to me and putting his hands on my shoulders. At this moment, I found some relief. Relief that it was with Gregory and not another member of the King Cobras. His comforting touch and his next words were a reminder I am not completely broken from the isolation and abusive treatment. He was the only one who was kind to me in this hellhole. Extra food here and secret conversations there. Conversations about his sister, tips on how to fight better, and life outside the walls of the warehouse. Though he has been reprimanded for his actions, his kindness is why the fire within me still blazes. Maybe not as much as it did before I found out that I was a freak of nature, but it's still burning, nonetheless.

"Hang in there, V. It will be over before you know it," Ash whispered into my ear.

"Why you bother being nice to that *freak* is beyond me," Gregory scoffed.

With the difficulty I was having with seeing, I could only assume the look Ash shot back said something along the lines of "It's a good thing you are the boss's son, 'cause otherwise, I would punch you right in the throat" because Gregory's laughter stopped immediately. Ash, aside from myself, was one of the few people who could defeat the big oaf and the majority of the other top boxers in The Pit. And as Ash gently guided me down the hallway, a not-so-slight smell of mildew lingering, I could hear Gregory's feet dragging behind us like a dog with his tail between his legs.

I've been down this hallway a thousand times, but the fluorescent lighting was so overwhelming I had to close my eyes in hopes that by the time we reached the elevator at the end of the hallway, the second serum would wear off enough for my vision to refocus. This was so frustrating, not being able to function like I normally do under both serums. Doubling the dosage? Really, Gregory? But I know neither of the serums will kill me no matter what the dosage is because they aren't designed to do so. Put me in a coma or knock me out for a few days, yes, but not kill me. Ash was kind enough to explain it to me when they first started using the second serum, but in the state I was in, this didn't make me feel any better.

Deep breaths, you'll get through this, and then you will show Gregory that doubling the second serum's dosage won't stop you from beating him, I thought over and over again.

I was barely aware that Ash and Gregory were still arguing or that we were already in the elevator. Regardless of how drugged out I was, every time I entered the elevator, I was reminded of those wood caravans that you see animals being transported with in the old black and white movies. And that's how I felt being in this elevator once one of the guys pressed the button to go up to The Pit, and we immediately lurched upward.

I closed my eyes as I tried to focus on the whirring sounds of the mechanisms when an unfamiliar smell started filling the small space. Regardless of how pleasant it was, I knew it wasn't either of the two guys. Gregory usually doused himself with expensive cologne, which always seemed pointless on nights he was going to fight. Sweat and cologne—not a great combination under the harsh lights in The Pit. And Ash usually smelled of ivory soap. No... *this* smell instead was that of the salty ocean air and campfire smoke. An oddly masculine mixture, but so incredibly intoxicating that it strangely alleviated some of the symptoms of the second serum I was feeling. I felt less dizzy, and when I opened my eyes, the blurriness was almost gone. And it seemed that the closer the elevator got to reaching The Pit, the more the smell filled my nostrils. But did this feeling of being less dizzy really have something to do with this unbelievably amazing scent, simply the movement of the elevator moving upwards, or both? Either way, I would soon find out—or at least I hoped so.

CHAPTER TWO

When the elevator jolted to a stop, Gregory lifted the gate open and then disappeared into the crowd of people. It wasn't unusual for there to be this many people standing in whatever free space they could find before taking their seats when the fight was about to begin; especially when I was one of the fighters.

Everyone wanted to see for themselves, up close, if I was truly a freak of nature or just some normal eighteen-year-old girl wearing prosthetics and makeup. I had grown used to the gasps of horror when they realized it was real, or believed Ross had spent thousands upon thousands of dollars on plastic surgery on me. I've had people invade my space by pulling on my ears or blocking me from where I was trying to go, just to put their grimy hands on my face.

Then there were the people, because the majority of them were criminals, who were here at The Pit not only to see the fight but also to network. But all of that didn't matter; it was normal for me as I struggled with trying to push the need to find out whether the source of the unknown scent was truly lessening the serum's effects on my senses. I needed to focus on the fact that Ross wanted a good show tonight for this mysteriously important guest.

I decided to momentarily focus on the fact that the fight wasn't going to start for another ten minutes and decided to watch some of the guards along the perimeter, as it seemed like a safer bet to not draw attention to myself; especially from Ross, who was keeping an eye on me through his peripheral.

However, with my heightened sense of smell, the scent seemed the strongest towards Ross's box on the second floor. Don't ask me why; especially with the incredible distance between me and the source of the scent and the many foul odors coming from all of the clientele. It was as though this intoxicating scenting pierced through the curtain created by the other scents and headed straight toward me. Which meant, I assumed, that the scent was coming from Ross's mystery guest.

Regardless, if word got around that I was doing something I wasn't supposed to do, like not keeping my full attention on the ring, he would take it as a reflection on him. Why? Who knows. It might as well be because the wind changed. So, keeping an "eye on me" while entertaining whomever he had in his box saved him the trouble. If he noticed something, he could send one of his men to nip it in the bud discreetly.

However, this decision proved to be futile because my desperation to find the source of this smell consumed my thoughts. I knew it shouldn't with all the reasons I just mentioned in regard to Ross watching and his own desperation to please the special guest tonight. I really knew I should concentrate, but I was super distracted. How could I not be, when every fiber of my being wanted to know the source of this intoxicating aroma and why it was mysteriously weakening the effects of the serum that was supposed to dull my senses and reflexes? I felt foolish for even bothering to look. What did I expect? A large arrow hovering over the source saying "Oh, hey! This is the person who smells so incredibly good?" No. Maybe. I don't know. Luckily, Ash's grip on my shoulder gave me a friendly reminder that snapped me back to the event about to occur and away from the ramblings of my own thoughts.

Focus, Vivila, focus! I thought. *Or you will be whipped more harshly than ever before, because there is someone important here that the boss wants to impress. Focus, focus, focus!*

I hadn't realized Ash was trying to get my attention until he was practically screaming into my ears; I was too intoxicated by that damn smell. Where or who was it coming from? I let my vision continue drifting, desperately trying to find the source. But the fight was about to start.

"V!" Ash yelled.

"Huh?"

"You okay?" he asked.

"I'm fine," I replied, nodding my head.

"You sure? I know you're feeling a little weaker than normal, but I need you to focus, *okay*?"

I nodded again.

"Okay. You can do this, V."

I didn't know how to tell him about the effect this amazing scent had on me without sounding completely mad or risking one of Gregory's lackeys possibly overhearing, so I just nodded again. Why his lackeys needed to be within earshot of me when Gregory and I fought was beyond me. *Don't focus on that, Vivila*. It won't help to focus on that. In an effort to focus on the present and not on yet *another* reason why Gregory annoyed me, I paid attention to the sounds produced by Ash fumbling in his jacket for the keys to my handcuffs. He then helped me to my seat before leaving to get a bottle of water.

As I sat there, I tried to concentrate on what I knew about Gregory's fighting strategies and techniques—but there was that aroma again, creeping in and distracting me. I had this strange feeling that it was coming from the elevated seating box where the boss usually sits, but I wasn't one hundred percent sure.

I was about to turn around and check when I noticed Ash coming toward me. Turning to face him, I noticed him shaking his head. Looking at the boss before a fight was a big no-no. It was a sign of mental weakness and nervousness. Both would not give the audience what they wanted to see. If the 'tourist attraction' didn't give them what they paid for, I would be given an extra ten lashes or no breakfast on top of the lashes for daring to look in the direction of the boss's high-rise seating box; especially tonight, with the "special" guest sitting next to Ross.

I will not look weak, I will not look weak, I thought, using the same coping mechanism I usually use to help calm my anxiety. Something about saying things three times seems to help. *Please let this scent continue to give me the extra strength I need. Please, please, please.*

In a continued attempt to focus on the present, I watched the judges as they took their seats by the ring. Then one of the King Cobras' doctors rolled in with his nurses, and both referees took their positions—one in the ring and one on the floor. It was time. And when the floor lights started to dim, the crowd of drunkards and gamblers started to cheer. I looked over to see Gregory taking off his hoodie and undershirt before pulling himself into the ring.

He scowled to make himself seem more intimidating and shifted his weight a few times to show the crowd that he was ready to win. I would have commented on how moronic he was acting but didn't because I knew if I did, even in a whisper, the jerk would rat on me to his dad, and then I would be punished in some way for it. Yes, I had gone days without food before and received a total of fifty lashes too, but with a special guest watching tonight, any name-calling might result in a more creative form of punishment... like being suspended by my ankles for a full twenty-four hours or something. Totally not worth it.

I looked back over to Ash and nodded. Then he helped me onto my feet, unaware that the source of the amazing smell was somehow continuing to lessen the symptoms of the double dosage of the second serum. Why was this scent helping? I couldn't say. But in this moment, I could care less and decided to use that to my advantage. Not against Ash, but against Gregory. I overdramatized how weak I was as I climbed into the ring, with Ash's help, and stood to look at Gregory from across the ring. I knew that it was working because the jerk was grinning, ear to ear, from the center of the ring by the referee. Ignoring Ash's last-minute words of encouragement, I "stumbled" over towards the two men. I wasn't trying to disregard my confusion, especially because I knew magic didn't exist. But this newfound strength was still amazing.

Now, these fights are scored based on the number of punches and effectiveness of the punches. It is not just the volume of punches, but the punches that have the most effect.[1] Usually, both opponents are of the same gender and weight class, but to Ross, I am the exception to that rule because I am his property and he can do whatever he wants with me. And as long as I keep making him money, the likelihood of me living another day is high. Lastly, in normal and legal bare-knuckle fighting, things like kicking, kneeing, elbows, wrestling, or throw-downs are not allowed. But here in The Pit, all of those things are allowed. The only things not allowed are biting and eye gouging. And, well, ideally, *no killing.*

With that in mind, when the bell rings, and the referee backs up, I know two things right off the bat. One, I need to keep up this 'weakling' charade for at least a few minutes before I can drop it because then Gregory is more likely to lower his guard. And two, despite the wearing-off effect of that scent, my best bet is to keep my distance. The second serum was still in my system, and my agility was still not at its fullest. If I immediately went in for a punch, Gregory would be able to grab me, and I would be at a disadvantage.

We circle each other for some time and I allow Gregory to get a few punches in. I drop to the ground each time before pushing myself back up. Blood drips down my forehead and into my swelling eyes; I quickly wipe it away along with the sweat. My ribs and shoulder hurt so badly that I lean against the ropes to catch my breath.

---

1 Policegazette, Bare Knuckle Boxing Rules Announced, July 17, 2016. http://policegazette.us/index.php/2016/06/17/bare-knuckle-boxing-rules-announced/

"Stop playing with each other and fight!" I hear a man in the audience yell.

Gregory, the moron that he is, throws his fists in the air in minor victory as he stomps over to me, about to try to end the fight by punching me in the stomach. Knowing that he usually steps forward before he punches, I kicked him right in the knee. He stumbled a few steps backward in shock and in pain, then without hesitation, I kicked him in the other knee.

The crowd fell silent with bated breath. Not that they hadn't seen me fight before, or even seen me fight Gregory, but seeing a small-framed sideshow chick having the upper hand on a larger-framed man was still a sight to be seen. They were getting their money's worth, even if that meant they had lost their bet on the outcome. Aside from a few coughs and groans coming from Gregory, this amount of quietness was a first for me. Nevertheless, I decided to cut through the silence with two uppercut punches—one under the left side of Gregory's chin and one under the right.

Gregory's head jerked from side to side, blood and spit spraying from one side of the ring to the other. Sweat was trickling profusely down both of our bodies and I couldn't explain why or what part of me decided to do this, but I threw one final blow right in his solar plexus. Both the crowd and I watched him curl forward before falling backward to the mat of the ring. I might have continued and just gone berserk on Gregory, regardless of the sound of the bell signaling the end of the fight, if both the referee and Ash hadn't stopped me. I had so much pent-up anger towards Gregory, Ross, and my situation in life that it all rose to the surface without my knowledge.

While I had indeed given Ross a great show for whomever he was trying to impress, knocking his son out like that was going to have some kind of repercussions. But I was unable to process or reflect on what they might be with how worked up I was. I had, sometime during the fight, forgotten about that wonderful smell and my desire to discover the source too. It wasn't until I was locked back in my room, thankful that my room was no longer flooded from last night's rain and beginning to calm down, that I remembered the scent again. The rejuvenating scent that aided me to win the fight when I had so much going against me. It had all been a blur.

Yet, alone in my room again and dreading what the morning would bring, I was also reminded of how poorly *I* smelled. I did my best to clean the blood and sweat off of me the best I could with a cloth and a glass of water on a wood crate that I used as a nightstand. I wondered if Ash would return so that I could use the bathroom and take a shower, but he never did. I didn't like the idea of changing into my pajamas, still gross and sweaty, but what choice did I have? The clothes I was wearing were damp and my pajamas were not. And if I laid my clothes on one of the many stacks of books, there was a good chance they would be dry in the morning.

Luckily, both of the serums were now fully out of my system, so I could shift back and start healing normally. It was unusual for them to wear off this quickly. Maybe that unfamiliar scent in The Pit was like some sort of magical spell. But why? Real magic doesn't exist, right? Not that I was complaining, for it was reducing the pain of changing into different clothes. And if real magic *did* exist, would it also increase the speed of my healing too? Looking over the sore and bruised areas where I had allowed Gregory to get in a few punches, the answer seemed to be a resounding "no." I was too exhausted to wait and see, so I decided to lie down on my bed and quickly fell asleep.

I was awoken several hours later to someone banging on the metal door. The morning light was blaring into my eyes from the part of the window not blocked by books, so it was hard to turn over and ignore whoever was standing out in the hallway. I just wanted to rest and properly heal—for once.

"V! Time to wake up. Boss wants to see you in twenty," Ash

said. I didn't respond. "Vivila! You need to get up now if you want a shower and to eat something."

"Yeah, okay," I finally said, reluctantly.

A numbing tickle washed over me as I felt the blood sinking to the base of my stomach. Though I had anticipated a punishment from the boss for knocking out his son and heir more quickly than he wanted given the special guest he had, a meeting this early couldn't be good. Yet, he didn't barge into my room during the night, so perhaps there was a chance that my punishment and lecture wouldn't be *that* bad. But who am I fooling?

Slowly rolling myself off my mattress, I fought against the sharp pain in my sides and the tender soreness of my muscles to push myself into a standing position. So, the intoxicating scent of last night most assuredly did not have "magical" qualities. I didn't have time to think about it anymore at this moment, so I wrapped one of my arms around my ribs and walked over to the stack of books that shelved the bag of toiletries. Slinging the towel over my shoulder, I was momentarily fascinated by the flock of pigeons cooing and bobbing their heads up outside the window. It was so nonchalant that I couldn't help but laugh a little.

Thunk, thunk, th-thunk.

"Come on, V! We don't have time for lollygagging."

With a deep sigh, I went to the door and turned around, my back and hands to the door. Regardless of how kind Ash was to me and whether another King Cobra member was with him or not, he was still a stickler for protocol.

"Ready!" I said, trying but failing to sound happy. It was downright prepubescent, regardless of how hoarse my voice sounded when I woke up.

A few seconds later, I heard the bottom window slide open and felt the handcuffs slide around my wrists. The metal was particularly ice cold this morning. Fall was coming soon, but these handcuffs had definitely been put in the freezer overnight instead of being put back on the hook by the door. One of Gregory's lackeys probably did it as payback. Not the most ingenious idea, but it was one that wouldn't get them in trouble with Ross.

After I was freed of the restraints and the window built into the bathroom's door was shut, the warm water from the showerhead felt like heaven as it trickled down my body. My muscles were able to relax, and I was overjoyed to finally wash the grime off of me. A simple and mundane act for any normal person, but this was one of the few things that made me forget how free I wasn't. My mind wandered toward the memory of the mysterious aroma as the warm water continued to temporarily wash away my surroundings and situation. I sniffed the air as if the physical act would make it reappear in front of me. I could almost hear the ocean water drawing and crashing in the distance. Feeling the pleasant temperature of the gritty sand between my toes. The blazing heat from a nearby campfire as its flames snapped and hissed. It was comforting, safe, and strong.

And yet Ross's word dominated repeatedly in my mind, abruptly putting the scene to an end: *"Daydreaming and imagination will get you nowhere, so snap out of it, or I will do it for you."*

It was what he always said when I wasn't paying attention to him or he caught me talking to myself in my room. And as much as I didn't want to, I knew he was right. Pipe dreams would only kill me—unless Ross did first. I need to forget about this wondrous scent. *Need to forget, need to forget, need—need.* My breathing felt heavy under the pressure in my heart. Even after I turned off the water to the showerhead and my body stood wet in the mostly moldy stall, this forced thought of forgetting the magical aroma crushed me unlike anything had before. Above the betrayal of my parents selling me away. I felt a part of my whole soul being torn in half by trying to give up hope on never finding the source of the scent.

I couldn't explain why. I just did. I felt whole again in a way I've never felt before. All my life, I had felt like an outsider, even before that fateful day in gym class—like I didn't belong. Not with my peers, my parents, or anyone in general. I had always felt small and insignificant. But the pipe dream of feeling accepted and meant for something greater still lingered. This scent making me feel strangely whole again, reminding me during my first year here at the warehouse—and maybe the years leading up to my arrival at the warehouse—of those wishes of one day not being made to feel like a nobody, or that there was somewhere I belonged. And whatever that scent did to ward off the effects almost gave me hope of fulfilling those desires. Silly, right? Naïve, too. But what experience did I have in the last six to eighteen years that would tell me differently? Hope was just another pipe dream to be had.

When I was dressed, knowing I wouldn't be given time to put my toiletries back in my room, I placed them into my little ripped toiletry bag and folded it nicely over the sink and gave two knocks on the metal door to signal I was ready. A tray of stale bread and a glass of orange juice presented itself through one of the small doors. It wouldn't be the first time I had eaten in the bathroom, and it definitely wouldn't be the last. I wasted no time in consuming what was on the tray not just because I was starving but also because I knew how much Ross had no patience for tardiness. Knocking twice on the door again and turning around, I put my hands behind my back for my cold binding bracelets to be reintroduced to me yet again. After Ash placed the restraints on my wrists through the grated door, he escorted me to the elevator. Silence enveloped the enclosure so thickly, I thought the pressure in my heart would kill me for sure before whatever punishment awaited me.

Ross's office was on the top floor of the warehouse. It drastically differed from any other room in the building. I remembered when I was a child, I secretly watched *The Godfather* from the railings of the stairs when my parents thought I was sleeping. Believe me when I say that Ross's office is an *exact* replica of Don Corleone's. The room reeked of sophistication and class, two things that Ross was not. The emerald-green leather chair behind the desk was turned to face the unlit fireplace when Ash and I entered. The mahogany blinds pulled partially open, letting in little to no natural light. Puffs of cigar smoke floated above the chair. The mantel above the faux fireplace held a clock and a ceramic urn of Ross's father's remains.

Ominous were the three King Cobras members erect like statues with guns. On the desk, all the usual things—the Art Deco green shade lamp, the mug of writing implements, the brass ashtray, the open laptop, the photographs of his wife and children, and the steaming cup of black coffee; all seemed to be drawing attention and pointing to a piece of paper on the walnut and black leather desk mat. A piece of paper that would soon determine the outcome of the situation I found myself in and one that made me both curious and nervous.

CHAPTER THREE

The mysterious paper was flipped over, which caused beads of sweat to start dripping down my face. While I was curious about what was written on the other side, I wasn't going to be the first to speak and ask about it, lest I wanted a punishment worse than the one I was most likely going to be receiving any minute now. And so I remained quiet, staring at the paper.

"That was quite the show last night," Ross said, not turning his chair around to look at me.

I said nothing.

"Gregory's injuries were so bad, Doctor Hall had to take him to the hospital. *My son* will be bedridden for at least three weeks!" he continued, raising his voice to an uncomfortable volume. He continued, "Fortunately for you, the special guest we had last night has not only offered to pay for my son's hospital bill, but has also offered a sacrilege amount of money. All he asks for in exchange"—he flipped around violently in his chair, staring dead into my eyes—"is you."

I couldn't believe what I just heard. I highly doubted the extent of Gregory's injuries would require him to be bedridden for more than a few days or a week, but again, I said nothing. Curiosity lingered heavily in Ross's eyes as he studied me, trying to see whatever this stranger saw in me that would result in this offer. He was almost calm and collected, which was totally unlike him, but it was something I had come to recognize as the calm before the storm. Although I had seen this demeanor several times before, each time I naively prayed for the storm to never come. I intently watched as he lifted an eyebrow like he was just unable to discover what this stranger saw in me. I jumped a little when the storm of rage hit as Ross bolted from his chair. The force at which he had stood up had made the chair collide against the wall and caused the ceramic urn on the mantel to smash on the floor.

When he was a mere inch away from my face, Ross glowered. My eyes darted back and forth between him and what I could see of the ashes and shards of the broken urn. My heart began to race in such a way that only Ross could make it as I felt the heat radiating from his red face onto mine. His innate ability to instill fear and control always left me wanting to curl into myself. But I will not let him get to me. *Not today, not today, not today.*

"What would a man like Aldric O'Connor want with you?" Ross snarled.

"I—I don't know, sir," I stuttered.

"You don't know? YOU DON'T KNOW why a man like Aldric O'Connor—who won 'Man of the Year' in *GQ* magazine four years in a row for strides against animal cruelty and owns half of the most luxurious hotels in North America—would want a piece of trash like you?"

"No, sir," I said as steadily as my nerves would allow. Although it took every bit of strength I had not to divert my eyes away from the man who owned me, this did stop my body from quivering in utter fear and dread. I wanted to run—run back to my room and cower in the corner furthest from the thick metal door. I prayed he didn't have a gun. You would think after six years such an act would be pointless—and it was. But for whatever reason, I prayed anyway.

"Don't lie to me, Vivila Gulmon!"

I didn't realize Ross had a gun in his hand until the butt of his gun's handgrip struck my temple and I immediately fell to the floor. *I should have known. Should have, should have, should have known.* He **always** carried one. The edge of the magazine clip must have scraped into my skin because the warm stickiness of blood dribbled down my face. Between the booming, erratic pulsing of my heart throbbing and my whole body quivering in fear, it was hard to tell if I was purely imaging things due to the state I was in, or if I was truly bleeding. Even as a groan escaped my lips, I still wasn't sure, so I closed my eyes tightly, praying to be back in my room.

I may be a freak of nature, know I how to fight, and I may not be very worldly... but I'm not stupid enough to fight back against the man who owns me. I desperately reached out in my mind again for the memory of the comforting scent of the salty ocean air and campfire, praying it would give me the strength I needed to get through this. But this attempt was foolish, for how could a memory save me in this moment? I reopened my eyes and saw that Ross was still towering over me.

But I was so lost in trying to calm my nerves, I barely heard Ross's next question. I couldn't say, "What?" or ask, "Could repeat your question again, sir?" That was a sure way to get shot—if you were lucky. Not shot in a dead way, but in a it-will-take-more-than-a-couple-of-days-to-heal way, mixed in with no-food-until-three-days-from-now way. No, the best course of action was to wait until Ross repeated the question, which he always did because he hated unanswered questions... *really* hated it. I'd rather not go into those gory ways at this point—I'll just leave it to your imagination.

"Who is Aldric O'Connor to you?" the leader of the King Cobras asked again through gritted teeth. "And how did you manage to defeat my son so quickly when he doubled the dose to dull your senses, hmm?"

"I don't understand what you mean, sir. I don't know this man," I answered as docile as I could and without reacting in complete and utter shock regarding the news that he knew his imbecile of a son had doubled the dose. Of course he knew. *Stupid! Stupid! Stupid!* But that's not what was really freaking me out, and not what could get me in more trouble than I'd ever been in—and that's saying A LOT. And in true me fashion, I did what I always did to help calm myself down: I repeated the truth in my head, what I wished was the truth, or something I didn't want to be true, as if it would make the anxiety-ridden situation *go away—Go away, go away!*

I don't know this man. I don't know this man. What in the world is he talking about? Do I know this man? No! I DO NOT KNOW THIS MAN—but if I expect to make it out of this room alive, I need to play dumb.

I was speaking the truth when I said I didn't know this Aldric O'Connor, but it didn't seem to matter to Ross. Oh, how I wished I could be anywhere else right now. It was a pipe dream, and one I would have thought would have vanished by now. After six years, I had resolved in knowing I would most likely be in this warehouse until both Ross and Gregory had died... or until I did. The latter seemed to be coming to fruition with Ross's strong desire in knowing why this unknown man would want me. Ross paced the room, muttering obscenities about my worth or lack thereof. He clearly thought I was too stupid to understand his question, which was proven by his next reworded question.

"How do you know the youngest and most successful entrepreneur in this state?" Ross demanded.

"I don't know, sir."

He kicked me in the stomach and I curled my body to protect myself.

"I said don't lie to me, Vivila!"

"I'm not!" I screamed.

But before Ross could kick me again, he is stopped by Ash's hand on his shoulder. He turned his attention away from me to my relief.

"How could she know who this man is when we don't allow her to have access to a television, the internet, newspapers, or the latest magazines?" Ash said as calmly as he could.

"Because he's a freak like her! All freaks know each other!

The world may not know it or want to admit it, but I do. And to think, I wanted to do business with him and form an alliance."

"Not to be rude or impugn your intelligence," Ash interrupted with some hesitation, "but how would you know that, sir? Supernatural beings don't exist aside from her. I mean, neither she nor her adoptive parents knew about her true identity until six years ago."

"I was adopted?" I asked without thinking, preemptively cringing as I awaited what would most likely be the next punishment.

Damn my curiosity. As surprising as this unexpected reveal of my parents actually being my *adoptive* parents was, it would be nothing compared to the blow I knew I was about to receive for speaking without Ross's permission. Would he strike me in the temple with the butt of his gun? Light a couple of cigars to burn several random parts of my body? Or would it be something new? I didn't know what punishment was coming, for he had done everything in the book—and then some.

"Did I say you could speak!?" Ross leaned down and screamed in my face before turning his attention to Ash for his insolence in taking my side. "And you better watch your tongue, boy."

With those words, Ross combed his fingers to the back of my head until he had grabbed a good chunk of my hair and jerked downwards. I unconsciously yelped from the gesture. If my hands were not bound, I would have brought them up to lessen the incredibly uncomfortable tightness. But as it was, I had to endure the foul warm breath protruding from Ross's rotting mouth upon my temple. I tried to keep my breathing stable, but failed miserably. Why did this Aldric O'Connor have to take an interest in me? Did he really think Ross would agree to such a trade?

This guy may be rich, but there was little chance he wielded the same amount of power as Ross. And had he really not realized that by making such an offer, he had inadvertently made things worse for me? As I looked over to Ash, whose focus was on Ross, I noticed his mouth about to open to speak again. Whatever Ash was about to say was going to make things worse for me.

Please, Ash, don't say anything that may enrage Ross any further, I thought as I wished to God I was telepathic, as absurd and fantasy-based as it was to wish for a nonexistent ability. *Oh please, please, please... don't say anything.*

"Boss, it really does seem to be a fair trade," Ash said, breaking the silence.

I screamed again, my feet scrambling to move fast enough as Ross dragged me by my hair until he stood mere inches from Ash's face. Well, at least I imagined so, for I could no longer smell Ross's horrible breath and my lower back brushed up against Ash's shoes. I gasped in agony, which was a huge mistake because Ross's grip briefly tightened, lifting me high enough to bring me to my knees, and then he released my hair by shoving my head toward the hardwood floor. I wasn't sure if I should have been relieved that my head didn't actually hit the floor or if it was simple dumb luck. Regardless, the tension building in the space was so suffocating, I thought I was going to faint; especially with how much my scalp throbbed in pain.

"A fair trade? A fair trade! Twenty-four hours, Ash! That's all that young punk gave me to agree to both offers and hand her over," Ross bellowed.

"Well, yeah, boss."

"Well, yeah, boss," Ross said mockingly. "My golden ticket! *The* reason people come to The Pit instead of somewhere else. FAIR?"

Ash said nothing.

"You're lucky I owe your father my life or I would shoot you where you stand! You hear me, boy?"

"Yes, boss," Ash said sheepishly.

As quickly as Ross had moved to be mere inches away from Ash's face, so was the return to mine. The barrel of his gun dug into my temple and the God-awful stench of his breath clouded invisibly around my face. I could feel my last meal rising to the back of my throat. I did my best to hold it back, for vomiting anywhere near Ross's presence would only get me in more trouble. Ignoring the blood trickling down to my chin and with the tip of Ross's nose grazing my brow, I focused on the small bit of sun peering through the blinds. It was little things like this that helped me mentally prepare for the unpredictable whim from the man standing so uncomfortably close to me.

"You would like that, wouldn't you? A little happily ever after for ya," Ross hissed. "Lest you forget, adoptive or not, your parents sold you to me, and you ain't going nowhere. You worthless, hideous freak! Even if I decided to give you over to this rich punk, he would grow tired of you. Maybe use you to satisfy his needs for a little while, but grow bored of you, nonetheless. I'll laugh in his face as he tries to pawn you back over to me before I kill him. You lousy freak! And if you ever try to make my son look poorly in The Pit again—I don't care how much money you make me, you'll wish you'd never been born, do you hear me?"

I blacked out for a moment as the butt of his gun struck the back of my head and I hit the floor at an alarming rate. Yet indescribably to me, my shaking fear transformed into a pulsating rage, spreading so quickly that I felt myself starting to shift. It was as though all of my hatred and pent-up anger had had enough of being terrified of Ross. While I was uncertain how long this would last before I was reminded why he was somebody and I nothing, all I could think was *You're lucky that I'm bound by handcuffs!*

With a dismissive hand gesture, resolved, he had once again established he was king of this decrepit castle and he was now bored with the situation and would rather focus his attention on something more interesting. Ross returned to the chair behind his desk and spun himself away from me without saying another word. Well, he might be done, but I sure as hell wasn't! I yanked and pushed against the chains of the hand-cuffs with all my might. I could feel the metal start to bend and pull apart, regardless of Ash's hands wrapped around both of my shoulders to help me to my feet, which took more effort than he was used to—because I was going to attack Ross and possibly end his life without caring about the consequences. It was a level of uncontrolled anger that I hadn't felt since I was twelve and it pulsated through my veins with such momentum that I nearly scratched Ash as I continued to pull the handcuffs apart while he guided me out of the office towards the elevator.

Perhaps it was just as well that Ash had gotten me out of there before I'd done anything or said anything I would later regret because if I had successfully attacked Ross without being shot at by the other two King Cobras members or by Ross, my "owner" would have gotten exactly what he deserved. However, that wasn't the main train of thought, or *any* cohesive thought for that matter, running through my mind. No. Because I had already started to shift, and I was experiencing pain unlike any I had ever felt in a long while. It was as though I was being torn apart in every direction by a pack of wolves who hadn't eaten in weeks. My skin losing the war with both my wings and tail clawing their way out. The drums of agony thumping fervently from the inside of my head outward.

My knees buckled, nearly taking Ash down to the floor with me. Though as it got more and more intense, I started to forget he was there with me. I couldn't tell you if Ross or any other King Cobra member stepped out of the office to see what was going on, nor could I tell you if I was screaming or silent. Even after the sweet relief of the wet, soft feathers of my wings filling the space between my arms, unhinging the remaining metal restraining me, and moving down my back. I turned to face Ash, my now freed arms wrapping around his chest as I began to lose consciousness and awareness of the other parts of my shift and the world around me. I pleaded in my head for the pain to just stop, stop—stop.

Then everything went dark and the pain became nonexistent. I could only hope, when I fell to my knees and before I went unconscious, that Ash would return my embrace, cradling me from any further harm to myself. I could only hope to find myself in my room when I awoke and that the self-induced force shift would be a sufficient punishment for Ross. But who am I kidding? When I slowly came to, I was surprised to see the vast space of The Pit below me. *This is not my room. This is not real. This is not real, not real, not—real.*

My mind was groggy and my body still felt filleted with pulsating pain; I exhaled and closed my eyes a few times to better focus on what I was seeing. I tried to lift my hands to my eyes but found they were restrained once again with what felt like a thicker metal than that of the handcuffs. Why this was and why my hands were numb, my mind was struggling to concentrate on for more than a few seconds. The strange angle at which the cuffs rested had cut off the blood circulation to my wrists. I jerked my body to and fro, finding my spotted white and brown wings hadn't retracted.

I was still in my freakish form, which had never happened before. Usually, if I were in this form before falling asleep, I would wake up normal. Why hadn't I this time? Oh, my head. Had I been injected with the serums? Is this why I hadn't shifted back? As my snow white, panther-like tail swooshed from side to side, I realized my feet were bound too. Slowly, my vision became clearer and I could see I truly was in The Pit. Yet, if I truly was in The Pit, then why was I so high up?

I'm, I'm—in the boss's seating box, I thought in a bit of a panic. I jerk my body from side to side again, though I knew it was in vain.

And in the moment, the all too familiar obnoxious laughing from Gregory and his lackeys broke the silence as my mind slowly slipped in and out of consciousness.

I heard one of them say something to the effect of, "That's how you crucify an angel."

Another said, "More like a fugly demon!"

The explosion of laughter continued.

Whatever they said next sounded like the adults in a *Peanuts* cartoon because I blacked out again. I knew Ross and Gregory to be cruel, but they had never been this savagely ruthless. I wasn't anything special, regardless of my freakish "true form," so what form of punishment was this? Defeating Gregory in front of a potential client deserved thirty lashes or no food for a week... not this. Or did this have more to do with the offers from his potential client—from Aldric O'Connor? *I am no one. I am no one—I am—no one.* And if what Ross said was true, that this Aldric guy was a freak like me—highly unlikely as that may be—then it wouldn't be too difficult to find a replacement in my absence, right? Again, I'm not anyone or anything special.

They say that dreams are your brain's way of processing all that has happened during your waking hours. I don't know if that truly applies to a freak like me because my dreams are simply reminders, flashbacks if you will, as to why I am nothing. As I continued to hang, strapped to the boss's box above The Pit and unconscious, my dreams somehow had a way of replaying what had occurred in Ross's office before bringing back the key moments of my past that had led to my current situation. Lucky me, right? Starting with the terrified looks on my classmates' faces, cowering against one another at the far corners of the gym. Under their looks was a need to stare intently at me, as if by making sure what they were seeing was real, they could determine whether I was a threat to them too, not just to the taunting group who I'd attacked. Or did they continue to focus on me because our teacher was staring at me too, and having one adult on their side would make their parents believe what had happened?

The blood staining my hands and the glossy floor around

me... The panic and disgusted looks on my parents'—*adoptive* parents'—faces when they hurried to school to pick me up. It was the first time they didn't dare touch me, as though I was some creature with a contagious disease from some third-world country. The broom that the woman who I thought was my real mother used to escort and prod me into Ross's maniacal grinning hands. The abuse I received, both psychological and mental, these last six years. Ross dangling a hope for a better life—a life I would most likely never experience. Ross's possessive claws digging further into me. All because this Aldric had offered to relieve the burden from Ross's shoulders. The burden that is me. Even in my dream state, I could feel real tears forming.

CHAPTER FOUR

I couldn't tell you how long I was actually out for because I wasn't exactly sure! It felt like half a day had passed, but it could have only been half an hour. An hour? Two hours? But the unfamiliar noises as I slowly came to were enough to startle me into being fully awake.

Clank! Cl-clank! Tssssshhh!

Bang! Bang! Bang!

"Where the frick are they!?" Gregory yelled.

"I don't know, man! I can't see a damn thing," one of his lackeys yelled.

"Well, don't waste your bullets until you d—"

Thump.

"Gregory?"

"Call the boss for back up. Matt?"

Whack! Thump! Thump!

With all the heavy smoke filling and rising around The Pit, I didn't have a clear idea of exactly what was going on below me. I could only guess that all of the continuous thumps I kept hearing were either bodies or some of the freestanding punching bags falling to the hard cement floor.

From behind me, I suddenly heard Ross's voice.

"Who the f--- do you think you are? Step away from my property, boy!"

"What are you going to do about it, old man?" an unfamiliar voice asked overconfidently and slightly muffled, like he was wearing a mask.

Don't provoke him! Don't provoke him! Whoever you are, you really don't want to provoke him! This is what I wanted to say to this stranger, but the words seemed to retreat to the back of my throat instead of coming out.

Ca-ca-clink-ink-ink! Tsssshhh! Bang! Bang! Growl. Whack! Whack!

"Ahhhh—" Ross screamed.

Thump!

Regardless of the presence of this heavy smoke now rolling from behind, I was annoyingly again losing focus—losing consciousness.

No, no, no. I must stay awake long enough for the smoke to dissipate and see how much damage Gregory and his lackeys received—and Ro—ss too, I thought. *Or—or maybe—ee they are de—de—.*

When I started to regain consciousness again, I found myself unable to open my eyes and amidst unfamiliar smells. It was clear I was no longer tied above The Pit, and the bed which I seemed to be lying on was the most comfortable mattress I'd been on in a very long time, so I could deduce I wasn't in my room either. The room I was in was free of mold to the point that it was completely sterilized. Yet, I wasn't sure if I should be pleased or frightened that I wasn't back in my room at the warehouse. I extended my keen hearing to find any clues to determine which answer was the correct one. Silence stood dominant, with the exception of the two separate rhythmic breathing patterns similar to that of rolling ocean waves. I wasn't alone.

While the fear started to drain the blood from my face and made my heart race, I needed to wake myself up before planning a course of action. I needed to know if I had been kidnapped from one hell only to be awoken to another. Were the sources of the breathing friend or foe? Though with the exception of Ash, I'm not sure if I can differentiate between the two anymore. To quote one of the many books I've read,

"Anyone can betray anyone."[2]

I need to wake up! I thought. *I need to force my eyes open and* **wake up***! Why can't I wake up? Wake up, Vivila!* **WAKE— UP!**

Suddenly, I caught a whiff of a very familiar masculine scent, but I couldn't figure out why it was here or where I knew it from. All I knew was that I didn't want the scent to go away, and breathing as much of the smokey and salty air was the most warm and inviting scent that somehow... I felt safe despite being in an unfamiliar setting. I foolishly thought it would heal me, this strange sleep-like trance that I seemed to be trapped in, as it had healed me before, right before my fight against Gregory. Wait! As it had healed me before? Be- fore—before—how is that possible? This—this was the smell from the other night! The one that pulled me out of the haze and helped me win the fight. But why? Why is it here? And for some strange reason, unbeknownst to me, I wanted to pray to whatever god existed in this heaven for it to be real and to never leave me again.

"Though the sleeping gas you had the pack members use does play a small role, it is only a single sprinkle of the problem, not the whole cake. She is extremely malnourished and weak from the beating she has most recently received," an unknown woman's voice said. "It is clear that she hasn't fully shifted very often, which may also explain her current condition. We need to be careful about how we introduce her to the pack members. We can't be sure how much she knows about both her own and our kind..."

Pack members? I **have** *found myself in another hell, but what sort of gang would refer to their other members as "pack members"?* I thought. *I must be delusional in my current state. Whatever that state may be.*

"Can she truly not know what she is?" asked an unknown man.

---

2 *Red Queen* by Victoria Aveyard

"That I cannot say, Alpha Aldric," the woman replied. "She may be aware that she is different from other people, but that's it. The traces of two unknown substances found in her system are also curious. One looks a lot like Subcinc-octovotus serum, which causes the body to shift partially, and the other seems to resemble a sedative, but it is unlike anything I've ever seen. I'll need to run further tests to be sure. But because she has been made to fight often, with these two serums constantly put into her system, her natural healing abilities have a hard time mending any and all injuries correctly. Though I believe the serums have finally flushed themselves out, so she should be fully healed soon."

Alpha Aldric? I thought. *I may not be worldly, but no one in the King Cobras gang ever referred to Ross as 'Alpha.' Wait! It's him! It's him! The source of that magnificent scent!—but how? Why? Oh, who cares, Vivila? It's him! Yet, what does this Alpha Aldric want from me? And what is Ross going to do when he discovers his 'special guest' is the one who took me? And what natural healing abilities does this woman speak of? I heal quicker than anyone I know, but that doesn't make it 'normal.' And what does she mean the serums are finally flushed out of my system? None of this makes any sense...*

Regardless of the many questions that flooded my mind, none of them seemed to truly matter at this moment because I finally had a name for that intoxicating smell. *Alpha Aldric. Alpha Aldric, Alpha—Aldric.* I repeated his name in my mind several times with different inflections, as if he might hear me calling for him. I know that sounds silly, but hearing his name sent butterflies to flutter around in my stomach. His voice was so husky and sultry, I yearned for him—for his touch, in a very primal way. Yet my racing heart, mimicked by some screaming contraption beside me, went from being overjoyed to foolishness and fear.

I mentally shook myself back into reality, though I wasn't thrilled about it. Am I in some sort of coma-like state as well as being in a strange environment with quite possibly another gang? And I'm naively ignoring these facts because I have the name of the person who possesses this wonderful smell? How is that even possible? Clearly, I am fully conscious to be able to hear all of their conversation. Why can't I open my eyes? Or speak, for that matter? A knot formed in my throat to the point where I didn't know if I could swallow or breathe any longer. What *does* this connection I share with this man mean exactly? And it appears they know I'm a freak—so what do they plan to do with me? WHAT DO THEY PLAN TO DO WITH ME?

Be-beep! Be-beep! BEEP! BEEP!

"What's going on, Doc?" Alpha Aldric asked in a tone that held both concern and anger.

"She's starting to wake up. Your presence and her realization that she is in a strange environment seems to have triggered a heightened emotional response."

"If she is 'waking up,' then why aren't her eyes open?"

"I don't know! I'm doing the best I can with the little knowledge I have of Winged Ailuranthropes! It was a disheartening sight when she was first brought in here. I didn't know what was her blood and what was someone else's. There were so many different scents on her and her clothing was in shambles; I had to throw them away. Then, trying to figure out what she was because her body was automatically shifting back to her human form—Alpha, look, I know how important it is for you to be here beside her, but it might be a good idea for you to leave until she does open her eyes. We don't want to *overwhelm* her right away. Especially when we don't know the full extent of the King Cobras' abuse and how it has affected her."

I've never been called a 'Winged Ailuranthrope' nor do I know exactly what that entails. That seems like a made-up word disguised as a real "scientific" one. And from how the doctor said it, she makes it seem like there are more freaks like me and that Ross may be correct in his accusations of Aldric being one too... but that's impossible. Ross was lying! Ross was lying—he was lying just to play with my emotions. Yet my heart was continuing to pound rapidly as I waited for Alpha Aldric to answer—to prove Ross to be false. Yet, it was quiet. So very, very quiet that it made me believe that neither of the two people were going to reply. This is crazy. I must be crazy. These people must be crazy. The words spoken between them seemed to be genuine and heartfelt, but was it that way because they knew I was listening?

Then again, they didn't seem to be aware of my consciousness until my heart started to pick up speed and that screaming contraption started to make that weird noise. Shuffled footsteps paced from where I lay to another part of the room and back again. Then, the familiar sound of a needle's plunger being pressed down, followed by a gurgling squirt of liquid into something above me. I must have been connected to whatever the doctor injected the liquid into, because a euphoric sensation of calmness washed over me. And after a few seconds, my heartbeat returned to normal.

"You're right, Agatha. I'm sorry," Alpha Aldric finally said with such a different demeanor than he'd displayed moments before; immense authority to one of utter vulnerability. "I'm just so glad to have found her. I—I don't want to lose her before I have the chance to get to know her."

"I'll keep you updated," Agatha said.

Footsteps drifted and faded away from the room, unfortunately taking the intoxicating scent with them. It vanished from the room—and took with it my ability to breathe comfortably. It was almost as if all the oxygen had been sucked out of the space when this Alpha Aldric left, leaving me to wonder again, to fear again, of never being near him—again. I might have a name to the scent, but I may never have a face to both. And without the power that his presence and scent had given me to be able to listen to what he was saying, I soon drifted back to sleep. For the life of me, I couldn't tell you how long I slept. Days? Weeks? Months? But it was the best rest I'd had in a very long time.

I've never been one to dream, so I didn't expect to start now, but I desperately tried to imagine what this Alpha Aldric looked like. Though I failed to produce anything more than a dark shadow in my mind, I suppose I was doing so in an attempt to calm my mind of my feelings towards this strange connection he and I seemed to have. I worried that because I was only able to conjure a dark shadow, the connection was all in my head and not real. Yet that didn't seem correct, though I couldn't explain why.

When I finally awoke, bright white fluorescent lights surrounded me so intensely that I had to cover my eyes with my hands. I was taken aback as I felt hard plastic, followed by a bending tube, brushing against my eyes. I looked up to fully examine what was attached to the back of my hands. Both hands? What a strange method to bind a prisoner. Ross would never waste time to bind someone with such a flimsy material. It raised my curiosity further to see that I was wearing a white gown. And as my vision continued to adjust to the harsh lighting, I searched the room for any sign of someone here with me, but I was alone. Now would be as good a time to escape as any. These people may have saved me from Ross, but that didn't mean that in my sleep I had forgotten the possibility of them being worse than Ross—crazier than Ross. Especially with them throwing around words like 'Alpha,' 'pack members,' and 'Winged Ailuranthropes.'

First, I glanced over to the box contraption mimicking my heartbeats. What was the purpose of this? None of the old medical journals in my room ever mentioned a mechanical box such as this. I could guess, but a whole lot of good that would do me. Then my eyes drifted to the elevated metal tray with needles, scalpels, vials of blood, and a jar of coconut oil. Were these things meant to be used to get answers from me?

I had seen tools such as these when passing the King Cobras' interrogation room. But I never saw a jar of coconut oil being amongst them. I only knew one use for coconut oil, and in my experience, it wasn't used as a torturing device. At least not that I was aware of—unless Ash lied to me.

He said it was "a curly hair staple" when he had snuck me a jar two years ago. Apparently, his sister had curly hair similar to mine and used it all the time to help control and moisturize her curls. However, when Ross finally received word three weeks later of this luxury having been given to me, I was denied food for a week and Ash had been docked a few days' pay. So why did this Alpha Aldric and Agatha have a jar of coconut oil on this medical tray of equipment?

I didn't know, and I really didn't have the time to ponder the reason behind the coconut oil any longer than I already had if I planned on making my escape. I also felt pretty foolish taking the time to wonder about it when I didn't know the obstacles that lay ahead of me in order to escape. Disconnecting the long tubes to my hands and then removing the adhesive wires from my chest, which inadvertently caused the beeping box to scream in one long continuous *beeeeeeep*, I began to push myself off of the bed only to be distracted with how clean and shiny the light teal tiled floor was. Aside from Ross's office, perhaps, I couldn't remember the last time I had seen a floor *this* clean. I could almost see my battered, ugly face in it.

Vivila! I thought annoyingly. *Now is not the time. Move, move, move! But where?*

I looked past the drawn back white curtain, which partially covered a cushioned mahogany-stained wood chair, to the open door to make sure no one had heard the box contraption screaming yet. Though the hallway on the other side of the door seemed void of sound, I didn't think it wise to make my escape in that direction. I didn't know where the hallway led, nor did I know how small or large this place was. Air blew from behind me, my naturally white curls sweeping in front of my face. Turning to see where this blowing air was coming from, I noticed two windows by the wall with a metal dresser and bookshelf. Unfortunately, although they were fully opened, they were too small to climb through.

Damn—Damn, damn, damn! I thought with growing frustration.

I focused my hearing once again towards the door. Nothing. Now's my chance. Creeping quietly and quickly towards the door, my thigh accidentally bumped into the wooden chair, causing it to groan. I stopped, my face and body starting to go so incredibly pale; I must have been the same color as my gown. I might not have heard anything when I got out of the bed, but if six years with the King Cobras had taught me anything, it is to never assume anything. I waited next to the chair and only a few yards from the door—very, very, very quietly and very, very, very still for what must have been ten minutes, though it could have been less. Had I not bumped into the chair, if only I *hadn't* bumped into the chair, I might have already been in the hallway.

When I didn't hear a single noise in the hallway, I let out a huge sigh of relief. I looked down at the gown I was wearing, not thrilled at the idea of wearing it because it was a bit too revealing in the back—but realized I didn't have much of a choice. I quickly scanned the room behind me once more and grew a bit frustrated. I couldn't see my clothes anywhere. They weren't much—dirty, with holes in them—but they were mine. I worked hard to earn those clothes and I couldn't help but feeling even more frustrated to see my clothes missing.

Looking under the bed in search of my clothes, from the corner of my eye, I spotted something on the wooden chair I had failed to notice. Folded neatly upon it were clean clothes and boots. Slowly, I crouch down and crept toward them on my hands and knees. At first glance, there didn't seem to be a single sign of wear to them. My fingers hovered over them; I feared that if I touched them, I might discover the clothes and boots to be a mirage. I didn't bother to think about the convenience or the reason behind the clothes. I was so entranced with these brand new clean clothes, I failed to notice one other thing—one very *important* thing.

CHAPTER FIVE

I was startled by the sudden sound of heavy footsteps running down the hall toward my room. I frantically began looking for another way to escape, but was well aware there wasn't one. Even if I sucked in my breath, there was still no way I would be able to fit through either window. The only option I could find was to quickly hide behind the tall filing cabinet. Perhaps with windows being open, they would think I had slipped through one of them despite their size. Shit! I'm running out of time. Oh, why did I bump into the chair? The still beeping contraption wasn't helping either... With every footstep becoming louder, my heartbeat raced faster and my palms became sweatier.

I slid behind the cabinet, though with the failure in opening the window, I knew it would only be a matter of seconds before they found me. It was a foolhardy idea, but it somehow made me feel like I had some semblance of control. If they had guns, there would be no way for me to take on both of them. Even if they didn't have guns, I had never been in a fight where the odds were two against one. Regardless, I tried to remain as still and as quiet as possible until I could better assess the approaching situation.

Don't move. Don't breathe, I keep telling myself as I heard the owners of the running footsteps enter the room. I wasn't sure if I should consider myself lucky that it took them this long to realize I was no longer connected to the still beeping box. I waited for the sounds of the heavyweight of guns being pulled from the fabrics of their pants or the click of the slide or hammer readying within their hands as they entered. Sounds I had grown accustomed to, now and again, living in Ross's warehouse.

While I heard something that resembled the first with one of them, I did not hear the next expected sounds. And as much as I was trying to control my breathing and movement, I couldn't control how fast my heart was racing.

"Where is she?" asked an unknown woman.

"Vivila?" asked a woman who sounded like the Doctor Agatha woman.

"My brother isn't going to be pleased if he finds out she disappeared."

"Beatrix!" the doctor hissed.

"Well, he will be, *Ag-a-tha...*" I heard Beatrix say the doctor's name mockingly.

"She's here. I can still smell her. She's just frightened. And you would be too if you woke up in an unfamiliar environment—"

She can smell me? They must be pretty close to be able to smell me, I thought to myself, my whole body trembling in fear. *Why haven't they fired off a few bullets to scare me into revealing my hiding place?*

"I was just saying."

"Shh! Vivila, sweetheart? It's okay. I know this must be very overwhelming, but I promise you're in a safe place and no harm will come to you. We're here to help you."

"Great wolves! You sound like my mom," Beatrix remarked.

Agatha must have shot Beatrix an ugly look because when she spoke again, it was in a completely different manner.

"I'm sorry, Vivila. I'm just really excited to properly meet my big brother's ma— To, uh, finally meet you. Won't you please come out from wherever you are hiding? You must be really hungry from sleeping all week. Let's go upstairs to the kitchen, just you and me."

"H-how do you know my name?" I asked without thinking.

"Aldric got your name from the King Cobras leader, when he demanded your freedom," Beatrix said. Her words seemed to end at a pause, like she was trying to choose the right ones, but finding it very difficult to hold back the information that she really wanted to say but for some reason couldn't.

Though I had heard her answer quite distinctly, I hadn't realized *how* hungry I was until Beatrix mentioned it. My stomach growled so loudly that there was little doubt as to where I was hiding. While both of the women sounded genuine and I wasn't entirely positive that they weren't armed, I wanted to see how close they actually were. Holding my breath and trying to squeeze through one of the windows didn't sound so stupid anymore. They were acting like they were offering me the key to the wardrobe that would allow me free access to Narnia, when I knew perfectly well there wasn't any key to Narnia—or a Narnia for that matter—and nothing came for free. These two women were trying to manipulate the situation to work in their favor like I wasn't wise to their plans. While I was naive to a lot of things, I wasn't in this moment. My hunger pains be damned. I thought about kicking the filing cabinet, guessing it would buy a few seconds of time. Though if they did have guns, knocking over the cabinet wouldn't have done me much good. I peered around the side of the file cabinet and saw that the two women were still standing by the door. Cautiously, I stood up and peered a little further out, noticing that they were definitely not armed.

This confused me. My brow knitted so close together I thought I might induce a headache, as I saw that they both had their hands raised in surrender. Why would they do such a thing? There had to be an ulterior motive. Based on the knowledge I had gained from fighting in the ring, I wasn't going to make the first move. But neither were they. I saw no void of emotions, like I had seen with the extra King Cobras members in Ross's office the other day—or last week? Gosh, I really don't know how much time had passed. This isn't good.

Nor do I see any contempt in their eyes for having to look upon a freak of nature. All I see is genuine concern. But it couldn't be for me, could it?

Am I dreaming? I must be dreaming. I am dreaming, I thought as I pinched my arm.

I felt a bit like Lucy from the book *The Lion, the Witch, and the Wardrobe*—naïve, innocent, and always wanting to see the good in everyone. Well, maybe not the last two. I don't think I'd qualify as innocent anymore after severely injuring my fellow classmates and killing some of Ross's fighters. Six years of constantly being let down has completely destroyed my ability to see the good in people... Ash aside, of course.

But I wanted to be more like Lucy, especially in this moment. How, though? I mean, it was so unreal to see these two women in nonthreatening positions; I was convinced I was dreaming. If these two are for real, then I have found the wardrobe leading to Narnia—to a world beyond the horrid war zone that has been my reality. Wearily convinced that I wasn't, I looked at both women—I mean **really** looked at them.

The woman closest to me was unfathomably beautiful. She appeared to be close to my age, about nineteen if I had to guess, and her olive skin and long black hair were both glistening and flowed with the summer's breeze in the warmth of the sun's light. Although she wasn't exactly tall, her body was made up of refined curves which were accentuated by the tight and slightly revealing clothing she wore. Then there were her eyes. I have always believed you can tell a lot about someone's personality through their eyes.

Almond-shaped dark brown eyes expressed her outspoken and tough exterior, but something told me that underneath she was also very passionate and loyal to the people she cared about. I couldn't help feeling both strangely envious and intimidated at the same time by this girl. Here was a prime example of what a teenage girl was supposed to look like and who had the sassy, moody attitude of a typical teen with many people wanting to be with her. Yet, I knew I would never be like this person in any of the ways I've described. I would always be nothing more than an ugly and worthless freak, undeserving of two words that had become so foreign to me... unconditional love.

Based on the stethoscope hanging around her neck, I assumed that the other woman, who stood with her hands still raised in a nonthreatening manner, was the doctor. She looked to be in her early forties, with thick shoulder-length wavy chestnut brown hair with a few strands of white that she put up in a loose ponytail. If I were in Narnia, she would be Mrs. Beaver, for there was something maternal about how she held herself, in a way that made any tightness in my muscles seem to unconsciously and immediately relax. Perhaps it also had to do with how serenely lost I was in her muted green eyes that were so large they were almost perfectly oval. Her slightly form-fitting T-shirt hung delicately over her ample figure. She wore tight jeans tucked into suede Timberlands. The outfit seemed so informal in comparison to her occupation and the image I was building up in my mind.

Why was she not wearing green scrubs or a white lab coat, like I had seen on the King Cobras doctor and doctors from my childhood? And not that I've seen many women over the past six years; other than in old magazines, books, and the few that came to watch me fight. Nonetheless, her choice of footwear fascinated me. Timberland boots seemed to be more fitting of Beatrix's hard persona. Her boots also seemed to be more fitting for hiking or hard labor, not tending to sick people.

"Wh-who are you? What do you want with me? Where am I? Where's Ross? Why haven't his men found me already?" I blurted the questions without thinking before recoiling back behind the filing cabinet. It was then that I became acutely aware of the warm throbbing pain in my neck. I reached up to touch it, but immediately retracted my hand. Even though there was a gauze bandage taped around part of my neck, the wound still stung. The doctor must have removed the tracking device while I was sleeping.

"You are quite safe. The King Cobras will inflict no harm on you any longer," the doctor said. "My name is Doctor Wade, but you may call me Doc—or Agatha. This is Beatrix, the sister of our—boss. As to where you are, well, you are in Ambler, my dear. Roughly a half hour from where you were rescued."

"Rescued? Why—why would you do that?" I asked from behind the cabinet. I didn't mean to sound as rude as I did. I shut my eyes tightly, waiting for them to rush over and strike me—to punish me in some way for speaking without being given permission. *Here it comes, here it comes, here it comes!* I screamed in my head. Though I was aware I had spoken out of turn twice without reprimand, it still surprised me as I dared to open my eyes again and listened very carefully. No movement was made in my direction.

"We want to help you without wanting anything in return. I can only speculate that this must be a new concept for you, but please give us the time to prove that our intentions are honorable," the doctor said calmly.

What if I'm wrong? I thought. *What if this Agatha person is not like Mrs. Beaver and is the White Witch?* Instead of giving Turkish delights and the promise of the title of King of Narnia like the White Witch did to Edmund, Agatha is offering me clothes, a meal, and promising the two women's kindness has no hidden agenda. Though I have no way of proving it either way, not right now at least, if anyone truly deserves the title of the White Witch, it would be Ross and Gregory, the dwarf driving Ross's sleigh. So to speak. And even if I'm not wrong, the doctor's words are like sugar, too easily dissolved by water or broken apart, so I'm keeping my guard up because one can't stay in Narnia forever. Eventually, the adventure has to end and reality resumes once more.

"Yeah, come on," Beatrix chimed in. "Why don't you get dressed and we'll grab something to eat like I promised."

My head cocked to one side in curiosity as I watched Agatha's gentle guiding hand suddenly reach for Beatrix's forearm; then, the two of them walked slowly towards the door. But before approaching the doorframe, Agatha turned her attention back to me and said, "We'll go back in the hallway so that you may get dressed with some privacy. Would that be all right with you?"

I wasn't sure what I had to lose at this point or why she bothered to ask if I would be okay with this. Shouldn't it be the other way around? All I could do was nod in compliance. When Agatha closed the door behind her, for reasons unbeknownst to me, I stood and stared at the door for some time as though I was studying it as an opponent before deciding to walk over to the chair with the folded clothes. Well, maybe not completely unknown. This was all new territory for me—clean environment, presented with clean clothes, and a genuine, kind attitude towards me.

I stared at the clothes not only because they were new and I had been afraid they were a mirage, but also because I wasn't commanded to put them on. This may seem ridiculous, but when you've been conditioned to eat when you're told to eat, to get dressed when you're told to get dressed, and to take a shower when you're told to take a shower, a simple allowance to dress when you want to throws you totally out of whack.

But again, what did I have to lose? Anything I did have to lose was already taken by Ross. Carefully, I first picked up the clean shirt, and got a whiff of the most heavenly, heavenly, heavenly floral aroma. I buried my face in the shirt, allowing my imagination to be transported to the meadow where the flowers lived in harmony. I could almost feel the warm rays of the sun on my skin and touch the petals stretching out from beneath the fabric. And as I pulled on each article of clothing, the warmth and aroma of the clothes surged throughout my whole body to the point that I nearly felt normal—nearly.

The reflection of the fluorescent lights above from the mirror by the door captured my attention next. It had been nearly two years since Ross had the ones in my bathroom removed and I had seen myself in a mirror. I wondered if I would still be able to recognize myself. I was sure I'd look a little older and my hair would look more like a savage wild animal's than a normal human being's. It would be no wonder why Agatha and Beatrix took a nonthreatening stance. If I looked like I thought I did, I wouldn't blame them for thinking I might attack them or go completely crazy at any minute. As I slowly walked towards the mirror to confirm my suspicions, I saw no wild animal or monster, just a hollow shell of a sad and pathetic girl.

My hair was indeed all over the place, but it was the dark rings under and around my eyes and how predominant my cheekbones stuck out that frightened me. The cuts and bruises didn't help either. Who was this girl in the mirror? Though I knew it was me, it took more effort than I thought it would to fight the urge to look away. It was no wonder I was as repulsive as Ross had always insisted I was. I touched the mirror with one hand and covered my eyes with the other as if I could magically erase the ugliness that was me, or discover by simply touching the mirror that it was all an illusion. If the latter were true, and not in my imagination, when I put both arms to my side, I might be beautiful. Stupid, I know, and when I did place my arms to my sides, the truth remained. I was not transformed into someone that another could love or accept. And this made me feel even more stupid.

Brushing such foolishness aside, because it wasn't going to change the fact that I was wasting time, especially with the two women waiting for me, I turned on the faucet to the sink below the mirror and splashed water upon my face like it would somehow wash away the gauntness of my face to something more normal. Yet as I ran my hands down my face to brush away some of the droplets from my eyes, merely touching the remaining cuts and bruises caused me to wince a little.

Well, I may not be able to magically erase how ugly I am,

and I am also aware how silly it was to think I could, but perhaps I could make my face even a bit less offensive by redoing my unnaturally white ponytail. I wanted to go over and reach for the coconut oil on the silver tray by the bed, but I didn't want to cause more trouble than I already had by unhooking myself from the beeping box and the tubes.

I would be lying if I said I wasn't startled by the sudden knock on the door and Agatha Doctor—Doctor Agatha—the Agatha person peering around the corner of the doorframe. Her huge smile, while seemingly warm, made me incredibly nervous. I had barely finished tying my hair back when my hands immediately dropped to my sides. It was difficult to maintain eye contact as she slowly entered the room again. I knew I must have done something wrong for her to come back in. She did say that she and Beatrix would wait in the hallway, didn't she? I was taking too long to get ready, wasn't I? *Oh God, oh God, oh God!* I closed my eyes so tightly it hurt a little as I waited for the punishment for having made them wait as long as they did.

Here it comes. Here comes my punishment... These were the thoughts running through my mind. My eyes were still shut, not letting an ounce of light in. I waited for confirmation that I had gone from one hell to another.

"I realized—" Agatha started to say.

Here it comes!!! I thought, biting down on my lower lip so hard I was certain I would break the skin. "—that I hadn't removed the needles from your arms," Agatha continued. "I can't imagine they are very comfortable."

"What?" I said in surprise, opening my eyes as I looked directly into the doctor's eyes, searching for some sign that she was kidding.

"Would it be okay for me to approach you to remove the needles that connected you to our equipment?" Agatha asked calmly.

My brow furrowed as I stared at her for some time, trying

to wrap my brain around the fact that I wasn't in trouble. I waited for the switch in mood—like Ross had done so many times. He would sometimes go from really nice to horribly cruel in a matter of minutes before striking me or making me feel insignificant somehow. It was one of his favorite tactics to torture me with. Yet, with each passing second and minute, to my surprise, the switch never occurred. It wasn't until a light breeze swept through the windows and across my shoulders, like it was trying to give me some form of encouragement, that I nodded in response to her question—however hesitant about submitting to her request. A switch was going to occur from nice to mean. It is going to happen, right?

CHAPTER SIX

Cautiously, and with bated breath, I obliged to Agatha's gesture to sit upon the bed, unable to keep myself from anticipating the switch from kind to cruel. I also cautiously obliged when she gently raised my arm with all of the needles in it. I desperately want to pull away, for if the switch happened, I didn't desire to be in her reach. I was so fixated on her every movement as she placed what looked like a cotton ball on the spot by where the needles went into my skin with one hand and dragged the needle out with the other. I intently watched her placing white medical tape on top of the cotton ball. And still, during all of this, in complete silence, the switch in her mood never occurred.

"There," Agatha finally says in a cheerful tone, my eyes drifting to hers at the break of the quiet. "Now that that is over, how about we get you something to eat?"

At the mention of food again, my stomach growls so loudly that I cover my midsection in hopes of shielding my embarrassment, though I can feel my cheeks growing red. I couldn't possibly hide both. *Oh God, oh God, oh my God!* I closed my eyes and held my breath as I awaited my punishment—for speaking without permission, trying to escape, my temptation in wanting to use the coconut oil, and last and most importantly, for my stomach growling in hunger. Yes, I had gone long periods of time without food, but I mastered not showing or hearing the pain of it from any of the King Cobras—well, at least I thought I had. If Ross were here to hear my stomach growl... I shuddered at the thought. I didn't know how things worked here with these two women, but I learned it was better to face the music than to delay it. Delaying only made the punishment ahead that much worse.

So, I quickly slid off the bed to my feet, turned my back toward her, clasped my hands together behind my head, and dropped to my knees. When I didn't feel the ice-cold metal harshly wrapped on my wrists or the scorching slice from a whip across my back, I became confused. More confused than her offer to remove the needles. But I didn't dare move. Not my head. Not my hands. Nothing.

The doctor continued to prepare the necessary equipment to remove the needles, as I did my very best not to move. If I'd learned anything from being owned by Ross, especially in circumstances similar to this, I'd learned that moving could result in punishments, including *additional* whips you didn't think you'd receive. Moving got you a week or so of no food. Moving got you the beating from hell. Moving got you in more trouble than you could imagine. And back to reality, I heard the *thunks* and *thuds* of Agatha walking in my direction until she was standing right in front of me.

Don't look up. Don't look up, don't look up, I thought.

I unconsciously jumped at the touch of the doctor's hands on my arms, warmly guiding me to my feet. Her hold on me didn't release until I cautiously met her gaze. The smile on her face was alarming to say the least. Where did it come from? What did it mean? Was there a form of punishment that is far worse than any I have received from the King Cobras? Why was she smiling? When the smile didn't falter from the doctor's face, I swallowed one small gulp and let out a heavy sigh.

When Agatha gestured toward the door a moment later, I was feeling slightly less unnerved about following her request. My guard was still up, and I wasn't ready to believe that I was in Narnia just yet—though the look of delight and pleasure in Beatrix's eyes as she saw me in clean clothes was testing the sturdiness of my guarded walls. Again with the exception of Ash, I hadn't been given this small gesture of kindness in such a long time that I nearly had the wind knocked out of me. I need to wake up. I need to wake up from the false Narnia before it's too late, and then I'll be completely broken instead of nearly broken. *It is false, isn't it? Isn't it? ISN'T IT?!?!?* Oh God, I just don't know. Their eye contact was making me so self-conscious that I had to avert my eyes. Their alleged delight in my company would only turn into disappointment, would it not? Especially with a practically broken and crazy freak like me.

Perhaps the two women would be disappointed at their "Alpha" for having sent "pack members" to rescue me. This may not have been the most logical or rational train of thought, but this was my first time outside of the warehouse in six years, and I didn't know how things operated outside of those confines anymore. Not that I ever did before. I thought I had loving parents and look where that got me. I'd been a disappointment and a sideshow prize my whole life—or at least that's how it felt. My eyes darted around the hallway, perhaps with thoughts of how to escape now that I had a slightly better idea of what this building was, or perhaps to distract myself from my self-deprecating thoughts.

With no windows in sight, aside from the ones in the room I had exited from, the hallway reminded me of the caverns under cathedrals I had seen in one of my books. I must be in a sort of Narnia because I had come to assume all basement hallways consisted of barely swept cement floors dusted by the peeling paint of the plastered walls, the insufferable smell of mildew, and harsh, occasional flickering of fluorescent lighting. But this! *This* was most definitely a cathedral in comparison. Polished, pristine, and cream-colored rectangular flagstone that was broken up by marbled and geometric shapes. Old-timey lantern-shaped light fixtures hung brightly and were equally spaced down the arched ceiling. Cherry wood framed the doors and faux wood columns. The space embodied warmth, strength, and dignity like no place I had ever seen.

"Viv? Viv?" Beatrix said.

"Hmm?" I replied absently.

"Is it okay that I call you that?"

"Hmm," was all that I seemed to be able to mutter, my eyes refusing to break from taking in every detail of my surroundings.

"So, what would you like to eat?" Beatrix asked, trying to sound upbeat. I may have only known her for a very short while, but her tone seemed forced for her personality. It didn't seem malicious because that sort of forced cheerfulness I was all too familiar with from the King Cobras. No, this was the sort of forced cheerfulness that appeared to come from a place of not wanting to scare me more than I already was, being in a strange environment.

"Whatever scraps that you don't want will be fine. Thank you," I replied.

I could tell that what I said must have been incorrect because when I finally looked back at them, the two women looked at one another in utter confusion and shock. There was an underlying pity in their gaze. *Stupid! Stupid, Vivila!* As they quickly composed themselves, their flabbergasted expressions were replaced with smiles and gestures toward the stairwell three yards ahead of where we stood. My throat tightened, embarrassed once again as I took a few steps back in the direction of the medical room. My vision made the walls seem to close in on me. I can't do this, *I can't do this without making a bigger fool of myself...*

"What do you plan to do with me? Why haven't you hand-cuffed me?" I blurted, my back hitting the doorframe with such force I fell to the floor. "Ross would never have tolerated this deliberate disregard of procedures, especially when it came to me. What do you want with me? What do you want with me?"

Pulling my knees to my chest, ignoring the sharp sting

shooting down my spine, I swayed back and forth as I purred to soothe myself. I used to purr all the time during my first few months at the warehouse but found it to be pointless when I realized I would never leave Ross's grasp. However, being that I was in a strange environment, perhaps it was okay to do so again. Hopefully, it is safe to purr again, I thought.

I didn't think I could stop myself from purring even if I wanted to. As large as the space was in the hallway, it never felt so minuscule. It didn't help that all I could see was blurred masses in various stages of grey. If only these two women would have answered my questions or punished me for my purring or the audacity of asking questions without permission in the first place. Even half of what Ross would have normally done if he had seen me in what he deemed to be a pathetic state—if only. I would feel I was regaining some semblance of control, of calmness. Amidst the tornado of anxiety circling my whole being, I barely registered the warm mass of knees down in front of me, the woman's hands softly running up and down my arms.

"Perhaps a little sedative to help calm her nerves, Doc," I hear the warm mass say, who I immediately identify as Beatrix.

I heard footsteps retreating into the room and returning moments later, followed by an all too familiar pinch in my arm from a needle. I could feel my anxiety slowly wash away, though my unanswered blurted questions still remained. Slightly foggy, and as relaxed as my mind and body now was, I could only hope I would now get the answers to them.

"Come on, my dear," Agatha said, helping me to my feet. "We plan to keep you safe, I assure you. You are our guest here. Nothing less. Alph—Beatrix's brother will give you the answers you seek in more detail soon enough. But right now, let's go upstairs and get you something to eat."

"Yeah, come on! We don't bite—much," Beatrix said with a bit of a chuckle, assisting the doctor in guiding me toward the stairs.

With a sideways glance, first to the doctor, then to Beatrix, I noticed Agatha scowl at Beatrix as though she wasn't pleased with Beatrix's comment. I said nothing after that, and neither did Beatrix.

Silence lingered as the three of us made our way up the stairs. Yet, I couldn't shake off this feeling that the two of them were holding an unspoken conversation. How? I wasn't sure. Perhaps they were talking and the sedative the doctor had given me was impairing my hearing. But that notion was quickly dismissed by the sounds of their shoes echoing between the walls.

My brow scrunched together as I looked back and forth between them, their expressions changing without reason and their lips unmoving. Even weirder was the fact that they seemed to be looking past me. Telepathy, perhaps? But that's ridiculous because that doesn't exist—does it? After more time had passed, I figured that I was reading too much into it and decided to disregard it for now as I continued to follow them. When we reached the top of the stairs, which opened up to what I presumed to be a very large living room, Beatrix temporarily released her supportive grip on me to raise and slap her arms at her side.

"I know!" Beatrix hissed at Agatha.

The two women briefly turned their attention to me, embarrassed expressions across their faces, before each quickly flashed me a grin. The odd change of looks caused more suspicion about whether the decidedly imaginary telepathic conversation between them wasn't so imaginary after all. I am definitely going mad. The weirdness wasn't made better when Beatrix explained how the room before us was their main living area, which I had already confirmed in my mind. It was nearly as large as The Pit. There were three curved couches arranged to form a crescent moon, which was very strange. Why would one living room need this many couches? All of them were a deep muted green.

Then there were at least seven spherical glass lanterns hanging from the ceiling too. A part of each of the lanterns was partially blacked out. Very, very strange. It took me some time to realize the lanterns were purposely depicting the different phases of the moon. Why? Did they worship the moon or something? Yet, as I looked over from the table in the middle of the crescent couches and the larger table behind the couches, both made entirely of branches, perhaps the décor alluded to nature worship or a deep-rooted connection to nature? Either way, the room appeared vastly different to the cathedral-like basement.

Oh geez! I hadn't realized how deep in thought I was nor the fact that both Agatha and Beatrix were no longer by my side until a sharp and distinct smoky, salty scent tickled my nose, bringing me back to the present and away from my over-analyzing thoughts. Oh, I hope, I hope, I hope Agatha and Beatrix aren't upset with me for lollygagging, but that combination of scents is so invigorating. Ross, Gregory, the King Cobras and the abuse were almost fading away in a heavy fog—a fog that was somehow making me feel empowered and free; two things I never thought I would feel, even in the confines of my own mind. And this particular "fog" could only come, as far as I knew thus far, from one person. My ability to breathe or focus on anything else was being held prisoner by my tonsils, as I dared to think of the name of this person—Alpha Aldric. A person I both feared and was intrigued with because I feared the mystery behind why the aroma had such an effect on me.

Frantically, I searched from where I stood for the source, hoping that it was Alpha Aldric. When he didn't appear, disappointment dug a hole in my chest, and even more so when the scent suddenly trailed away. Oh, I was most certainly *not* like Lucy from the *Lion, the Witch, and the Wardrobe*. Without the strong scent of Alpha Aldric, I felt more like one of the White Witch's collection of victims turned to stone, imprisoned and suffocating from how low I was on the social totem pole. My vision blurred, much as it had down in the basement, so I closed my eyes and tried to focus on the direction of the trailing scent. I could feel myself curling inward again, the weight of my breathing pushing me to the floor and preventing me from hearing Agatha calling my name.

Not again! Not again! And not here, whatever this 'here' is. Agatha did say the Alpha would answer all of my questions about why I was here and what they planned to do with me. Her promise to prove their actions to be honorable was empty compared to my unwanted and jabbing thoughts repeatedly telling me how worthless I was and how no one could ever truly care about me without fulfilling their own secret agendas.

I wanted to deny the power of those thoughts because of how kind these women had been to me and the fact that I was clinging to believe Alpha Aldric's words, when I was in a coma-like state, about not wanting to lose me before having a chance to know me—but I couldn't help reflecting on the lack of experience in normal girl stuff like how to act in a large social situation, putting on makeup, or dating. From what I remembered about what Ross had told me about Alpha Aldric, what could I possibly have to offer besides a good uppercut?

My lungs felt constricted under the foolishness for even imagining, for one moment, that this man, this Alpha Aldric, would dream to think of me in a romantic way. A man who might as well be a figment of my imagination for as much as I knew about him. A man whose only identifier was his scent and what little Ross had told me about him.

But oh, how foolish I am. There is a distinct possibility Alpha Aldric doesn't really want to get to know me because he is like Ross and wants to own me so badly that he sent his men to infiltrate the warehouse. And for what? The pleasure of watching me fight his men? Pleasures of the flesh? Oh, God!

"Vivila!?" Agatha said, lightly placing her hand on my shoulder.

"I'm sorry!" I blurted without thinking, jumping back to face her.

My vision suddenly became very clear from once again being surprised back to the reality of the present.

"I didn't mean to startle you again, sweetheart," Agatha kindly said. "The kitchen is this way. Would you feel better holding my hand? This is a very large house. It's completely understandable for you to be overwhelmed by the house's size."

I nodded, looking one more time around the main living room for a shadow or a disturbance to a rug or furniture—something. To prove my mind hadn't gone deeper into insanity and imagined the scent had been close—that he had been close. Though most likely for different reasons, both Agatha and I displayed an expression of confusion. I shifted my gaze from my knees to the floor, back to the lovingly patient eyes, then opened and closed my eyes a few times. This was an insanely stupid method I occasionally used with some deep breaths when I was trying to will myself to push emotions or unwanted thoughts away. There was a time and a place to allow both to run free without consequences, but in front of strangers was not one of them. Especially with how insanely stupid I must have looked in this moment, though Agatha didn't show she thought that... at all. She simply helped me back to my feet and guided me through the double swinging doors that opened to the kitchen.

And as large as I thought the main living room was, this room was nearly just as big. It had black and white checkered marble floor, which reminded me of a movie I had once seen that was set in the early 1900s. *Secret Garden* perhaps, but I don't remember, so I can't say for sure. A huge black granite island with white-painted wood cabinets and drawers. Though I only counted four chairs lined on the side closest to me, I swear it could comfortably fit fifteen. An eight-burner stove stood behind the island with a ring of pots and pans hanging high above it.

While I did notice the ample counter space with the double-bowled copper sink adorned with calla lilies and irises, my attention was drawn to the warm and inviting smell of lavender and rosemary by the wall of windows. If I were in Narnia, this kitchen would almost resemble the one Mr. and Mrs. Beaver would have in their dam. However, I decided to keep this thought to myself. I was already coming across as crazy with the hiding behind the filing cabinet, the meltdown that required a sedative, and my overall naivety with how the world works outside of the warehouse—I didn't need another reason for the two women to think I was completely bananas. Then again, who was I fooling?

CHAPTER SEVEN

The early afternoon light shone in through a paned door at the far end of the kitchen. On the other side of the door was a small garden of herbs and wildflowers. Any contemplation of wanting to escape, now that a door to the outside world presented itself, was momentarily put on hold because it felt like an eternity since I had seen nature's unyielding beauty. I nearly cried.

One of the many downfalls of living in the basement at the warehouse in the rougher parts of the city was that plant life seemed to be snuffed out by the cement and mankind's disregard. Though there didn't seem to be any boundaries—or at least none the two women had told me about yet—I nervously looked over to Agatha and then to the door. I know I had told myself that I had nothing to lose by following them out the door of the medical room in the basement, I know—but my mind was having difficulty in not following the rules laid out by Ross, even though I knew perfectly well he wasn't here and his rules didn't apply—well, *fairly* certain.

When Agatha gestured that it was okay for me to go ahead—to go outside into the garden—I was still hesitant to move for a spell; it seemed too good to be true. But after all, that was the theme of today: "too good to be true." Looking over at Beatrix, I saw that there was an underlying emotion expressing pity behind the neutral exterior. Pity toward the chained and terrified animal I must have appeared to be. Pity toward the sheltered child I was and not the young woman I actually looked. She wasn't wrong—if my assumption of what she was thinking was correct. For even as I felt safe enough to dare to move, I stumbled a bit like a newborn calf as I walked. I forced myself with little success to ignore any additional thoughts showing on the two women's faces while they watched me going around the long chestnut dining table and out the door.

Without thinking, I yanked off the boots from my feet one by one. They were stifling to begin with. Not only because I had grown used to not wearing any kind of footwear, unless I was fighting, but also because of the amount of nervous sweat that had puddled within the boots. The oblong slabs of the stone path winding throughout the small garden felt warm under my toes—a little *too* warm. Not that I cared as I lifted my head and closed my eyes to bask in the sun's benevolent rays. It was heavenly. Even if Alpha Aldric was just another Ross and decided to have me killed or lock me away in an even worse and smaller room than the one I had back in the warehouse, it would be worth it because I would have this moment to help me escape in my mind. There were so many new smells that were fresh and free of the horrid aromas that I had to blanket myself with for six years.

Slowly, I raised my head and opened my eyes. I noticed that beyond the fir trees that acted as a fence around most of the garden, the sky transitioned from a light blue to white to a fading gold. Whispering strings of clouds skirted above each subtle color change. This gang—or pack or whatever they are—must be very rich (if the massive size of what I had seen of the house thus far wasn't enough of an indication) because I had also never seen this much open land before. Yes, the fence of trees blocked the majority of the view, yet it still couldn't hide the vastness beyond this garden. The forest bordering the perimeter made it appear that perhaps they didn't own as much property as my imagination wanted. Surely, they had neighbors. Surely, I was foolish in thinking they didn't because of the length of time I had been kept hidden from the outside world... right?

And yet, I was in awe of it all. I fell to my knees, my hands cupping the budding roses before me. I didn't care if the plant's thorns pricked my skin; I was going to keep absorbing all of what this Narnia had to offer. I hoped the White Witch, which was Ross, wouldn't return, bringing me back to the winter of my enslaved six years. Please, please, please let Alpha Aldric be like Aslan and not the White Witch's lesser-known brother!

"Vivila?" I heard Agatha say from behind me. "Why don't you come back inside and I'll make you a sandwich."

A robin hopped along the flagstone path, cocking its head to the side at me before going about its business. I slowly turned my head in Agatha's direction, brushing my nose against my shoulder and briefly comparing the earlier "meadow" fantasy of the clean clothes to the reality of this garden's aroma. Though nothing could be compared to the physical presence of nature, and the smell of the clean clothes was a nice substitute, this bit of Narnia had come to an end.

"Is it okay for me to put the boots back on?" I asked, looking at the bottoms of my feet and then up at the doctor. The soles of my feet didn't appear dirty to me—but my definition of dirty was most likely different from either of the two women's. I didn't know whose boots were lent to me and I wasn't about to mess them up more than I probably already had.

As I looked into Agatha's eyes, waiting for her permission, I realized I had once again said something wrong and all I could think of was *Oh God*. My feet were absolutely filthy! There was no way she would let me back inside to ruin the pristine kitchen floors. I looked around me for a hose so that I could wash off my feet. I couldn't put the boots back on, of course. *What was I thinking? Stupid, stupid Vivila*. A garden as well kept as this must have a hose—an outside spigot. Out of the corner of my eye, I noticed the sun reflecting off of a shiny surface. Taking a leap that it was what I was looking for, I rushed over to it before Agatha was finally about to answer my question. Just my luck, a first since I woke up in this place—well, second if you count me not getting caught using the coconut oil. A brass spigot presented itself at the corner of the house and one of the walls of trees.

I wasted no time in turning the handle and washed off as much of the light coating of dirt on my feet as I could before my hands gently guided me upward and away from the running water. I reached for the handle so I could at least turn the water off, but was stopped again by the same hands that had pulled me up to my feet. I moved my attention backwards to see who the hands belonged to. It wasn't too much of a surprise to find it was Agatha, but it still didn't stop me from feeling foolish once again.

I should have waited—I should have waited for her to speak before rushing so foolhardy to the spigot, I thought, unable to look her directly in the eyes. *Oh, what she must think of me.*

"Vivila," the doctor said calmly. "Why did you feel the need to wash your feet?"

"I don't know whose boots were lent to me and I didn't want to ruin them more than I already had," I said sheepishly.

"But they are *your* boots."

"No, they are not," I said, my words sounding more like a protest than I had intended.

"But they are," the doctor reiterated, "because I am giving the boots to you."

"Why?" I asked, finally looking at the ample figured woman in front of me.

"Why what, honeybun?" Agatha asked.

"Why would you do such a thing, when I haven't done anything to earn them?" I answered, the wind slightly knocked out of me from the shock of her generosity.

"Because I wanted to, nothing more." She met my gaze with a smile.

A strong part of me wanted to question her "gift" of these boots, but I couldn't find the words to continue. Another part of me wanted to think that maybe what Agatha and Beatrix said about wanting nothing in return for their kindness was true. But unfortunately, I'm weak. Maybe not physically, but mentally—very much so. *Do what you do whenever Ross or Gregory acts nice to you; play long and keep your **guard up**.* That—that is what I recoiled into. I wasn't proud of this plan. I didn't like resorting to this plan, but I still didn't know these two women long enough to *not* resort to this plan.

If I ever learned to play poker, I would have the best "poker" face—not in the world... in every galaxy in all of space! All right, that's a little overdramatic, but you get the picture. Total composure and total control on the outside but weeping and decaying on the inside. Or, in other words, act dumb and compliant on the outside but ultimately—totally guarded.

"Oh, well thank you," I said, hoping my voice sounded normal and not robotic and forced. It really was nice of her to give me the boots and I wasn't so broken to be without heart, but it was all still very strange and new to me. Like I said, I just didn't know how else to react. I needed to play along until I could be absolutely certain of the two women's true intentions.

As Agatha stepped back and gestured to go back inside the kitchen, I took one last glance up into the sky and breathed in the many earthy aromas—some floral and some with a bit of a sharp bite to them—before turning off the water pouring from the spigot and following the doctor's lead. I carried the boots in my hand because the thought of putting them on, regardless of my pretend compliance, still made me feel uncomfortable. And I could only hope my wet feet didn't pick up any dirt along the way to and onto the kitchen floor. My rising anxiety at this thought had my heart thumping erratically with each step and my breathing growing heavy and shallow. I held my breath a bit to not sound like a wild animal.

Inside, Beatrix graciously offered the chair next to hers. After I carefully placed the wet boots by the door, I cautiously made my way over to her, my hands grasping the back of the offered chair in such a way as to ensure it didn't groan or mark the tiled floor. Especially so when I sat upon the chair and pulled myself closer to the table. An act of compliance and letting my guard down I may have been portraying, I also didn't want to give away that it had been six years since I had sat on a chair—six years since I had sat at a table for that matter. Neither of the two women seemed to notice. Beatrix was too preoccupied relaying how she wanted to take me shopping and show me around town with such an energetic speed I thought my head would implode. I didn't know how to respond, so I simply kept quiet.

When the doctor suddenly presented a ceramic plate holding a BLT. sandwich in front of me, my eyes widened at the sight of fresh food that wasn't rotten and hadn't been tampered with. I was, at first, afraid to touch it. Lowering my head, I sniffed the sandwich and then carefully allowed my fingers to skim the surface of the bread, forgetting momentarily how this must have looked to both of the women. That was until I saw Agatha sit down on the chair opposite me. Swallowing a huge gulp, I shot up from the chair I was sitting in. I would have said "my chair," but let's be honest, the chair didn't belong to me, nor did the savory sandwich before me. And yet neither of the two women made any movement to take the plate away from me.

I recalled a few times when Gregory had brought me a plate of fresh food. He stood with some of his lackeys to watch me eat it. The food would have live cockroaches stuffed inside or have a wire connected to a stun gun, and either surprise would result in hearty laughter and, of course, a complete shock to my system. Yet, as I lifted one side of the sandwich in front of me, there wasn't either. Looking over to both of the women, who stared at me with grins spreading across their faces, I concluded they must be waiting for me to ask permission or at least I assumed they were. I mean, why else would they be grinning? It could be because they were pleased to have my company.

Maybe they were one of those weirdos like Gregory who

enjoyed watching me when his lackeys weren't around. But this didn't seem to be the case here, or I hoped not. Though I didn't see an emptiness behind their shared expression, like the ones I had grown accustomed to by every King Cobras member except Ash, I couldn't determine which form of permission they desired. So I continued to wait, concentrating on the chirping of birds out in the garden as I did so.

The smell of the bacon alone was heavenly, but I didn't dare touch the BLT. I half expected both Agatha and Beatrix were growing tired of me constantly waiting for permission, though neither of them showed it. I wasn't going to let my guard down and idiotically take a bite without the go-ahead, despite my act of playing along with their "no strings attached" kindness. I am not that naïve—or maybe I am. I've been extremely sheltered these past six years and don't know how "normal people" interact with one another. This was just very confusing—very overwhelming... their kindness. There has to be a catch because there is always a catch, and yet when both of the women finally understood what was taking me so long to take the first bite, there was still no sign of a catch. No sign of a catch, like when the doctor removed the needles from my arms. It truly was a Narnia of paradise, if these women were for real—if this Alpha Aldric was for real. Whatever he looked like.

After Agatha and Beatrix gestured that it was okay to start eating, I finally took a bite and—oh my! The bread was so soft, the bacon seemed to melt with the mayonnaise, and the tomato was incredibly ripe and refreshing. The grease from the bacon and the juice of the tomato were dribbling down my chin. The sandwich was like nothing I'd had in such a long time that I had a hard time focusing on anything that wasn't this sandwich.

Out of breath by the time the last bite arrived, I became very self-conscious when I finally looked up to see both Agatha and Beatrix were staring at me. Had they been watching me eat this whole time? Was there food on my face? With my horrible table manners, specifically scarfing down the sandwich like an untamed wildebeest, it was no wonder they were staring. I could feel my face turn red and nervous knots forming in the pit of my stomach.

"Jesus!" Beatrix exclaimed, slamming both her fists so hard on the table I thought it would split in two. It didn't, luckily, but the grimace on her face appeared to demand the table do so regardless. "Did the King Cobras ever feed you? Those bastards!"

"Beatrix Helen O'Connor!" Agatha scolded.

"What?" Beatrix replied with so much sass that I was certain she would be punished for speaking out to a woman fifteen years her senior.

Was it because her brother was the leader and pulled rank because of it? Either way, I pushed my chair away from the table because if Agatha was going to reprimand Beatrix, I wasn't going to be caught in the crossfire. My movement appeared to have gone unnoticed—though I wasn't sure how that could be. The two women glared at each other like two wolves refusing to back down from an unnecessary fight.

"This is not how we treat a guest," Agatha said with disappointment. "If your mother was alive to see this rude behavior..."

Beatrix scoffed as both of her hands lifted in the air before slamming hard on her thighs.

"We don't know the extent of what she has gone through," Agatha continued, the volume of her voice escalating with her finger pointing at Beatrix.

"I was just saying," Beatrix started to retort.

"This is a very large house for just the three of you. Do the other members of your gang live elsewhere?" I asked awkwardly and out of the blue, mostly because it felt weird to be the subject of a conversation like I wasn't there. Though honestly, it wasn't the first time I was talked about as if I weren't there;

it was the first time I had been talked about as if someone really cared about me and my feelings. Well, with the exception of Ash, of course. And as strange as it was to blurt out a question amidst a suddenly rising argument, it was enough to silence the both of them. However, having the attention drawn back at me may not have been the smartest move. *Stupid! Stupid! Stupid me!* Both Agatha and Beatrix then glanced up at each other, seemingly having yet another telepathic conversation.

This time, I was quite certain I wasn't imagining it. As the uncomfortable silence continued to build, I decided the best way to possibly redeem myself was to go over to the enormous sink and wash both my dish and hands. My adoptive parents weren't exactly "Parents of the Year," even before they sold me to Ross, and cleaning my place at the dinner table appeased them, so hopefully it would appease the two women. Plus, I didn't know how long the unspoken conversation was going to last, and I didn't want to seem ungrateful. But before I could get up from my chair, Beatrix lightly placed her hand on my forearm.

Startled by the touch and fearful of accidentally dropping the plate, I stared at her hand for what felt like the same length of time as the telepathic conversation that the two women just had. The plate shattered into a million pieces, causing my heart to pulsate so violently that my body shook uncontrollably. The weight of my breath demanded that I curl into myself again and elicited a desire to hide.

"Viv-baby, relax," Beatrix said in a calming tone, moving from where she had sat on the chair next to me to squatting down in front of me. "Breathe —in—out—in! That's it. Good."

"You're not in trouble. Accidents happen all the time. Just stay where you are and I'll grab the dustbin and broom, dear," Agatha said, her hand resting on my shoulder before she exited the kitchen.

"I'm—I'm sorry if my question was inappropriate and I-I did-didn't want you to th-think I was ungrateful for everything both of you and Alpha Aldric have done for me," I stuttered, slowly lifting my gaze to meet Beatrix's. I wasn't sure if what I just said made any sense, but the words were out and I couldn't take them back. Oh, I was making so many mistakes today. They should just give me back to the King Cobras. I know how things operate there, but here—*oh geez, oh geez, oh geez.* Maybe if they would just whip me, I would calm down and stop making such idiotic errors. But why haven't they? It doesn't make any sense. Not at all. Not. At. All.

CHAPTER EIGHT

An apology, depending on what I had done in front of Ross, usually softened the punishment that would follow; especially if I spoke or voiced an opinion when I shouldn't have. And sometimes, I didn't know if I was going to get a punishment or a wrath of endless lectures and threats. It was as predictable as the changing wind direction, or rather the likelihood of seeing the wind before it came. With this conditioning of reminding others I was aware of being on the same level as a pebble in one's shoes, I awaited once again a similar reaction for doing the wrong thing. My already confused state was unprepared and taken to a new level with Beatrix's next words.

"Nonsense, you didn't speak out of line. You can ask or say whatever you want; especially with how much we are still strangers to you and you're still trying to figure us out," Beatrix said with a smile. "But how do you know my brother's name is Aldric and that he is the Alpha?"

"I heard it, while I was sleeping—so-sort of," I answered. I didn't know how to explain how I had been able to hear both Agatha and Aldric talk. I still wasn't quite sure myself.

"Fair enough," Beatrix answered.

"And your question wasn't inappropriate at all. I'm sorry if we made you think that it was," Agatha said upon her return to the room. "Alpha ordered everyone, except for the two of us, to not enter the pack house or sleep here until you had time to adjust and fully heal."

"May I ask another question?" I quietly asked.

"Girl—you can ask as many questions as you'd like!" Beatrix said as she combed her fingers through her long black hair and shrugged like what I had just said was common sense.

"Why do you call him 'Alpha Aldric'? I've never heard a gang leader being called 'Alpha' or a gang called a 'pack.'"

"That, my darling," Agatha replied cautiously as she kneeled down to begin sweeping up the shards of broken plate, "is something that would be best told to you by Alpha. Despite Beatrix being his sister, it is not our place to say."

"When will I meet him?" I asked.

"Soon," Agatha assured.

Not much was said after that. I was glad of that because it left little room for me to create another mistake and another meltdown. Agatha insisted on showing me to my bedroom, which was three times larger than the one I had back at the warehouse and on the third floor. And as I followed her, I couldn't help reflecting again on how strange it was that neither of the two women had shown any annoyance toward my many meltdowns thus far. Had I been back at the warehouse— well, never mind. I didn't want to think about that right now. I quickly switched subjects in my mind with Agatha's words of "soon." Why would Alpha Aldric put so much effort into "rescuing" a freak like me if he weren't going to introduce himself? Admittedly, this wasn't a new question that had crossed my mind, but "soon"? How soon was soon?

By the time I had asked myself that question, I nearly bumped into Agatha. She had stopped in front of the door and turned, I guess to see if I was still behind her. It was an ordinary wooden door. No mini sliding doors inlaid in it, like the door to my room back at the warehouse. I did notice a keyhole below the brass doorknob, a pretty flimsy mechanism if they suddenly decided to lock me in. I quizzically looked at the doctor, wondering why we were just standing in the hallway, but she merely smiled back and finally opened the door.

Peering hesitantly inside, my mouth dropped in awe as I

saw that the room was pristine and the furniture looked brand new—like everything else in this castle of a house. There was not a single plastic pallet on the floor like my bedroom at the warehouse. How would I keep the floors clean without them? I may have washed my feet with the water from the spigot in the gardens, but not well enough to make me feel any less uncomfortable. Yet, at the same time, I didn't want to appear rude, did I? I could hardly focus on what Agatha was saying as I took a step no further than the doorframe in fear that I might break something. I also felt out of place. Who am I kidding? I *am* out of place. This... this was meant to be my room?

There was no way I could accept such a gift of this stature. Though I told Agatha this, she waved off my nonsense and beckoned me to come into the room so she could finish relaying all the amenities of the room. She also tried to comfort me by saying I was a guest in this house and it would only be polite for me to be treated as such. Yet this was very overwhelming, especially when I heard I would have my own bathroom and "my" bedroom was across the hall from Alpha Aldric's.

"Well, I'll leave you to it," Agatha said.

I stepped out of the way as the doctor made her way out of the room, my eyes not leaving the marvel within. There was definitely no way I could accept such a gift as this room, particularly at the reminder of my bare feet having been outside. Neither Agatha nor Beatrix had said anything back in the kitchen, but I couldn't just assume it went unnoticed, could I?

"Feel free to explore," Agatha said, which startled me into facing her. "If you need Beatrix or me, both of our rooms are at the end of the hallway. Although I do have some work to do, so you may find me in my office down in the basement by the room you woke up in. Dinner will be ready around seven, if you get hungry."

I gave a short nod, hoping I didn't come across as looking like a complete moron, jumping in the air when I was just startled. Then again, looking like a moron may be inevitable.

Not that I like the idea. Oh God, I could feel myself growing overly nervous again—vision blurring, racing heart, need to curl into—I jumped back into the present when Agatha's hand gently rested on my shoulder again. What, is this her thing? Hands on the shoulder? It was kinda nice though... I blinked my eyes a few times to be sure the smile was not in jest.

"It's all right, dear," Agatha said. "Go on in. If it's your feet you're worried about... one, dirt is easily cleaned up on hardwood floors... two, there is a direct path from here to the bathroom without worry of touching the rug under the bed... and three, both the sheets and the towels are easily washed."

With a wink, she guided me into the bedroom before closing the door behind her. My brows knitted as I mauled over her words while I stood in the same spot for what felt like hours. Not just because of what she said, but because I just didn't know what else to do. It had been six years since anyone had given me the freedom to go anywhere unaccompanied.

Six years since someone presented me with common human decency without fear of being caught and reprimanded. The air in this room smelled sweet and light, unlike my room back at the warehouse, which smelled dank and heavy. This freedom, in a room this large, was just too good to be true, and it was causing the air to suddenly become suffocating. More suffocating than my mouse hole of a bedroom in the warehouse. I just needed to be sure.

I hesitantly reached for the knob with bated breath. My fingers caressed the metal before I pressed my palm to it and turned the knob. My imagination was shocked to find that the door was unlocked and when I slowly and deliberately pulled it open, I was surprised to also find that no one awaited me on the other side. Carefully, swallowing a gulp large enough to be the size of a ping-pong ball, I peered around either side of the doorframe. No one. There's absolutely no one guarding the outside? It must be a ruse...

A ruse. A ruse. A ruse! I thought as I quietly closed the door and looked about the room. *What if there are cameras in my room and they are watching me to see how I will react to being in a room as magnanimous as this? Why is my room across the hall from their Alpha? To prevent me from running?*

My chest was heaving and my heart was thumping so fast until it noticed the window on the opposite side of the room. I could use the door, but with how large this house probably was, I would get lost and increase my chances of bumping into Agatha or Beatrix. Flying seemed the best option right now. However, with my lack of any practice flying, that should be a big red flag, so I decided to dismiss the idea as being completely idiotic. Unconsciously, I started to bite my nails. When my claws weren't out, my very human nails were pretty nonexistent with the amount of time I spent chewing on them. My human nails still grew at an abnormal rate. But I tended to chew on them when I was reading a good book or, in this case, when I was trying to figure out what the best course of action should be that would result in the least amount of consequences.

However, the doctor *did* say they would prove their intentions to be honorable. While they hadn't done anything to disprove this, in fact they had been very kind, I just—I don't know. My brows squeezed together in confusion and in a slight panic as I frantically searched every corner of the room for cameras and bugs. Though I had no real idea what to look for. *But I need to be sure. I absolutely need to be sure!* When I discovered nothing beyond the room being simply an ordinary room—and a very luxurious one at that—but with absolutely no hidden surveillance or entrapments like what I might expect to find if I were still in Ross's possession, the realization that Agatha had spoken the truth... well, I felt quite foolish for having the need to check. But could you really blame me after the hell I grew to accept as my normal for the last six years?

I walked over to the window, careful to not step on the rug because it looked very expensive and I didn't want to give the two women, not to mention Alpha Aldric, a reason to regret welcoming me into their home by placing my unworthy feet upon it. As I carefully reached for the two handles and applied gentle pressure to push open the double-paned window, I noticed two birds on a nearby tree bickering. The second-floor roof shingled with U-shaped terra-cotta just blocked the garden I'd briefly kneeled in only moments ago.

Although the sun had already begun its descent below the horizon, and despite my keen eyesight, I had to squint to fully see what was beyond the first row of trees. There appeared to be either a path or narrow dirt road leading to a circle of houses, shingled in the same material as the second-floor roof. Was my first assumption of Alpha Aldric and his pack's property vastly correct? If so, then the idea of escaping is unwise. Where would I go? I have no money and limited knowledge about how to survive in the outside world.

I closed my eyes for a few seconds, inhaling deep and heavy breaths, trying to will my paranoia, if only for the time being. Was I looking for malicious faults in the two women? In Alpha Aldric? Yes, yes, I was. Total paranoia parallel parking annoyingly in my thoughts was occurring. It didn't matter how hard I tried to put obstacles in this feeling's path so that I could breathe easier; the paranoia simply wasn't going away. It was totally weird that this Alpha Aldric emanated that mysteriously healing aroma. There I go again, my thoughts going all over the place. And yet, if he was willing to go great lengths to have Ross hand me over to him, pay for Gregory's hospital bills, and then send his men to ambush the King Cobras to "rescue" me—if he were willing to do all that, why was he refusing to show his face to me? Not to mention the words he said while I was in that coma/deep sleep situation. He didn't want to lose me before he had the chance to know me? Now that he finally found me? What was that all about? What the hell is going on!?

I turned my attention from the nature outside my window to study the maroon-colored curtains with an abstract floral design; first with my eyes and second with my fingers. I suppose I did so as a distraction, away from the thoughts that were making me more confused than before. Thoughts surrounding not only the mysterious Alpha Aldric but also some of the things Agatha had said before she left me in this room. As my finger drifted down the textured fabric, the bumps rising and falling like small mountains, I wondered again how comfortable I should allow myself to get in a room as nice as this. Calling this "my room" caused my stomach to go into nervous knots. I had a room and knowing how Ross felt about parting with his property; it would be *my* room until he was done with me. This once again emphasized the question on how comfortable I could really be here, especially when behind the dark-colored curtain was a thin and translucent white curtain. Why would there be a need for a second...

A yawn escaped before I could finish the distracted thought surrounding the curtains. I wasn't aware of how tired I was until it suddenly washed over me. I weighed my sleeping options from the bed to the floor, and while the white comforter looked so soft and puffy with more pillows than I had ever seen neatly placed on one bed before, the floor seemed like a safer bet. If I slept on the floor, I'd be less likely to ruin such fineries. Had the mattress and bedding been on par with the ones I had slept in back in my room at the warehouse, I might have felt comfortable sleeping in this bed before me. But this bed looked brand new and did not look at all like it should have been thrown out fifteen plus years ago.

I remembered what Agatha had said about both the towels and sheets being easy to clean, but did I dare go into the bathroom to use the towels as a makeshift bed on the floor? I resigned to rest my head on the carpet below the bed, while my body curled up on the bare floor. It was close enough to my bed back in the warehouse and I fell asleep almost immediately.

In my dreams, I found myself deep in a forest so entangled

with thick branches that the full moon looming above barely shined through. Alpha Aldric stood in a spot that appeared to be miles away, though how I knew the moon to be full or that it was him lurking in the shadows I couldn't say. I didn't dare move or speak in fear that this shadow form of Alpha Aldric would vanish. Even though I was aware of this being a dream, I could still feel the night's wind whisking through the trees and through my thick, white hair.

I frantically pushed my hair away from my face as I watched him slowly walk closer to me, and closer—the ground crunching under each of his steps until he was mere yards away from me. Yet even with the annoyance of the wind, the tree branches above didn't move enough to allow more moonlight to shine enough so that I could finally see what he looked like. But that shouldn't have mattered. I mean, my eyes were adjusted to the dark, especially being a Winged Ail... whatever Agatha had called me. He should have been visible enough for me to make out some features, but for whatever reason he was presented as nothing more than mere shadow. No, no, no! This can't be. This is just unfair. Completely and utterly unfair. Why? Just one little visual to prove he was real and not some imaginary dark mass.

My frustration was reaching the breaking point as this dream continued. Not only was Alpha Aldric appearing as a black mass, but the silence was becoming unbearable. Should I be the one to speak? I quickly decided no. If Ross was correct on what he had told me back in his office, here was a man of great power, and the man's strange title of "Alpha" was proof of that. And though I knew this was only a dream and would hold no consequences in the waking world, I was still hesitant to speak. I still wanted to give a good impression—I *needed* to give a good impression. Why? I didn't know. Just as I didn't know why there was this strange and strong gravitation toward this man. It was like he was the yin to my yang. Whatever that cliché meant... All right, I knew what the expression meant—but not in relation to Alpha Aldric. It frightened me, there was no denying that. A man I didn't really know. Oh, why isn't he saying anything? Why? Why? Why?

Then Alpha Aldric spoke. His voice, though I couldn't hear any distinguishable words, was still as husky and sultry as I remembered from during my sleep down in the basement. It was almost as though it counterbalanced my light and airy voice. But why? Perhaps if I crept slowly toward him, closing the gap between us, I could hear him more clearly. The wind swept in behind me, encouraging me to move into the shadows with him. However, despite my excellent night vision, Alpha Aldric still only appeared as a black mass. Frustration built up from the pit of my stomach to my face like a heavy and steaming cloud. I'm not sure what motivated me to do this, but I raised my hand to touch him. If I could just pull him away from the shadows and closer to me, he would cease to be a black mass and I would see him at last.

But then, in the distance, marching closer and closer to where he and I both stood, a mysterious and sudden loud wood drum tapped once—twice—thrice. I turned my head in the direction of the drum for a moment—a millisecond of a moment. Was an army approaching—a gang? Though as far as I knew, drums were no longer used to sound the start of a battle. However, were this to be the start of an out-of-nowhere battle, I was somehow certain the two of us would overcome the...

I returned my gaze to the black mass of Alpha Aldric, the drum rapping louder and louder. I stood there frozen in agonizing shock at what I was unexpectedly seeing. The image caused the air in my lungs to feel depleted almost instantaneously. Alpha Aldric began to whisk away into nothing, as though he had been nothing more than a mirage made of sand.

"Come back!" I shouted, the sound of the drum becoming increasingly deafening. "Please don't leave me here!"

Survival from whatever was approaching was no longer a possibility. I could find a tree to climb, but never learned how.

I closed my eyes and focused with all my might to force myself to shift, for though I'd never had an opportunity to learn to fly either, it seemed like my only option.

TAP-T-T—TAP, THUNK!

My concentration was abruptly broken at the oddness of the last rap of the drum. All of my panic quickly changed to confusion. This no longer sounded like a drum or an announcement of an unknown battle, but a knock on a door. Then I remembered I was dreaming. *It's just a dream, just a dream, just a dream. Wake up! Wake up, Vivila.*

My eyes slowly fluttered open as I remembered I had only been dreaming—and the drum rolling away in the dark forest was actually someone knocking on the door. Yet, it did take me a few to remember I was still lying on the floor of this nice bedroom and not back in my room at the warehouse. It wasn't until I heard the knocking once again that I pushed myself off of the floor, noticing the towels nearby and throwing them under the bed. I walked over to the door slowly. As weird as the dream was that I had just awakened from, I decided it would be incrementally weirder for whoever was on the other side to see that I did not sleep in the bed.

"Wh-who is it?" I said. My voice was straining to get the words out.

"Vivila? It's Beatrix."

"Come—come in." I attempted to smooth my hair down.

Taking a few steps back, I watched the door creak open and heard the clattering of metal and dishes along with it. Though Agatha had said this was "my" room, I still couldn't help rubbing my arm from the guilt. Guilt from what may seem out of place since I hadn't done anything wrong—but as I had mentioned earlier, I felt very uncomfortable and out of place in this room; in this enormous house. I darted my eyes from the floor to Beatrix as I caught glimpses of her putting the tray in her hands on the dresser adjacent to the door. Perhaps if I move closer to the corner by the window, I can hide behind the curtain and disappear, I thought. I was most likely making a usually normal situation incredibly awkward. I could feel her eyes on me and it wasn't helping.

"Hey, hey! It's okay," Beatrix said, raising both of her hands in the air in surrender. "I'm just bringing you a tray of food since you missed dinner."

"Wha—what time is it?" I asked.

"Like 8:30," Beatrix answered, pulling out her phone from her back pocket.

"I'm sorry. It won't happen again."

"You don't need to apologize. We kind of sprung a lot on you for your first day. No biggie, okay?"

I nodded.

"My brother wasn't sure what kind of food you liked," Beatrix chuckled as she pretended to examine what was on the tray. "There's a little bit of everything on here."

"Thank you," I blurted with a squeak, like I was some pubescent boy.

"Don't feel obligated to eat it all, okay?"

I nodded before asking, "When will I meet your brother? I—I mean Alpha Aldric." I bit my lip, anticipating that asking this question again would finally be the one to get me in trouble with these people—this pack.

"I'm not sure," Beatrix said with a shrug and leaning her shoulder against the wall. "Maybe like when the Doc said, 'soon.' Usually I can predict when my older brother does things, but with you being his—uh-tsk—hmm, I don't know, Viv."

"His what?" I asked, growing more than a little annoyed with the cryptic-ness of these women's answers. His what? His, his, his—I was bewildered at what Beatrix was trying to say. How could I be anything to Alpha Aldric, when I was nothing to him—to anyone—except to Ross as a key source of income? This left me to wonder... why am I here?

CHAPTER NINE

I found myself fidgeting as I continued to wait for Beatrix to explain herself—if Beatrix *would* explain herself. My mind raced to every tangent to find answers that might explain this ownership by Alpha Aldric. I had entered into a new hell, possessed by a new owner, which made my heart sink to the pit of my stomach. I felt utterly foolish; however high my guarded walls still were and skeptical as I was of them, to have even a sliver of hope otherwise. But nothing surprised me more than when Beatrix finally spoke.

"He'll tell you when the time is right. I wouldn't worry about it. But anyway, I'll let you eat. Tomorrow, if you're up for it, we'll go shopping for clothes. No offense, but Doc's clothes make you look like a hot mess," Beatrix said with a chuckle again.

"You—you don't have to. These clothes are fine."

"Babe, relax. Great Wolf! They must have—uh, look. Don't worry about—" Beatrix said.

I had a feeling I knew how she was going to finish her sentence before she cut herself off. Bringing up her disgust, once again, about how the King Cobras treated me. Though their treatment wasn't right, it had become my normal. And yet, this time, her almost words released all my pent-up anger that I had been suppressing since my last meeting in Ross's office. It could have been due to how kind the two women had been to me thus far. It could have been due to Alpha Aldric thinking I was worthy enough to be rescued, though I still didn't know why. There was a chance that the three of them would truly be another version of Ross, and the doctor's words about proving their intentions to be honorable were similar to the lies Ross tended to give me—to hurt me and my self-esteem.

Whatever the reasoning for this release of pent-up anger, I was suddenly triggered—via her almost Freudian slip, by the remembrance of Ross's reminder that he owned me, he had no intention of letting me go, and the people who I thought were my real parents were actually not. It hurts enough to know that they sold me instead of loving and accepting me as their own. It was possible Ross was lying, but his words have a tendency to sting regardless. And there was no way I was going to forgive him for tying me to his seating box above The Pit like I was some damn trophy! I also didn't know what I would do if I saw his face again or if I would get away with it, but I wanted to do something to him. Something really bad that would cause him immense pain.

As my hands curled tightly into fists, I could feel my claws grow and dig into my palms. Even after I felt the blood begin to seep out and I heard the first drop hit the hardwood floor, my rage still grew—well, until the points of my wings and tail desperately tried to push through my skin like a million knives stabbing into my whole back. My knees buckled and my body slammed to the floor. My hands would have lessened the pain of hitting the floor if it weren't for the unexpected throbbing headache, particularly around my temples. I screamed for it to stop. Though it was extremely embarrassing for this to be happening in front of Beatrix, it was difficult to focus and to breathe. It was like I had been thrown into a huge vat of water and, because I don't know how to swim, it felt as though I was drowning.

"Sorry, my mouth kinda has a mind of its own. Viv, Viv, you need to calm down," she said. I could barely hear her speak. Her voice sounded almost marbled. "Breathe, Viv. I'll, uh, go get the doctor. I'll be back soon. Shit! Shit! Shit!"

I heard her awkwardly turn to run out the door and down the hallway, which sounded like a faraway echo. Sinking deeper in the waters of my own anxiety, a rope in the form of a very recognizable salty and smoky aroma stretched out like a lifeline just out of my grasp. The closer it came, the more the weight of drowning in water began to empty, and the easier it was to breathe and focus on the present—away from the entrapment of my own psyche. The pain that was present in my upper and lower back slowly shriveled. I wanted to question why this relief was occurring so quickly, but was too overjoyed that the pain was vanishing. I also wanted to question why he was present now of all times. Yet, I was growing too tired to allow my mind to ponder any further.

"Aldric?" I whispered without thinking about the possible consequences of addressing him so informally.

"Shh," was all he responded with. He gently lifted me into his arms.

I used to cry myself to sleep or simply pass out in somewhat similar moments like these because no one ever thought to comfort me. Not in the last six years, at least. Yet, here were two strong arms that could easily break every bone in my body, holding me like I was some precious gift. I tried to open my eyes and look up at him, but I saw nothing more than a blurred image. Just as in my dream, he was a black mass. But unlike my dream, he was solid and tangible. No drums to tap him out of existence, especially as he lifted me up, his heavy footsteps moving us to the bed with no risk at all of dropping me. As my anxiety continued to subside, my hearing grew clearer by the second, and with one swift motion, he pulled the comforter and sheets downward. The fabrics made a soft shushing sound.

"My feet," I muttered.

"Shh," he said again, the mattress shifting to accommodate both of us as he laid me down.

His one arm refused to let go of me while we slid under the

still tucked in sheets. I could feel his weight bowing behind me and his other arm snaking around my waist, pulling me closer to him. Molding to my shape, he held me. Held, held, held me in a way no one had ever dared to. With each breath he took pushing against my back, I knew I should feel uncomfortable and angered that Alpha Aldric was daring to invade my personal space without being formally introduced, and still so many questions left unanswered. But strangely, I wasn't. This was exactly what I needed, though I didn't know I needed it. And in his arms, the possibility of feeling independently strong and free didn't seem like a pipe dream.

In the morning, a cool gentle breeze brushed across my face and startled me awake. I was fairly certain I hadn't opened the window last night, or perhaps I had, but that was the least of my worries. The weight on the bed was significantly less than it had been before I drifted asleep. I looked over my shoulder to be sure, only to be disappointed in discovering he was no longer cuddling with me. It had been similar to being in Narnia again and sleeping next to the great lion, Aslan. Though, now that I was out of the wardrobe, as it were, the harsh reality of having never cuddled or slept in the same bed with someone, including the two people I thought were my real parents, saddened me. Even the few drunken times Gregory had tried to make inappropriate advances on me late at night; though he denied it the following morning. Advances I pushed to the dark recesses of my mind. But could I really be saddened about something I never experienced? Yes. No. And yet, sleeping next to Alpha Aldric last night still left a usual question to be asked... How was I ever able to sleep *without* him by my side? It was clearly a question he hadn't asked himself or perhaps felt similarly because otherwise, he would have still been in bed with me, right?

This bed—oh no! The remembrance of this fact mixed in with how dirty I must be was just the jolt I needed to get out of it. Well, *fell* out of it. My head nearly slammed against the hardwood floor as I did so. Nevertheless, my back stung to the high heavens as I turned to push myself up and into a sitting position, careful not to lean back against the bed. My shadow stretched to the space under the bedroom door from the morning light. I could hear the birds talking to one another. The fresh air reminded me, if the extremely soft bed hadn't already, that I was not in my moldy basement room back at the warehouse any longer.

Another question popped up in my mind because I obviously wasn't going to stop thinking about the strange appearance and disappearance of Alpha Aldric... Where did he go? I felt a terrible knot in my stomach rising up to my thumping heart regarding my foolhardiness, for I was disappointed about not finding a man I hardly knew to still be here in this room with me. Why would he be, and why would I even think of having any kind of feelings toward him? Yes, again, I was curious how his scent had healed me the night of my fight with Gregory and I had so many questions I wanted to ask him, which may have been the real reason I had tried to escape again. Well, aside from not having anywhere else to go. I definitely did not want to return to the warehouse.

But I just couldn't shake off this feeling of Alpha Aldric and I having known each other since we were in our mothers' wombs. That thought came with no factual basis at all. Pretty stupid, huh? Maybe not as stupid as staying in this house when I still wasn't certain if I could trust Alpha Aldric, Agatha, and Beatrix. I knew not to trust Ross and Gregory, but I could trust them to be themselves, if that makes any sense. I knew when they were lying to me, what to do and say to please their egos, or what to expect when I didn't. But with Alpha Aldric, specifically, I knew none of these things, and yet the pit of my stomach ached and my breath went shallow. I felt stupid, stupid, stupid.

I tried to shake off my foolishness and reinforce the walls around my heart with the knowledge that if what Ross had said about Alpha Aldric was indeed true, this man had a life, and one with many responsibilities to attend to. Responsibilities that most certainly did not include properly introducing himself to me or taking the time to answer my questions, though it was he who rescued me—sort of. Of course not. Maybe I should escape. Questions and my inexperience about how the world works be damned! But I quickly realized the thought was more foolish than the thoughts I had had this morning. Though the day was still early to brush aside such foolish and naïve thoughts, the chances of have more of these sorts of thoughts were pretty high. My annoyance of this knowledge of the inner workings of an anxious mind caused my breathing to temporarily grow shallow and my heart to start beating really fast. I could feel the tips of my fingers begin to tingle as they normally did when I was about to have a panic attack. Oh, how I wished I could just curl into a ball and banish my rising anxieties. Then everything would be better.

"Vivila, sweetheart?" Agatha's maternal and cheerful voice interrupted my racing thoughts from the other side of the door.

I jumped at the unexpected sound of the doctor's voice. Thankfully, she wasn't able to see the blood rushing to my cheeks or had opened the door and caught me being lost in my own head before. I tended to pace back and forth, my hands gesturing my thoughts. You would have supposed I would have stopped both with the amount of times I had been ridiculed or punished for doing this back at the warehouse. Every time I thought I had stopped this behavior, Gregory and his lackeys would show up on the other side of the door—and remind me that I hadn't through one of the small sliding doors within the door to. I guess that's why they say, "old habits die hard." The saying was especially so now. I was fairly certain this door wasn't locked, and I wasn't going to be ridiculed or punished, but I still stood where I was and I was still embarrassed at the prospect of being caught lost in my thoughts. When Agatha knocked again and opened the door, I couldn't help averting my gaze and rubbing the length of my arm with my other hand.

"Good morning?!" Agatha said, as she peered inside the room.

"Good morning," I say with a weak smile.

"You must be starving, my dear. You didn't touch your dinner," Agatha said. I heard her lifting and dropping the tray's dome lid.

"I'm sorry," I said, hoping my growling stomach wasn't giving too much away.

"There is no need to apologize. All things considered. Did you sleep well?" Agatha asked calmly.

I nodded.

"I believe Grace put clean towels in your bathroom, so if you want, you can take a shower. I'll have Beatrix lend you an outfit, and then you can come into the kitchen for breakfast."

"Who—who's Grace? And why do I have my own bathroom?" I asked, trying not to sound rude or ungrateful, but also I had completely forgotten about the connecting bathroom.

The latter was a question I had wanted to ask her yesterday. However, Ross's voice played in my head. "*Curiosity is a weakness. To give into it is foolish.*" But I needed to know the extent of what I was allowed to ask, despite my hesitation around the fact of only consciously knowing them for a day. Hesitation because it was just too hard to believe she, Beatrix, and, as much as I was now trying not to think about him, Alpha Aldric, were all doing this out of the goodness of their hearts. With my protective walls up and pretending to play along, I waited for her response as my eyes slowly moved to meet hers.

But Agatha's eyes held no judgement—instead, I found endless patience, which seemed so unfathomable... and slightly uncomfortable. Unnerving as this seemingly lack of a hidden agenda was, it was also making my resolution of keeping my guard up really difficult. If this were proof of Agatha's intentions being honorable, however small, then it would be the punch to knock the wind out of me.

So, as I continued to wait for her answer, I took in as much air as I could in preparation for the possibility of bad news—of anything negative really, like I'd been conditioned to expect for the last six years. Perhaps I thought I would feel better if I could put the doctor in the same category as Ross and Gregory... the world would make sense again. I would breathe easier knowing that this person Agatha may or may not be pretending to be would forever exist only in fantasy land. Is this crazy of me to say? I don't—I do—know. Maybe. God help me—if He exists. Please help me.

"All the rooms have private bathrooms attached to them," I finally heard the doctor finally say. "And if you ask me, I think yours is the nicest. Next to the Alpha's... well, like I said, I'll let you take a shower and I'll see you downstairs in the kitchen."

"How do I, um—" I started to say but stopped because it was a stupid question. 'How do I work the bathroom?' is what I wanted to ask. Not that I didn't know how to use all the bathroom stuff, of course; I would be a baby if I didn't—nervous laughter... *Oh, this is embarrassing.* I just—I just didn't know if I would know how to navigate my way around this bathroom. A bathroom attached to a breathtakingly immaculate bedroom inside a mansion that is a million-gazillion nicer than what I'm used to... Hopefully, you get the picture of why I was extremely nervous to ask what I wanted to ask, so I decided to simply point in the direction of the bathroom.

"Nothing to be embarrassed about," Agatha said with a smile, gesturing for me to follow her to the bathroom. "I can't imagine what your bathroom situation must have been like, but I can assure you that you'll still be able to manage just fine."

I relaxed a little bit until I noticed how large this bathroom was. Manage just fine? Manage just fine?!?! That was a bit of an understatement. For one thing, the showerhead was completely separate from the bathtub and enclosed not by curtain but with glass panels. Why would someone not want the showerhead and bathtub together? It looked like such a waste of water and pipes. But the tub—oh my goodness, an actual *tub*! I hadn't seen one of those in what felt like an eternity. I'd almost started to believe them to be extinct. Wood paneled walls painted a light shade of grey, which contrasted the dark grey painted wood cabinet below the sink and the granite top. The floor was made up of tiny square tiles. I don't even want to think about how much time it took to lay those all down so perfectly. I dared to walk into the space, which was cool to the touch. I was in complete awe. I almost forgot the need to breathe until I nearly choked for air.

"Well, come on, dear," the doctor said calmly. "I have three boys and there is no way you'll dirty a bathroom to the same extent as they can."

As I slowly walked further in, I watched her turn the showerhead on. She rotated her hand, standing a good enough distance to not get too wet, and waited for the water to reach the right temperature before giving me a wink and exiting. I waited until I heard the bedroom door close, then I stripped off all of my clothes and stepped in.

The pressure of the water was constant and heavenly as it ran along every inch of my body. Not once did it scold me or spit off and on due to faulty plumbing like the one I had used back at the warehouse. I didn't dare use the bar of soap sitting on a small porcelain shelf because for the past six years, I had been made to use the shampoo to wash both my hair and my body. Ross didn't want to spend more money on me than he had to, so he gave me some odorless, cheap shampoo that had most likely been bought at a dollar store. Yet, this shampoo had a wonderful floral aroma to it. I had never wanted to spend hours in the shower as I did in this moment. It was a small glimpse of normalcy and I wanted to bask in it as long as possible—but I didn't want to have Agatha and Beatrix waiting for me longer than they had to.

I dried myself with the white towel hung outside the glass

door and returned to the bedroom. It wasn't until after I had pulled the T-shirt over my head that I finally remembered the cuts on the inside of palms from my claws last night. I had been so disappointed in finding Aldric gone and enthralled in the luxuriousness of the bathroom that the whole incident was temporarily stripped from my mind. I healed relatively fast in comparison to normal people, and the crescent-shaped redness was a reminder of this fact. There was a particular thing Agatha had said to Alpha Aldric during my coma-like state down in the basement that wouldn't leave me alone: that it was due to being subjected to the serums for the past six years that I hadn't been healing as fast as I should have.

Was that true? I mean, it would explain why some of the injuries had left scars or permanent reminders, while others hadn't. Knowing myself, I could spend hours contemplating this new discovery, and time was not on my side because once again, Agatha and Beatrix were waiting for me in the kitchen.

CHAPTER TEN

Aware of the possible time constraint on how long the two women were willing to wait, I quickly braided my hair in such a way as to slump it over my shoulder. Then I went over to the side of the bed where I had stashed the towels I had used for sleeping on the floor and refolded them. I was thankful that Agatha hadn't said anything about them being gone when I had followed her into the bathroom earlier. After putting the towels back, I exited the bedroom. Agatha may have said that it was "mine" for the duration of my stay here, but it was difficult in claiming the room as such. Were it dingy and uncomfortably small, barely furnished, like the one I had grown accustomed to back at the warehouse, then maybe I would feel more okay saying it was "my bedroom."

Closing the door behind me as quietly as I could manage, though it still seemed to whine slightly and there weren't any signs of people in the hallway who might be offended from it shutting loudly, I momentarily stared at the door directly across from where I stood. I knew right away that it led to Alpha Aldric's bedroom because the doctor had told me last night it was his room—though I thought nothing of it until now. It would explain how he got to me so quickly. But this led to another unanswered question: Why was I purposefully put in a room across from a man quite possibly as powerful as Ross? Was it so I wouldn't try to escape? Or to ensure that the King Cobras wouldn't be able to recapture me?

But the latter didn't make sense because that would mean

Alpha Aldric would be some sort of superhuman capable of heightening heat and reflexes. The only such being I know of that actually exists... is me. There was no way Alpha Aldric would be able to take on Ross's men all by himself because of this rea—*Clunk.* Crap! I hadn't realized how long I had been awkwardly staring at Alpha Aldric's door until I heard something drop on the floor on the other side. It could have very well been a brush or a shoe, but it was enough to startle me back to the present. I looked to either end of the hallway, once again grateful that no one was around to see my cheeks growing red out of embarrassment.

Now it could have been how overwhelmed I was last night, but this house seemed to get larger by the minute as I turned in the direction I assumed would lead me to the kitchen. Gregory had given me—well, rather *thrown* at me after he lifted the grate above my bed for better aim—a book about the history of the haunted Winchester house. While I'm sure he stole it as a cruel way to scare the living daylights out of me, I found it quite interesting. The book had pictures of the labyrinth-like layout. Yet, its complexity appeared to be nothing in comparison to this house. Although this could also have to do with it being my second conscious day here.

I closed my eyes and tried to remember the direction Agatha and I had ascended the stairs from; the bedroom door was on the right—or was it the left? The right? Ah, geez. Why did I think that would work? Reopening my eyes, I noticed there was a crossing hallway not twenty feet from where I stood. It's a start. My stomach growled and though I knew how to ignore it, with the panic enveloping me as my heart formed a pounding knot the size of a golf ball and my breath shortened, I wasn't certain I would be able to ignore my stomach's need for food. Especially if the crossing hallway proved to get me more lost. This could also have to do with the prospect of receiving unspoiled food like yesterday's BLT.

Oh. why didn't someone wait for me? I thought, deciding

to make a right. *Maybe they are starting to realize that I wasn't worth rescuing because I'm not. I'm not, I'm not, I'm not.*

Walking in the direction of the crossing hallway, two sets of stairs presented themselves: one straight ahead and one to the right, which had a landing before forking off into another set of stairs and another hallway. I decided on the stairwell straight ahead, for it seemed to be the one least likely to get me more lost than I felt, though I soon found out that it too had a landing like the stairwell on the right. However, when I reached the bottom, a room resembling a gym presented itself. It was twice the size of the warehouse's, which I didn't think was possible. Cleaner too, which I could believe based on the cleanliness of what I had seen of the house thus far. There was a weird contraption in the center too. It was curious that the lights were on, especially with it being empty of people, but all I could focus on was the repetitive thoughts racing through my mind: *This isn't right, this isn't right, this isn't the right way. Backtrack, Vivila. Backtrack.* Turning around, I raced back up the long stairwell to the intersecting hallways.

I should have just stayed in the bedroom. I've surely pushed the women's patience to the breaking point now. I had reason to believe this, the two women hadn't given me any reason to believe this—yet. But rational thinking was far from my mind as I raced down the other sets of stairs, my heart thumping out of my chest and beads of sweat running down my face. At the bottom, I realized I was in the same hallway by the room I had woken up in, or at least I hoped it was. After a few twists and turns, I was relieved to find it was indeed the room I had woken up in. I used my usual coping mechanism of repeating things three times in an effort to make the situation be true or false by thinking—*This is good. This is good. This is good.*

Confident in knowing how to reach the kitchen from here, I made my way up the same stairwell Agatha and Beatrix had taken me up yesterday. Relief washed over me when I saw the large living room at the top. My hands dropped to my knees as

I panted from all the running I had just done, my heart no longer racing from the panic of being lost. After a few minutes, my breathing had become even again, and I mentally prepared myself to finally get an answer to my question about whether I had pushed the two women's kindness and patience or not.

I wasn't quite sure how much time had passed since Agatha had left me in the bathroom, but it seemed like hours. Though I knew perfectly well how Ross would have handled my tardiness, I pushed the thought away. It was particularly easy to do—as I cautiously approached the kitchen—when the incredibly enticing, earthy smell of coffee filled my nostrils. Truth be told, I hadn't had coffee since I'd snuck a sip from the man I thought was my real father, and that was six years ago.

"Good morning, my dear," Agatha said warmly as I entered the room.

"I'm sorry," I blurted. I could only hope I didn't sound as exasperated as I still felt from all the running I had done to get here.

"What do you have to be sorry for?"

"I—I got lost. I'm—I'm sorry," I said, struggling to get the words out.

"Beatrix!" Agatha yelled as she turned to face Beatrix.

"I thought she would have remembered how to get here. She's not stupid," Beatrix said, teetering between genuinely guilty and defensive.

"It's her second day awake since her coma," Agatha said sternly, slapping her hand to her forehead. "And it's a big house."

"I know that! But she figured it out, didn't she?"

"No thanks to you!" Agatha redirected her attention to me and said, "I'm sorry for shouting like I did. I didn't mean to frighten you."

I shook my head to indicate that it was okay, though in truth it had shaken me—just a bit.

"Ready for a day of shopping?" Beatrix cheerfully asked me, clearly attempting to change the subject.

I didn't know how to answer the question without sounding rude, but had we talked about going shopping? I couldn't remember. I couldn't even muster a nod in acknowledgment because I just couldn't remember. Nonetheless, just picturing having to be around so many people and spending money that I hadn't earned or possessed made me very nauseous and clamming for air. I wished I hadn't dared to leave the bedroom to try to find the kitchen; I was really wishing I hadn't left that room. For unlike the crummy lowlifes that attended the fights back at the warehouse, the mall would be filled with nicer people—*normal* people. At least, I imagined it would be. *I'm not ready, not ready, not ready.*

Plus, the clean clothes that had been laid on my bed were more than generous and would suffice until they had worn themselves out, which would hopefully be in a year. If I'm still here, that is; otherwise, the new clothes would most likely only last a few months. But oh, how I wished I stayed in my room. I felt a gentle hand upon my shoulders forcing me to retreat from the imprisonment that was my mind and back to the present.

"I didn't know how you liked your coffee, so I left it black," the doctor said, guiding me to a chair by the table and then placing the steaming mug next to the plate of eggs and toast. "But there is cream and sugar right over here...and you *can* say no to shopping by the way."

"I-I've never really had coffee be-before," I stuttered.

"Never had coffee before?" Beatrix asked in surprise. "Next to shoes and pizza, it's like one of life's necessities."

"Beatrix," Agatha hissed.

"Sorry," Beatrix said sarcastically. "But it is. And who says 'no' to a whole day at the King of Prussia mall, or as I like to call it, the 'Queen of all malls' because of how ginormous it is."

"She has every right to say no," Agatha said.

"Wha-what about Ross and the rest of the King Cobras?" I asked.

"Girl, don't you worry about that," Beatrix assured me. "Only neighboring packs know where this pack house is. Plus, I drive like a wolf on its prey."

I found it curious how many wolf analogies and terminologies were still being used. Yesterday was one thing, but it still confused me. Even as I dug into the eggs and listened to both the women's conversation, my mind was trying to piece together everything I had learned since I became conscious enough to try to make sense of it all. But my conclusion didn't make sense either and, and I decided I would reflect on the matter another time and simply try to enjoy the women's company for now. This was all a new concept for me, and one I couldn't help but remain guarded about.

Curiously, I stared at the coffee for some time before wrapping my fingers around the cup's handle. While not as hot as the cup itself, which I rounded with my other hand but immediately retracted, it was very warm. My thumb made small circles around the smoothness of the ceramic material. I suddenly became extremely self-aware about how stupid this must have looked if they'd momentarily drawn their attention away from each other and to me. So, I decided I try to recall what my adoptive mother had told me about how to make hot liquid less hot. I think it had something to do with blowing on the liquid.

God! I feel like an infant right now! In all fairness, yesterday's BLT aside, I can't say that I remember the last time I had a hot meal, let alone a hot beverage. There were a few times when my meals would be put in the freezers, hours before the tray was slid through one of the windows on my door. Unless it was Ash's turn, but even then he would only be able to give me the food at a lukewarm temperature. *Gasp!* I feel like a broken record too! For even in my own mind, I sound like a sheltered looney. I can't behave—I *won't* behave... Correction, I have to *try* to behave as though I were back in the warehouse. Lost in my head instead of trying to pay attention to and learning the social cues from these two women because, like I said, I wasn't sure how long I'd be here.

I sighed, biting my lower lip, and lightly blew on the coffee before carefully bringing the cup to my lips to take a small sip. While it wasn't terrible, the taste was still bitter, overbearing, and unfortunately, still so scorching hot that I nearly burned my tongue. It took some effort to prevent my involuntary reflexes from dropping the cup. I really didn't want to make a mess of myself, especially in front of them. From the corner of my eye, I noticed Agatha sliding over a small pitcher of what I assumed to be the creamer she had mentioned. The pitcher was soon followed by a tiny bowl of sugar with a silver spoon partially buried into it.

"Th-thank you," I said meekly.

"You're welcome, dear," Agatha said. "Don't worry about going too heavy on both. We have plenty more."

I'll admit, I was extremely grateful that she had seemed to have anticipated my unspoken question. The cream and sugar did make the coffee more pleasurable, and the scrambled eggs were absolutely delicious—not bland and without random bits of hair or dirt—*but* I felt uncomfortably guilty about leaving the plate and whatnot on the table. Regardless, Agatha waved me away, insisting that I should go have fun shopping. Yet, as I nervously followed Beatrix through the living room toward the garage, my mind seemed to want to wander toward Alpha Aldric again.

He remained a black mass, as he had appeared in my dreams. I couldn't figure out why I was so torn in my feelings toward him. Everything in me was telling me to remain guarded, like I was trying to be with Agatha and Beatrix; and with the exception of Ash, Alpha Aldric could quite possibly be like every other man in my life for the past six years. I suppose it scared me, this feeling I just couldn't shake off. That weird connection I had mentioned earlier in the bedroom—as well as the unanswered question of why his scent had aided in wearing off the effects of the second serum prior to my fight with Gregory. Oh, why do I feel like such a broken record, pondering the same few thoughts again and again? It will only lead to trouble, possibly being the final straw to break the rest of what little self-preservation I had left. Perhaps I should try to escape.

By the time that thought had crossed my mind, Beatrix and I were in the garage. And while I thought the gym in this mansion was huge, this parking garage was even larger. It could have been my nerves causing me to misperceive what I was seeing. It seemed as though my heart was thumping out of my chest as I continued to take in this space. My palms were so sweaty that I rubbed them along my clothes in an attempt to dry them. How much space did three people need and what would necessitate a garage that sort of resembled ones I had seen at the King of Prussia Mall with my parents—adoptive parents—before the dodgeball incident?

Unlike the rusty and dirty cars held together with duct tape and garbage bags, a gentle breeze being all that was needed for them to fall apart—like I was used to seeing outside my bedroom window at the warehouse—the cars in this garage were unbelievably pristine and in excellent condition. There had to be at least twenty, if not more, cars of various sizes and colors. Was it strange of me to think that I thought maybe the shopping excursion was suspicious and foreboding?

Although I still wasn't looking forward to the shopping excursion, and a huge part of me wanted to make a run back to the bedroom and lock the door, that didn't mean I wasn't in awe of the beauty of each car. And yet, I couldn't shake the feeling that Agatha and Beatrix were going to have me be responsible, for the length of my stay, for maintaining the cleanliness of these cars as a way to earn my keep. Why wouldn't I think this, when my parents had made me feel like I had to earn my keep with the countless amount of chores, alongside the ridicule about my behavior once company had left? Then there were unfathomable and horrid tasks to earn food or new-ish clothes with the King Cobras.

One of the nicer tasks Ross had me do was clean The Pit's equipment and floor with a toothbrush and grungy bucket of soapy water. Loads and hours of fun there. With that said, how could I be expected to accept the whole "kindness without ulterior motives or expectations" thing the two women were trying to prove to me? Nonetheless, I hadn't realized my mouth was agape until Beatrix turned to speak to me.

"Well?" Beatrix asked, amused.

"Hmm?" I said, figuring it was the safest answer to make without being rude or too obvious that I was once again lost in my thoughts.

"Which—" she said, wagging her finger back and forth.

Did she really expect me to pick a car like I would with a lineup of books? Were they all hers or her brother's? I should have just stayed in the bedroom. It may not be as safe as I felt in my bedroom back at the warehouse, but at least it didn't require me to make choices I shouldn't be allowed to make. But with how long it had taken me just to find the kitchen earlier, I suppose I didn't have much of a choice. My heart thumped like a million right hooks to the stomach, and all I could muster was a shake of my head and a few steps because I didn't know what the right answer was. The idea that shopping was code for me having to clean these cars was becoming more like a reality and less like some crazy assumption.

I became more suspicious when Beatrix let out a laugh and gestured for me to follow her to a sporty dark blue car. She then asked for me to get in the passenger seat while she went to grab the keys to the vehicle. Though I shouldn't have been surprised at this point, there was not a lick of filth or piece of garbage inside. I felt like running as I obliged and took a seat. It had been six years since I had been in a car, and being in such a small, enclosed space was causing my already high anxiety to go into overdrive. My hands began to tingle and close in on themselves. No matter how many times I tried to wave the feeling away, it just wouldn't leave.

Please let it be a tutorial on how to clean the car. Please tell me Beatrix wasn't serious in going shopping! I screamed in my head. I felt as though I were in a sauna the longer I waited for Beatrix to return. And in this moment of wanting to be anywhere else, for unknown reasons, I wished with every fiber of my being for the great Aslan that was the mysterious Alpha Aldric to be present, or at least his magically intoxicating aroma to banish the panic attack I was having. It was incredibly silly, not to mention stupid, to wish this.

I cannot grow attached. I cannot grow attached. I cannot grow attached to a man I don't know.

CHAPTER ELEVEN

I was about to find the courage to get out of the car when the driver side door creaked open and Beatrix stepped in. *Damn it!* Beatrix only offered a smile before she turned the key and revved the engine, which did not make me feel any better. I stared at her as though my life depended on it—but in truth, it was to help me focus on anything that wasn't a reminder of the small, enclosed space and the anxiety racing with my heartbeat. It took me a bit to register why she was tugging on her seatbelt and making quick glances in my direction. She was trying to communicate that I should put on my seatbelt.

And though I finally obeyed her suggestion, my anxiety went into overdrive with each sharp turn as the piercing squeals of the wheels echoed tenfold against the cement walls and pillars as we made our way out of the garage. I think my claws may have come out from how hard I was gripping both the arm rest and my seat, despite my attempts to not cause permanent holes in the leather. Everything in my line of vision quickly turned into blurred blobs of color. Even the knobs, buttons, and Beatrix herself were becoming one big surrounding Jackson Pollock painting.

When the sun appeared from beyond the confines of the garage and glared a vivid red-orange, all I could think was *This is too fast, too fast, too fast.* I could feel the eggs and toast turning into a gut-wrenching pain, and I was sure I was going to puke. The only time I'd liked going fast was when I was knocking Gregory out in the ring. But this was much too fast, too fast—

"Too fast!" I shouted at the top of my lungs, my eyes closing firmly shut.

Beatrix slowed the car down and pulled to the side of the road. It was then that I could feel my ears starting to elongate and my tail and wings desperately wanting to push through my skin.

Don't transform, don't transform, I pleaded to my body as I heard Beatrix get out of the car to come over to my side of the car. Just like outside of Ross's office before I had been "rescued," I felt a million knives stabbing me all over as my wings and tail tried to pierce through my flesh. I didn't have Ash to catch me, and I nearly hit my head on the dashboard. *Not here, not here.*

"Vivila, calm down. It's okay," I barely heard her say, as she laid her hand on my shoulders. "I'll drive slower, I promise."

And then, nothing. Everything went black. Now I could have been dreaming, however real it felt, but two strong arms and the all-too-familiar wondrous aroma of the salty ocean air and campfire smoke swooped me up. I felt like I was floating on a cloud, being healed and feeling whole again, when I was nothing more than incurable broken shards. I couldn't tell you how much time had passed or how I ended up back in the room that Agatha said was "mine," but as the dream I thought I was in came to an end, I heard three very distinct voices conversing. Well, almost distinct. In truth, my brain felt a bit discombobulated as I slowly woke up, though I kept my eyes shut in an effort to get my mind back to neutral.

"You're pushing her too hard," I heard Alpha Aldric scold, though his voice sounded far away, and it was difficult to concentrate on anything with the fog that filled my mind and the pounding of my heart. But as I tried to push through this state in an effort to come back to some form of clarity, it also sounded like he was trying to keep his composure. "Perhaps it was foolish of me to have asked you to help her adjust to living here."

"Oh, come on," a voice sounding an awful lot like Beatrix, except higher pitched, said. "The mall isn't that bad and no one in the King Cobras would have been there. And from what I've heard, she could mostly likely knock them out with one swing. You asked me to get her some clothes. I don't know her style, let alone her size. All I know is that Doc's are swimming on her—no offense.

"She's been held captive for the past six years, Beatrix. She doesn't know what her 'style' is," Agatha yelled. "From what I observed from her behavior, she's been made to wear the same clothes every day until they are barely covering her. My guess is she's also had to earn the right to get 'new clothes,' and I don't want to even begin to contemplate how—"

"I know she was held captive!" Beatrix shouted. "I'm sorry, okay? I probably shouldn't have driven as fast as I did, but how was I supposed to know she was having a panic attack, let alone passing out because of it? Yes, she looked overwhelmed—"

"Beatrix, just stop," Alpha Aldric said, exasperated, as though Beatrix had said something similar only moments before I had regained consciousness.

I tried to remain still. I needed to remain still. My need to remain perfectly still came partly because I wanted to hear more of what they were saying. People tend to show their true colors when they think no one is listening or when the people they are talking about aren't around. At least in my limited experience. The other part of me wanted to be as still as possible because there was something very soothing and rejuvenating about Alpha's voice. Regardless, my plan must have been successful because the three of them continued their conversation.

"Go to the mall," Agatha said, sounding just as tired of Beatrix's excuse as the Alpha's. "If they don't fit, then we'll worry about exchanging them when the time comes."

I heard Beatrix scoff, followed by footsteps walking away.

"Well, she seems to be doing better," Agatha continued. "Her claws have finally retracted. She should wake up soon."

"Have a tray of food waiting for her," Alpha Aldric said.

"Of course, Alpha," Agatha said.

That was the last thing I heard before I drifted back to sleep. Yet as I did so, something bothered me. Maybe I was wrong in being suspicious of these people having ulterior motives and having my walls up. However, those two things had kept me alive for the past six years. I had been so bent on comparing them to Ross and Gregory, I just couldn't believe people with genuine kindness actually existed. My plan to remain still during their conversation about me—to discover their true nature—was successful, but it wasn't what I expected. And that is what really bothered me—scared me. It still seemed too good to be true and yet, it was true.

When I finally awoke, the sun was high in the sky as it shined through the open bedroom window. I couldn't tell you how I felt because I wasn't sure myself. I pushed myself up and looked over to the door. A covered tray of what I assumed was the food Alpha Aldric asked the doctor to have waiting for me was on the dresser. I also noticed five shopping bags on the floor, which made me feel a bit uncomfortable. Moving from the bed to sit on the large windowsill, I let my mind drift into the nothing filling my chest. As I looked out the window, watching the clouds pass by and change shape along the way, a few birds raced across the sky.

I don't know if I would say I was becoming at peace with this knowledge of genuine kindness from the other three people in this very large house. I don't know if I could say I was at peace with the knowledge that they cared about what I'd endured with the King Cobras. I don't know if I was at peace at all. Ross would surely try to find me at any cost to have me back. He would kill me for the impertinence of daring to leave him, even though it was beyond my control or doing. Did Alpha Aldric have the means or the manpower to protect me? I still didn't understand what kind of gang leader would refer to himself as "Alpha" or his gang members as "pack members."

What I did know was I needed to get out of this room, despite my confusion and the grumbling of my stomach. So, I slid off of the ledge of the windowsill, happy at least to not be wearing any shoes. One, because it felt freeing to go shoeless without worrying about dirt or sharp objects lying haphazardly on the ground like I would back at the warehouse. And two, I really needed time to myself without the stuffiness of this room at the moment—which seemed to amplify my worrisome thoughts—without alerting Alpha Aldric, Agatha, or Beatrix to my whereabouts with noisy shoes. As I made my way toward the door, I lifted the cover off the tray to see a turkey and cheese sandwich with pickles on the side. Tempting as it was to take a bite, I would just have to hope the food would be here when I got back. Placing the cover back over the food, I exited my room.

Choosing the way opposite of the one I had earlier, I started to notice how many paintings were of huge wolves. Even the lamps on the walls had canine motifs within them. Not to mention the heavily-marooned wallpaper and short-width elongated rug with yet even more wolves, alongside a few birds here and there. It was very strange. Not to mention the many doors I passed along the way. One of the doors opened a crack. I looked from one end of the hallway over to the other. When I was certain no one was looking or coming my way, though I hadn't heard or seen anybody since I'd left the bedroom, I peered in. A window on the far wall let in the natural light. The window seemed to have a view of a courtyard or something, though I didn't have the courage to fully walk into the room to be sure. This room, however, seemed to be someone's bedroom. Whose, I didn't know, but if I had to guess, the room looked to belong to a guy. Guitars, men's underwear, combat boots.

These people may be genuinely good people, but they appeared to have a lot more people living in this large house than they were letting on. And taking the wolf terminology and decorative designs a little too obsessively. Continuing my journey down the hallway, I followed the curve until a small fork presented itself as a few stairs upward and a long curved downward set of stairs. While the first was well lit and less like Alice following the rabbit into Wonderland, I opted for the latter. I figured the railing would offer enough navigation alongside my naturally heightened vision that I wouldn't have to worry about falling—or at least I hoped so.

Even in the pitch darkness as I reached the bottom, I cautiously ran my hands along the wall until I could just make out a form that resembled a light switch. I was utterly relieved to discover it was most assuredly so. But nothing could have prepared me for what lay behind me as I turned around in this oddly circular room. I saw nothing but books. Hundreds upon hundreds of books. I hadn't seen this many in a very long time and on shelves no less, not stacked haphazardly upon a dirty pallet-covered floor. I had also never seen or been in a room that didn't have four sides. A circular room? I just didn't think those existed until now. Well, the prior wasn't exactly true. I had seen pictures of the White House's Oval Office. But even *that* room wasn't as beautiful as the one I was standing in. My knees nearly collapsed under this wondrous awe.

Walking toward the closest shelf, I flipped through a couple of books and noticed none of the pages had been ripped out nor were there signs that the books were starting to mold. Yet, low and behold, in whole hardback, was C.S. Lewis's *The Lion, the Witch, and the Wardrobe.* It was unlike the copy I had back at the warehouse, for one of Gregory's lackeys had torn the paperback book in half before burning the other half in front of me, so I never knew how the story ended. I certainly wouldn't be allowed to bring the book back to the bedroom with me, so I walked over to a large mustard-yellow couch in the center of the room and sat down. I couldn't tell you how much time had passed, yet with each turning of the page, I finally understood what occurred after Peter, Susan, Edmund, and Lucy met with Mr. and Mrs. Beaver, the hardship the four children met, the war, and Aslan's sacrifice.

Though as I neared the end of the book, I was still no closer in knowing what 'Turkish Delight' was or why Edmund would request such a mysterious treat from the wicked White Witch. I couldn't help remembering all those many nights back at the warehouse, wishing I had had a wardrobe to escape from the world I was trapped in, if only for an hour. This house and the three people I had met thus far within it could be my wardrobe, my Narnia—if there wasn't the looming fear of Ross dragging me back to that hellhole that had once been my bedroom. I was so immersed in the world of Narnia and my own thoughts that I didn't immediately notice the scent of salt and campfire smoke entering the space.

"Reading anything good?" asked the familiar husky and sultry voice.

The book slipped from my hands and onto the floor with a small thud. I didn't dare look up at him lest he disappear into thin air or his appearance, now that my vision wasn't prohibited, or... or— God! I don't know. Had I fallen asleep again? and was simply dreaming he was here? I quickly pinched my arm. I was most definitely not dreaming. Both the small redness appearing and the slight sting around the pinched area were proof of that. My heart started to race and my hands seemed to shake so uncontrollably that I placed them firmly upon my lap, my fingers tucked into nonexistent space between my thighs. But unless I spoke, I would either faint or look insolent.

Speak, Vivila, speak! I screamed in my head. But for whatever reason, the words wouldn't leave the tip of my tongue.

Out of the corner of my eyes, Alpha Aldric gradually walked over to where the book had dropped and kneeled to pick it up. His skin was olive and the hair on his muscular arms was a heavy black. If his large bare feet were any indication, the Alpha must be over six feet tall. I wanted to look up at him to see whether he was as tall as I imagined him to be. Plus, giving him eye contact would only be polite, especially now that I was certain of not dreaming. But I was scared, nonetheless, for no other reason than I was nothing and that never held any power—which I assumed came from a higher self-esteem, which I lacked greatly.

Deep breaths. You can do this, you can—do this, I thought, closing my eyes for a moment in an effort to collect myself.

"*The Lion, the Witch, and the Wardrobe*," he said nonchalantly. "An interesting choice."

"Why?" I blurted without thinking, my eyes focusing intently on each fiber of the rug under my feet. I did that to hide how flushed I was from speaking out of turn and the excitement of finally meeting him in person—consciously and not in a weird coma-like state. He'd radiated warmth and power when he had leaned down to pick up the book. Not to mention how his intoxicating scent sent shivers throughout my whole body.

And while I also finally knew the trueness of his nature as well as his sister's and the doctor's, having lived under Ross's thumb for as long as I did had me cringing at the idiocy of asking without being given permission. There was a huge part of me reminding me that this man was the Alpha, the boss of this gang—this "pack." There were rules like not speaking or looking at a man of power without permission. There were rules. There *are* rules... aren't there?

My complete embarrassment about my unconscious yet simply blatant disregard, nonetheless, of proper conduct in this house, in this "pack," was inexcusable. Or perhaps, it could be just a little. I no longer knew how to interact with people outside affiliations of the King Cobras. Perhaps. But I truly didn't know why the book I had chosen to read was an "interesting choice." I just had to hope, as I waited for Alpha Aldric to speak again, that I wouldn't be reprimanded for my nativity.

"My mother used to read it to my sister and me when we were kids," he answered with a hint of intrigue in his voice. He took a few steps back from me. I could hear him open the book and flip through the pages, and then I felt his eyes shift to look at me. "It was a favorite of hers."

"Was?" I asked—but as soon as the question left my lips, I knew instantly why he was using the past tense. His mother was dead. This realization was another reason not to try to look up at him again—not yet, anyway. My cheeks felt flush with embarrassment. Perhaps if I quickly apologize, I can make up for my foolish question, I thought. "I'm sorry."

"No need to be sorry. It's a fair question," he said calmly. "She died eight years ago from leukemia."

"I'm sorry," I said again, not knowing what else to say. I looked at the books on the bottom shelves, for it seemed the best way to hide my embarrassment. Oh, why am I still refusing to look at him?

"It was a long time ago." And then, after a brief pause, he asked, "Do you mind if I sit across from you?"

He's asking my permission? To sit in a chair in his own house? And why hasn't he reprimanded me for speaking out of turn earlier?

"Of course, Alpha Aldric," I said, self-consciously.

"Just Aldric," he said as the chair sighed at the touch of his weight. "I would ask how you know my name or my title as Alpha, but I'm sure either my sister or Agatha has told you."

"I overheard it when I was comatose in the basement," I blurted.

I didn't think it was possible, but I'd never felt more out of place than in this situation in the library with Aldric—thus far, anyway. Perhaps it had to do with his status or how intoxicating his aroma was. Regardless, I kept my eyes fixated on the dark red oriental rug under my feet. I could feel him staring at me, studying me as the quiet lingered.

"Hmm," Aldric said, more amused than anything else. Silence lingered for a span of what felt like an eternity, causing the air in the room to seem extremely heavy before he continued. "You know it's rude to not look someone in the eye when they are trying to converse with you."

Closing my eyes once more to take a few deep breaths, I turned my attention toward him as I slowly lifted my eyes from his feet to the dark blue slacks with a perfectly ironed line up the middle, to the grey T-shirt that hugged his athletic build, to the scruffy beard along his square chin and around his small, thin lips. From there, my eyes glanced upward to the long narrow nose, then quickly observed his once-shaved sides ending near the top of his head where a long section of his black hair flopped over to one side before I finally settled on his large, drooping hazel eyes. His looks were so serene and everything a man should strive to be. He stole my breath.

You're being weird, you're being weird, you're being weird, I thought, averting my gaze.

"I look that bad, huh?" Aldric chuckled.

"No—I, um..." I bit my lower lip to stop myself from saying anything more that might make me more awkward.

"I'm just kidding, Vivila," he said again with a chuckle.

I gave him a weak smile.

"Do you mind if I read aloud for a bit?" Aldric asked calmly, casually turning the closed book back and forth.

He wanted to read aloud to me. He **wanted** to read aloud to me. I don't know why, but it both overjoyed and confused me at the same time. *Don't be awkward, don't be awkward, don't be awkward. Answer him, Vivila. Answer him now!* But I couldn't. Ross could have magically appeared with a gun at my temple like he had done many times in the past, and I still couldn't form my mouth to say anything to him. It was like Aldric had some power over me and it was causing me to be completely flabbergasted for no reason. Absolutely no... reason.

CHAPTER TWELVE

I shook my head. Again, this asking for my permission thing—
even to read me part of a damn book—made me a little self-
conscious and uneasy... however aware I was of there being
no ulterior motives. It was becoming annoying that my mind
drifted, whether I liked it or not, toward the rare times Ross
showed any form of kindness. Well, if you could call it that.
Promises of buying me "new" clothes, though they weren't
really new—just clothes that had far fewer holes in them than
what I was wearing at the time. I would quickly learn, in order
to receive them, I was to clean The Pit with nothing more than
an old toothbrush and a rusty bucket of water. My hands were
wrinkly and sometimes blistered, and my knees reddened
by the time I had finished several hours later. Regardless, I
couldn't help curiously watching Aldric lean back in the chair
and open the book.

"And soon after that a very strange person stepped out
from among the trees into the light of the lamppost," Aldric
read aloud. "He was only a little taller than Lucy herself and
he carried over his head an umbrella, white with snow. From
the waist upward he was like a man, but his legs were shaped
like a goats[3]—"

His voice was so incredibly enticing and warm. Aldric could
read Tolkien and have my full attention. And yet, his voice was
also very soothing to the point that I didn't remember when
exactly my feet had rested against my butt or the moment I'd

3 C.S. Lewis. *The Lion, the Witch, and the Wardrobe.* 1950

placed my head on the armrest. I believe it was right around Edmund's first encounter with the White Witch that I had unknowingly fallen asleep. Now, it could have just been in my dreams—though I don't think it was—but I felt myself being swooped into Aldric's arms and carried up the stairs. His calming aroma of the ocean air and campfire filled my nostrils and soothed my soul once more. It was as though the scent made any troubling dreams vanish. I took comfort in knowing that whatever dreams I would have during my slumber, the ominous black mass I had associated with Aldric would never return again. For I now knew what he looked like and there was nothing that could erase his beautiful image from my mind. After carefully laying me under the silky softness of what I assumed was the top sheet and comforter, he placed an endearing kiss on the top of my head.

When I awoke in the morning, the sun shined on my face and the birds were twittering just outside the window. As I turned to face the room, still feeling a bit out of place and unworthy of being in a bedroom as nice as this, I took pleasure in the weight of his scent still on my clothes, pulling the neck of the shirt up and over my nose like a security blanket. A smile crept to the corners of my mouth, but it was short-lived. Why hadn't he shaken me awake or scolded me for falling asleep in the middle of his read-aloud? Was it even stranger that I was acting so giddy over his scent on the shirt I was wearing? I knew his and the two women's intentions were vastly different from Ross's. But then why was my anxiety suddenly rising causing my fingers to tingle and my breath to be swallowed? No, no, no. He's not like Ross. He is *not* like Ross. I'm overreacting, overreacting, overreacting. Stop it, Vivila! Stop it! Stop it! Stop it!

Suddenly, I heard a knocking on my door and I fell off of the bed in surprise, dragging the bedding along with me. Though it wasn't an aggressive pounding, I had been so lost in my own thoughts, my mind was finding it difficult to veer back into a calm and logical state. Peering just above the mattress, I waited for the person on the other side of the door to make another move; whether it be another few knocks, voicing their presence, or walking away. I hoped for the second option, but with how startled I was and everything, I kind of also hoped for the third.

"Hey girl, it's Beatrix," a familiar voice said. "I just wanted to check up on you to see how you are doing. Can I come in?"

I nodded before it hit me that she couldn't see me. I smacked my head with the palm of my hand.

"Yes," I said with a slight squeak.

The door creaked open and Beatrix stood within the door-frame with a curious look spread across her face. However, the longer she stood there looking intently at me, the redder my face got. It would take no less than a miracle to save me from this embarrassment. A miracle that I was certain would never come. And Beatrix continued to stare at me, shifting her gaze momentarily to the sheets and comforter loosely hanging over the bed and onto the floor, then back to me before speaking, which wasn't helping me feel any less embarrassed.

"What are you doing on the floor?" she asked in concern.

"I'm sorry," I replied, hastily withdrawing myself from the sheets held on me so that I could stand up.

"You need to stop saying sorry for things that you don't need to be sorry for," Beatrix said, shaking her head.

"I'm sor—it's a habit..." I said, extra cautious not to apologize as I nervously nibbled my lip.

"I should be the one apologizing. I didn't realize I had startled you," Beatrix said, studying how the bedding was pulled to one side. She leaned further into the room, lifting the tray cover, and noticed the untouched food. Turning her attention back to me, and I suppose in an effort to change the subject, she continued, "You must be starving."

Though I wasn't entirely, I nodded to be polite. I pushed myself up to stand in front of her. Though with how tangled I was in the bedding, it wasn't as graceful as I was trying to be.

"Oh! Before I forget," she said, twisting her waist back toward the hallway and presenting a few shopping bags, "I'm not sure if it's your style, but they should fit—well, hopefully."

Placing the bags just on the inside of the room, Beatrix smiled and gestured that she would wait outside the room, then closed the door. I just stood there, staring at the bags as though they were prized jewels... or perhaps a baited trap. Finally, after staring at the inanimate objects for what felt *way* too long for the average sane person, I went into the bathroom to wash my hands. The last thing I wanted to do was to ruin the clothes with my hands. Silly, I know, but it seemed less crazy than grabbing one of the towels to help look through the bag. Yet when I reached the sink, I decided while I was in the bathroom that I might as well just take a shower. An even crazier idea, but if you lived in the same hellhole as I did with the King Cobras, you might do the same.

The only comforting thought, if you could call it that, about these crazy actions was that this was only day three of knowing these people and away from Ross. And as much as I wanted to believe that the only person standing in my way was me, not Ross, I just couldn't—or could I? I was about to make my way over to the bags when I heard Agatha's voice outside the window, which redirected my attention. It wasn't my business, I know, but when I heard my name, I tiptoed toward the window, my back flattened against the wall to keep from being seen—or at least I hoped so.

Carefully peering around the corner, I noticed the doctor was talking into some thin rectangular device, which I assumed was a cellphone. Although it wasn't like any I had seen before. Both my adoptive parents and Ash had flip phones. Ash had accidentally used it in front of me four years ago before he and another member of the King Cobras were about to lead me up to The Pit. He was just taking last minute bets from those who were running late to the warehouse; but he didn't have one after that, or at least *I* never saw it again, but Gregory taunted me for three grueling months that his father had smashed Ash's phone and it was my fault.

I confronted Ash about it on one of the rare occasions he snuck to my room to talk, but he kept changing the subject. This particular and peculiar cellphone Agatha was using fascinated me because it seemed so futuristic in its thin, rectangular shape, like something I would have possibly seen in the original Star Wars trilogy. All of that distraction and I nearly forgot she was talking about me... nearly, but not entirely.

"I agree. But I still don't think it is wise to worry Vivila more than we need to," Agatha said with a sigh. "But how do we expect to earn her trust if we're not being hon—that's not what I'm referring to and you know it—of course not, Alpha. I—yes, I will ask her. What time should I tell her to expect you?" This pause was way too long for my comfort. "Okay, bye-bye."

What could be so worrisome that it kept both Agatha and Aldric from telling me the whole information? Yes, it was reassuring to hear that they wanted to earn my trust, just as it had been to hear their intentions were actually genuine, but it still left me a little perplexed. I may again sound like a broken record, but no one, aside from Ash, thought to earn my trust. At least, not in this manner. I had been so used to being like Edmund and his interactions with the White Witch. People, including my parents and classmates prior to the fateful dodgeball incident, promised me such wonderful and sometimes simple things. Then I learned they had no intention of following through with their promises because I had helped fulfill their own agendas.

And then there was the last part of what Agatha had said. My heart fluttered at the thought that Aldric wanted to meet with me—intentionally and not by chance—which I didn't fully understand. Not the meeting with him, but my feelings. Oh, how I wished I could understand this need to be close to him. He and I had only met face-to-face for the first time last night, but I had this indescribable feeling that started the night of my fight with that idiot Gregory.

KNOCK KNOCK!

"Vivila, you ready?" Beatrix asked after she rapped on the door.

"Almost," I said, a bit embarrassed that I had been so lost in my own head that I was not only still in my pajamas, but I hadn't even tried to put on one outfit. What if the outfit I reached for didn't match at all? Do I even care if I match?

I could feel the blood rush to my cheeks. It wasn't like I had actually gotten caught over listening to Agatha's conversation, but it still felt like I had. I fumbled to get over to the shopping bags, nearly skinning my knees as I tripped. Socks and hardwood floors—not a good combination when you're in a rush, I guess. My adoptive parents' house was all carpet, with the exception of the bathroom, kitchen, and garage. And anytime I did encounter a hardwood floor, I had been wearing shoes. Regardless, I suppose this was as good as any time to learn. Although I still felt incredibly stupid.

"You okay?" Beatrix asked from the other side of the door.

"Yes," I said, trying to sound like I hadn't just tripped all over myself, though it probably wasn't worth the effort given the noise my body had made and the involuntary grunt. I also hadn't realized how much the palms of my hands were throbbing from trying to prevent my fall until she had asked her question.

I decided, for the sake of reducing the chances of tripping a second time, I would make the rest of the short distance by scooting my butt with the aid of my hands pushing against the floor. And while I had seen this sort of movement done many times by my next-door neighbor's dog back when I was still living with my adoptive parents, it still seemed like the safest bet—although I felt quite silly doing the maneuver now.

I quickly pulled out what I needed from the bag. I didn't care if the outfit matched, for I'd never cared before and I wasn't going to start caring now. However, I did want to look presentable; especially with how overgenerous these people had been to buy me clothes. I prayed I wouldn't do anything to ruin them. I also wanted to look presentable because of the prospect of seeing Aldric again. Had Beatrix not been waiting for me to get dressed, I may have pondered the strangeness of this even longer. But as it was, I hastily put on what I had taken from some of the shopping bags. Then I checked the mirror above the dresser to make sure my hair wasn't a frazzled mess.

I did look presentable, and I almost felt as though I were a normal eighteen-year-old girl. Indifferent instead of grateful that the clothes I was wearing weren't covered in holes, sweat stains, or dirt. Indifferent instead of uncomfortable with how revealing the clothes were or that three of the five pairs of shoes had high heels. I had seen my adoptive mother wear this type of shoe when she and my adoptive father went out, leaving me with a babysitter who was only four years older than me. And if I were a normal teenage girl, checking my hair in the mirror would be followed by putting on my makeup.

But I'd never worn makeup, nor did I know how to put it on. I don't know if I should have been sad or angry at the woman who I thought was my real mother. She never thought to teach me how or let me watch her put hers on. Had she known my true nature before that fateful day in gym class? I didn't know. For I also didn't know how a normal mother and daughter acted with one another, but I would like to think they would have experienced this unknown world of makeup or other normal girly things together. My chest ached at the void of all the experiences I'd never had because I was indeed not a normal eighteen-year-old girl.

When I finally opened the door, Beatrix was standing right in front of me and looking every bit of what a normal teenage girl should look like, and more. Though I still wasn't sure how old she actually was. She looked to be my age, but she could have been a few years older. Her long hair fell perfectly down and around her shoulders, glistening from the sun's light despite how far away she was from the window and me standing mostly in the doorframe. Her clothes were formfitting and highlighted her best features. Features that I had for certain not been blessed with. However, when I looked down at her shoes, I understood why there had been a few pairs of high heels in the shopping bags.

"How can you walk in those?" I asked, although I hadn't realized I had said that aloud until I heard Beatrix giggle. I was about to apologize, but remembered what she had said about apologizing.

"You get used to them," she said matter-of-factly.

As I looked up to meet Beatrix's eyes, her lips looked almost nonexistent, as though she was trying not to ask something she thought might upset me. And yet, I could nearly read her thoughts—or perhaps it seemed like I could because of what I had been dwelling on before I had opened the door; the subject of my thoughts still in the forefront of my mind. I had watched my adoptive mother put on her heels and walk around in them, but she had always said I was too young to try hers on or for her to buy a pair for me.

I remember telling her many times how most of the popular girls wore those types of shoes all the time. Her response was always the same: *That's the problem with kids these days. Always trying to grow up instead of appreciating being a child. It doesn't help that their weak-minded parents cave into their children's every whim.* Even now, I wasn't sure what she meant by that.

As Beatrix's expression softened, I watched in curiosity while she suddenly scanned me from head to toe. I suppose that just as I had taken in her whole look, she was examining mine. However accustomed I was to opponents sizing me up in the ring, it was nothing compared to what Beatrix was doing in this moment. I pulled the shorts I had put on down so they would cover more of my legs, though not by much, and placed my arm across my chest to cover the little bit of cleavage I had.

My eyes darted from her to the floor to what I could see of the hallway as I waited for her to say something—anything. I hadn't realized I had been holding my breath until she smiled and stretched out her hand for me to take it. I stared at her hand for what felt like several minutes before I finally mustered the courage to put my hand in hers.

Beatrix turned to face the hallway and proceeded to guide me down the hallway, the same direction that had led me to the circular library. We passed the open bedroom door I'd peered in yesterday and went into another bedroom. I didn't have enough time to fully take the room in before she dragged me into the connecting bathroom, but from the amount of leopard print, scattered clothing, and accessories, this bedroom must have been hers... or at least I hoped it was.

With the amount of doors I had seen, it appeared that many people lived here—if the bedroom I had peered in yesterday and the one we had just entered, to get to the bathroom we were now standing in, were any indication of the number of people that were here. But then, that begged the question of where the other residents were. I recalled Agatha saying Alpha Aldric had requested that everyone not be in this house until I was healed and ready. This may be silly for me to be curious about, but if the bedroom connected to this bathroom wasn't Beatrix's, would the owner be upset we were here, rummaging through their things? Well, Beatrix was doing the rummaging in a cabinet under the sink. I was just standing awkwardly by the doorframe. I just had to hope that the owner of this room and bathroom wasn't going to suddenly enter anytime soon.

CHAPTER THIRTEEN

Beatrix cursed under her breath about not finding a jar of some sort as I examined my surroundings. As my mind wandered, I started to understand another thing Agatha had previously said. This bathroom, in a similar style to the one adjoining the room I was staying in, was not nearly as large. A much nicer version of the bathroom I was made to use back at the warehouse, the showerhead was above the bathtub. However, this bathroom wasn't tidy—not one bit. Clean for sure, but undergarments were draped over the curtain rod and the towels were haphazardly folded on the rod by the sink.

"Sorry for the mess," Beatrix said, returning her attention to me and a small yellow tub in hand. "I don't usually let people come into my room—that often—unless they're a hot guy. Just kidding... kind of."

I laughed along with her, hoping I didn't sound as self-conscious as I felt. It was just yet another thing in a long laundry list of why I was anything but a normal eighteen-year-old girl.

"Well, anyway... When was the last time you used a hair mask?" Beatrix asked.

"A hair what?" I asked.

"A hair mask," Beatrix reiterated. I was thankful that she didn't sound annoyed at me for not knowing what she was talking about. "It helps to bring moisture into frizzy and damaged hair."

"Damaged?" I asked, raising my eyebrows. Was my hair this way because it matched how I felt on the inside? However, the question was quickly dismissed as Beatrix continued to explain the use of this 'hair mask.'

"For those of us who constantly dye or add a lot of heat to our hair—or in your case, have naturally curly hair," she said as she gently guided me to my knees in front of the bathtub.

While I obliged her request, I was still confused. This is why she led me here, to give me hair care tips? I knew I should be overjoyed, or at least I thought I should be, at the prospect of doing something "normal" teenage girls do, but I instead felt awkward and self-conscious. Although... would I have felt less of either had she simply remarked on whether the clothes I chose matched? Probably not.

Regardless of the awareness of the genuine kindness of Aldric and Agatha as well as Beatrix being true, I still couldn't understand why she cared to help me with my hair. I was no one—no one special, and yet, I was starting to get an inkling that I was more than just a mere guest to them. But that was stupid. I quickly pushed away the foolish notion, focusing on Beatrix's gentle pressure on the back of my head with her hand causing my face to be perpendicular to the basin of the tub. Then, she softly flipped my hair from the back to the front, followed by the groaning squeak of the faucet being turned on, Beatrix slowly pouring water over my curls, and lastly running her finger through my hair with what I presumed was this alleged 'hair mask.'

"What about coconut oil? Would that be considered a hair mask?" I asked, feeling it would be a betrayal not to remember what Ash had said about coconut oil and curly hair.

"Coconut oil is—great," Beatrix said, sounding a bit distracted. "However, if you overuse it, it can do the exact opposite of what you want it to."

I didn't say much after that, just short affirmations to show that I was listening to what she was saying. In truth, I mostly kept quiet because while waiting for this so-called 'hair mask' to sit, I kind of wished she would pull me around the house by my hair or cut it all off with a knife instead of making me feel like a live doll or a lost puppy. Insane as that most certainly sounded, I would have felt a whole lot more at ease than I was. Even when she finally rinsed, combed, and blow-dried my hair, any pleasure of feeling like a normal eighteen-year-old girl was shattered as Ross's voice filled my mind.

"Nobody could ever love or care about you. You are a thorn in my side. Just looking at your hideous face revolts me—revolts everyone who looks upon you. What? You think because no one has said so to your face that it is not true? You should be thanking me for being nice enough to tell you the truth. You worthless piece of garbage. The only reason you came into this world, the only reason you are still alive, is because you make me money. If you ever try to escape, I will find you. No matter how hard you try to hide."

"Vivila? Vivila!" I finally heard Beatrix say as she lifted my chin to look at her. "Are you okay? What's wrong?"

"Nothing... nothing. I'm okay," I said. It was a lie, but she didn't need to know that. Especially after all of her hard work in helping me with my hair. I didn't want to seem ungrateful and have another meltdown that may require her to run and find Agatha. I was extremely relieved she didn't press any further, but gradually led me to the mirror so that I could see the result of what she had done to my hair.

From the hideous mess in the mirror down in Agatha's medical room only a few days ago, to the reflection appearing before me now—I almost looked normal. Almost. There were still dark circles under my eyes, my cheeks were still gaunt, and I still wasn't pretty by any means. But my hair... well, it didn't look like it belonged to a forgotten and broken animal—something I still was inside. My curls fell in perfectly controlled ringlets down and around my skeleton of a figure. I could feel the tears already making their way over my lashes and down my sunken cheeks before I could stop them.

"Thank you," I finally managed to say, unable to pull my

gaze away from my reflection.

"No worries," Beatrix answered. "Let's head down to the kitchen. I don't know about you, but I am famished!"

I nodded and turned to follow her back out into the hallway, unsure if I was really hungry or how long Ross's words would linger in my mind. And as we finally made it to the correct set of stairs that would lead us to the kitchen, I crossed my fingers that the uncertainty of the two would resolve themselves prior to entering the kitchen. Especially the prior, as we began rounding the bottom of the stairs and quickly passing the large living room and a strong whiff of something warm, sweet, and cinnamon-y filled the hallway, the aroma becoming stronger when Beatrix pushed the kitchen door open. The aroma of whatever Agatha was pulling out of the oven was almost as intoxicating as the scent that seemed to exude from Aldric whenever he was near... almost.

"Good morning," the doctor greeted the two of us before briefly looking at me with a slight tug of her own hair and a warm smile to communicate that she liked what Beatrix had done to my hair. It made me blush, for I was still getting used to receiving genuine compliments about my appearance. So much so that I was a bit flabbergasted about returning the greeting.

"Mornin', Doc," Beatrix said.

Though I immediately wanted to ask what she was talking to Aldric about on the phone, I held my tongue and answered with a good morning of my own. I took a seat next to Beatrix. I had decided, with determination and however unhopeful I still was, to not let Ross's words ruin the pleasure I was starting to feel in the presence of these two women. More particularly, to what was on the plate Agatha placed in front of me. She said it was called a "cinnamon bun," something I had never had before.

My adoptive parents were very strict when it came to sweets. Unless it was someone's birthday, I was never allowed to have any. It's not that I had never seen a cinnamon roll before, I just never knew what they were called. They, along with every other candy or pasty, were simply called 'cavity sins.' My adoptive parents weren't particularly religious nor had I ever heard this term outside of my parents, but it was a term I had thought was common until my peers started to make fun of me for using it. Just when I had thought "Albino Girl" was the worst nickname I could have been called.

Regardless, I intently observed the two women, Agatha taking a seat directly across from me, to see what the correct way to eat the large pastry was. With a fork in one hand and a knife in the other, Agatha divided the roll into smaller bite-size pieces. Beatrix, on the other hand, seemed to pull the roll apart with her fingers as if she were peeling apart each layer of an onion or unraveling a ball of yarn. As intrigued as I was by both methods, I didn't think I would favor having the gooey substance within and the white icing on top on my fingers, so I reached for the fork and knife.

Staring at the cinnamon roll before me for a bit longer, ignoring the idle conversation Agatha and Beatrix were having with one another, I plunged the fork into the roll. And after gliding the knife through the pastry, I slowly lifted the fork toward my mouth. I was pleasantly surprised to see the gooey inside and the bit of icing staying relatively where they were, especially with the wisps of steam rising from the piece of the roll. I half expected both to droop like honey, maple syrup, or what I remembered of them. Yet neither seemed to do so until I placed the piece in my mouth, releasing a wonder of sweet cinnamon goodness that melted on my tongue like butter. I savored the simple yet magnanimous flavors for a few moments before finally chewing and swallowing. I didn't want it to end, yet soon enough, the plate before me laid empty.

"I thought maybe today," Agatha interrupted my silence, "if you are up for it, of course, we might take a stroll around the grounds or you can explore them yourselves. There are easily marked signs along the paths that Alpha Aldric has had put up for your convenience, so you shouldn't get lost. Then tonight after dinner, the Alpha has asked me to ask you, if perhaps you would like to meet him in the library, so that you two can continue reading where you guys left off. You're not obligated in any way—"

"Wh-why would he do all of that for me?" I asked, suddenly struggling once again not only to get the words out, but also trying to understand why Aldric, along with these two women, kept giving and doing things for me that I didn't deserve. Not by a long shot. Was this what Agatha's and Aldric's conversation on the phone had been about? True, I was excited about the prospect of seeing him again, more than I thought I should be about someone I barely knew.

But despite knowing how true all three of their hearts were— the clothes, the hair mask, the cinnamon roll, and now the easily marked signs for me, all for me... well, it made that ridiculous notion I had earlier of being more than just a "guest" appear to be a reality. A reality of this Narnia-like place less like the coming of Aslan and more like the tyrannical reign of the White Witch. I could feel my heart race erratically and a weight pressing on my chest, which made breathing a bit of a struggle.

I didn't mean to sound ungrateful by any means, but something negatively triggered in me and made all of this too much to handle. Had the reasoning for all of this been because Aldric expected sexual favors or to finally punish me for thinking these gifts were for free, I might have felt more at ease. But as it were, as... it... it... God! I can't find the strength to finish the train of thought. Fire, alongside the feeling of a thousand knives piercing every inch of my body! The pain, the pain, the pain—sucking the ability to breathe with each wave. I thought the agony outside of Ross's office and in the car with Beatrix was bad. It was nothing compared to this.

I couldn't tell you when I pulled back from the chair or

how I ended up in a corner of the kitchen, but my wings and tail wasted no time emerging out of me, which caused my knees to buckle from under me and the room around me to be nothing more than dark grey masses. In an effort to suppress the surging pain of shifting and the high anxiety I was in, the warm stickiness of blood trickling down my back, I grabbed a hunk of my hair on either side of my head so tightly that I almost feared I might rip it out. Yet, it was the least of my worries. I couldn't breathe. I just couldn't breathe no matter how desperately I tried to reach for some air—any air.

"This is too much," I whispered without realizing I had until I was aware enough to hear footsteps zig-zagging from one side of the room to another before approaching me. Though I could have simply imagined the help I desired. What I did know was that I had started to rock back and forth between, or perhaps during, weaving in and out of consciousness.

When I suddenly felt the all-too-familiar pinch of a needle to my hip, the excruciating pain I was in began to subside, the shift retreating. However, with the amount of energy it had taken to shift and fight the shift, my whole body collapsed like a plush doll. My eyelids felt so heavy that I immediately gave up trying to keep them open.

"Get the Alpha!" I barely heard Agatha demand. Both she and Beatrix sounded as though they were trying to speak underwater.

"But he's in meetings with the other packs all day and a Skype meeting with the closest pride!" Beatrix said, a little panicky.

The doctor must have glowered at the olive-skinned beauty because I heard footsteps running out of the kitchen. I could just hear the fabric of the doctor's clothing shift as she kneeled in front of me and I felt her hands lightly moving up and down my arms. With all my might, I wanted to fight this, but it seemed like an impossible task when I was losing more and more focus on the present.

"Vivila? Vivila?" Agatha said soothingly, though her voice still sounded like it was coming from the deepest depths of the ocean. It was quite possible that she wasn't saying anything, and that it was all in my mind—wishing was she saying the words I longed to hear in this moment. Though, for as well read as I was, I don't think I would string together the words quite like the doctor, which quickly made me erase the possibility of it being all in my mind, despite some lingering doubts.

"You're in a safe place. Breathe, honey," she continued. "No one is forcing you to do anything you don't want to do, okay? Alpha Aldric is a good man. He doesn't expect anything from you, except to keep you safe, okay? Breathe. The sedative should help you calm down soon. We just want you to know that not everyone is like what you've been used to with the King Cobras. That may be hard to believe right now."

I wasn't sure how much time had passed, but the sedative did calm me down just like the doctor said it would. Though with how much energy it had taken for me to accidentally start to shift, I was pretty exhausted anyway. As things began to refocus and the illusion of sounds and Agatha's voice appeared less far away, a pair of hard sole shoes entered into the kitchen carrying an intoxicating scent I knew to be Aldric. Like a weight I hadn't realized was on my chest was lifted, I felt as though I could breathe easily again.

And as ridiculous as it may sound, believe me, I didn't know how nor did I care because of how good it felt, as my broken spirit and my shattered heart felt complete by his presence. It was as though my whole being could tackle anything. It frightened me, yes, but Aldric's heat melted my erratic mentality as he drew closer to me. The compassionate pull along my arms so that I could once again stand relatively on my own two feet curiously provided the strength to move on from the incident. I closed my eyes and leaned into him for support because I wanted to—*needed* to soak up as much of his energy as he would allow as the two of us started to walk toward the welcoming aromas and sounds of nature.

"I have her," Aldric said over his shoulder. "Thank you for getting me. Please inform Beta Cillian that he can fill me in the proceedings of today's meetings tomorrow."

"Yes, Alpha," both women responded.

It was weird how much I trusted him despite my conditioned behavior from the six years locked in a room somewhere in northeast Philadelphia. I wanted to finally ask him about this weird connection between us, but I didn't know if I had the strength to do so yet. Even if I did, what if it was only me who felt it? Which brought up another recurring question about why he had bothered to send his 'pack members' to rescue me. I decided for now I would simply bask in the rejuvenating qualities of being near him with the hope that my usually anxious mind wouldn't ruin it.

And by the time I finally opened my eyes again, the two of us were deep in the forest lines. He stopped walking when I murmured what I hoped was coherent enough, that I would like to be put down. Luckily, my murmur was coherent because Aldric carefully and somewhat reluctantly put me down on my feet, keeping his hands gently around my waist in case I fainted again. I slowly and cautiously turned around to see that the mansion could just be seen behind the cover of the trees. My brow furrowed as to why he had brought me out here. I looked upwards, taking in the surroundings, to trees reaching toward the sky. It was a dream. It must have been. I had never seen trees stretching their branches in every direction as though to pay homage to the sun that shined down like shooting stars before. Even when I lived with my adoptive parents in Upper Darby, I couldn't recall trees positioning so freely like the ones encompassing us. Nor did I recall leaves exhibiting this array of colors because of how the light was shining through and around them. From yellow to a dark green and every color in between. The patterns, the patterns, the patterns of the different layers of those leaves.

A huge nest was wedged between three thick branches on one of the broader trunk trees. With my keen eyesight, I became fascinated by the colors and patterns of the lint and ribbons which were woven in with various sizes of twigs. The birds would need to be very large to need a nest of this size. How far both birds must have also traveled to gather all the materials to make a home for their future children. The time and effort to construct a nest so beautifully intricate. An example of the unconditional love parents are supposed to give their children. An example of something I was robbed of. Did my real parents prepare for my coming into the world, or were they impatiently waiting for me to be born so they could finally be rid of me? A question that may never be answered...

CHAPTER FOURTEEN

A wind suddenly swept from high above amidst the acidic hole of what I lacked in parental love as I continued to watch the mother bird feed her young and the large nest swayed. The tree branches and leaves brushed up against one another, producing a sound of a thousand whispers—a thousand secrets—reminiscing the many upon many unanswered questions I had. The more the wind blew through the rest of the forest, the more it felt as though it was stealing the air in my lungs.

That was until I suddenly heard thudding crunches by where Aldric stood, which caused my gaze to be redirected to the wonders in the area around the earth's floor and a sudden appearance of a creature not ten feet from where we stood. A doe. I could recall seeing a herd of them in my childhood when my adoptive parents had taken me to Valley Forge to teach me how to ride a bike. Yet I had never seen one this close before, casually grazing until she became aware of us and she gracefully dashed away. I wish I could be as graceful as this doe, as *free* as this doe, and as at peace with nature. I could feel the tears filling my eyes again. Not from fear or anxiety, but in a mixture of burning awe. Maybe one day I would be. Maybe.

As if he could sense the turmoil and emptiness I was feeling, Aldric slid his hand into mine and gave a little squeeze. This wasn't the first time he had shown me kindness or touched me. He had comforted me during my first conscious night in the mansion when I had a complete meltdown and he had been nothing more than a dark shadow in my mind and in the overwhelming fog blocking my clear line of sight. He had picked me up, carried me to bed, and lain next to me until I had fallen asleep. It was the best and strangest sleep I ever had. Could I call it an act of affection? No, I suppose not. It was merely a method to calm me down and nothing more. Then again, I couldn't get those words I overheard during those moments when I was in a weird coma-like state and I couldn't will my eyes to open. Something about him needing to be near me, finally finding me, and not wanting to lose me, but that I needed time to adjust because they didn't know how much psychological damage the King Cobras did to me. Oh, if only they knew, then Aldric *really* wouldn't want me.

Wait! Did I want Aldric? I couldn't deny how incredibly handsome he was when he surprised me in the circular library. More importantly, did he want me? Despite what I'd overheard, I still wasn't sure. Yet, the moments that led the two of us here, our fingers intertwined with one another and his thumb making soft circles near the top of my hand... It was such a simple gesture, it made me wonder if he did. With how little we knew each other, I'll be honest when I say a large part of me wanted to pull away, out of instinct—out of a need to protect myself, both psychologically and physically. But there was a small part of me, which was ever so slowly gaining momentum, that didn't want to pull away. For as I briefly glanced down at our hands woven into one another's, the tears obscuring my vision, a strange and tingling energy was running up and down my arm. It was as though we were not only sharing an unexplainable energy, but Aldric was taking my pain and the void in my heart into himself, lessening these feelings for me.

And without words or movement, when I looked into his eyes I felt the peace I was looking for. Seconds felt like hours and minutes like eternity as we continued to stare at one another. Nature and all the beings who lived within it went silent. The rise and fall of my chest as I breathed in his intoxicating aroma was matched in perfect synchronization. It wasn't until he stepped closer, closing the gap between us, that I snapped out of the unrealistic dream happening between us and pulled away from him.

Stupid, stupid, stupid, Vivila, my mind screamed at me, Ross's words paraphrased in a loop. *"Nobody could ever love or care about you, let alone this successful and handsome man in front of you. None of your parents, neither adoptive nor real, wanted you. You're trash and nothing more. Why did Aldric rescue you? Because of the only reason you came into this world, to make a profit off of you and nothing else. You're a worthless piece of garbage and should have been left in that crummy hole of a bedroom back at the warehouse."* I am worthless, worthless, worthless!!!

"Vivila!" I heard Aldric say to me before I realized he was standing in front of me, his hands on my shoulders. "I won't let any harm come to you."

"How can you make such an empty promise?" I asked bitterly. I wasn't sure where the anger was coming from, or maybe I was. Either way, the anger was out and there was no way to be rid of it. At least not anytime soon. "You rescue me without telling me why. You stayed in the shadows up until recently in the library. Do you plan to use me for your own personal pleasures? To make a profit off of me? I am nothing but a freak of nature. And Ross will find me again, sooner or later."

My claws extended, and I used this as an opportunity to escape from Aldric by digging them into one side of his arm. But instead of releasing, he held on stronger and intently waited until my eyes met his. Even through the tears streaming down my face, I could have sworn his once hazel eyes glowed yellow like a wolf's. But that was impossible. I tried to wipe my eyes on the side of my arm before looking into his eyes again. Still, his eye color remained the same. I would have asked about why his eyes were a different color, but the anger within me still coursed fervently. I wasn't going to let my steaming anger get in the way of achieving my goal in receiving the answers I have been longing for just because of my bewilderment of Aldric's sudden change of eye color in his wolf form. It was still very bizarre nonetheless, causing my whole face to scrunch up in confusion.

"Please," Aldric started to say, slowly releasing me and stepping back, his hands raised in surrender.

I wanted to run, but the fact that he didn't return my anger with anger like I was hoping he would—for it would be similar to how Ross would have responded... The fact that Aldric acted as though the deep cuts I had inflicted upon him were nothing more than mere scratches... his sincere tone... I wanted to run, but I just couldn't get my body to move.

Did he cast some sort of spell on me? No, no, no, that couldn't be because magic didn't exist, right? The only mysticism and freak of nature I knew resided in me; so, no—magic does not exist. But seriously, why couldn't I move from where I stood? Intrigue in what he wanted to tell me? No, for that was right up there with nonexistence of magic. But then—how else could I explain the sudden change in his eye color?

"If you could just follow me," Aldric continued, a slight hint of nervousness in his voice, "there's a place I would like to show you. It's very dear to me—I'll explain everything there, I promise."

"Why can't you explain it here?" I blurted, becoming increasingly suspicious of his behavior and desire to take me elsewhere all of a sudden.

"Please," Aldric simply answered as he raised his injured arm for me to take hold of his hand.

I stared at his hand as though I had never seen a hand before. Could I trust him? Could I? You would think I wouldn't have metaphorically taken a few steps backwards because I had already learned how true his heart was. And yet, I just couldn't return the gesture. It confused me and was still so new to me. It was as though he had already trusted me, but how? Why? I studied every line in his palm, which wasn't a difficult task to do given my heightened eyesight, until he spoke again.

"I'm not like Ross," he said calmly, gently. Aldric didn't sound annoyed or angry; there was such sincerity in the tone of his voice—and when I dared to look into those beautiful hazel eyes, it was there too. His next words almost brought me to tears, for no man apart from Ash had ever said anything like this to me and meant it. "I don't think you're worthless, nor do I plan or have any desire to profit from you. I was in the shadows, as you say, not by choice, but because Agatha said it would be vital to your recovery—despite what you mean to me and long I've searched for you. I'm twenty-four years old and I know that isn't old, though it is six years older than you, but... but..."

"Searching for me? Why?" I asked in almost a whisper as my anger started to dissipate.

When what felt like more than a few minutes had passed, though it was most likely only half a minute, with no answer from Aldric, I asked my question again, my anger building momentum again.

"Why? Why were you searching for me? Why? Why, Aldric?"

"Because we're mates!" Aldric yelled, the anger in his voice coming more from a place of frustration than pure annoyance. However, his next words quickly shifted into a state of self-consciousness and almost vulnerability. "I'm a werewolf and the Alpha... the leader of the Red Rose Pack... my sister and the doctor are werewolves too."

"Werewolves don't exist!" I shouted back. I could feel the blood draining from my scrunched-up face due to a weird mixture of panic, confusion, and anger. I was readying to go into fight-or-flight mode, though that concept appeared to be an impossibility at that moment. Super frustrating because I couldn't explain why. "Nor does magic, though I can't explain why I am unable to run, even though I want to. You're crazier than I am if you expect me to believe in you being a fictional creature. And mates? What the hell does that mean?"

I didn't know what to make of what he was saying. Nor did I think I was prepared for whatever answers he was about to offer. He wasn't Ross, but he could be far more dangerous if he truly believed he was a werewolf. And yet, as crazy as this sounded, a naïve part of me wanted it to be true. It would almost be a relief to know I'm not the only freak—No, no, no! This is madness. Complete and utter madness. And mates? What in the world did he mean by that? Again, this is all a totally crazy period. His accent is as American as mine is. He might have an extremely Irish name, if you include both his first and last names, but that still didn't explain the use of the word "mates."

As my chest heaved and my heart thumped, and as overwhelmed and confused as I felt, I finally found the will to turn and walk away from him. No answer would make this situation better. I could hear him calling for me to stop and to come back, but I didn't. I was going to keep walking until this madness no longer existed, or at least that's what I was going to keep telling myself with every step. I'd go past the mansion of a house and maybe into the great unknown... whatever that phrase meant, and regardless of how terrifying traveling alone sounded given I had no clue how to survive on my own.

However, I barely made it five yards away from where I had left him when a massive black wolf leapt over me, blocking my path, causing some of the tendrils of my white hair to whoosh forward. In an effort to back away and flee, I ended up falling right on my butt. A wolf, but larger than any wolf I had ever read about, whose stance was so domineering and intimidating, I contemplated whether I would be able to defend myself if this wolf decided to attack me. Yes, I knew how to fight, but in the controlled setting of the ring in The Pit. Fighting techniques that consisted of trial and error, the heightened senses of being a freak of nature, and most importantly, knowing my opponents were *human*.

The longer this massive wolf and I stared at each other, the more I noticed the wolf seemed to have the same hazel-colored eyes as Aldric. There was also no indication in his eyes that he would actually attack me. Then the wolf slowly lowered himself until he was lying upon the forest floor as if to give me another reason not to be frightened of him. Could this be Aldric? No, no way!

But then the wind blew from the direction of this abnormally large wolf, sending an all too familiar scent of salty ocean air and campfire smoke. If that weren't strange enough, when my eyes drifted to the wolf's front legs, I noticed four deep cuts in the exact spots where I had dug my claws into Aldric's arm. And though the wounds appeared to be rapidly healing, which was odd too, I continued to stare at the arm until the cuts disappeared. Could this *really* be Aldric, or was it a strange coincidence?

"Aldric?" I asked breathlessly, as my eyes finally rose back to meet him.

Did... did the wolf just nod? How is it possible for a wolf to actually understand what I'm saying? Wolves, from what I've read, aren't capable of understanding human speech. Fluctuation of tones and sounds as a method of understanding humans, but not actual words. I realize I'm not entirely human and wolves, to my knowledge, aren't usually domesticated. But this wolf nodding back at me could only mean that the animal was truly Aldric—as crazy as the whole situation seemed to me.

I carefully stood up and walked over to Aldric, needing to touch his fur for confirmation that it was really him and not an illusion. However, when my fingers reached toward the patch of fur by his cheek, I stopped. Was this okay? Would he find my gesture to be an insult because of his status as Alpha or think I was doing so like I would a common dog? But his coat reflected so beautifully in the sun's light through the trees that it almost looked more brown than black. It looked soft—as soft as what I imagined cashmere would be. As I admired his coat, I felt Aldric's cheek press into the palm of my hand. And beyond my comprehension, I felt the relief I had always been searching for. The curse I thought had been placed upon only me. The curse of being a Winged Ailuranthrope or whatever I had heard Agatha said I was. Maybe I wasn't brought into this world to make people like Ross money. Tears filled my eyes once again.

Gradually, I moved my hand along his jawline, studying the direction in which his fur grew. I was suddenly startled, to say the least, when Aldric started to purr. It was a sound I never thought a wolf would ever produce, and I retreated self-consciously, for I couldn't help feeling as though I had done something wrong. And when he darted behind me into the cover of some trees, I wanted to run or curl into myself. I had done something wrong, and it took the air from my lungs. Try as I might, I was having a hard time retrieving the air back into me. That was until I felt two very human and masculine hands upon my shoulders.

I wanted to turn to face the person I hoped was Aldric but couldn't. I was too ashamed because here I was almost acting like some of the female escorts of Ross's criminal clientele who would want to pet me like a stray animal or gawk at me like those poor animals caged in zoos. Maybe it sounded extreme and untrue, but after seeing him dart away from me like he did after I touched him in his wolf form, I couldn't help feeling guilty and feeling like all those women, nonetheless.

"Vivila, look at me," Aldric said, not as a command but as a hoped request. "Look at me, please."

I did, but I averted my gaze and nibbled on my lip. His fingers gently guided my chin upward and didn't slide away until my eyes finally met his.

"You did nothing wrong," Aldric said calmly.

"No?" I asked in disbelief.

"Of course not," Aldric answered. "I apologize if I startled you. I just didn't know any other way to prove it to you."

I continued to stare into his now hazel eyes as I tried to process once more what had just been revealed to me without any definitive thoughts or emotions. I knew I had voiced my relief in knowing I wasn't the only freak of nature, but my brain still felt scrambled, almost. I guess I was saddened by the sudden realization that Aldric, Beatrix, and Agatha had known their true nature since birth, had known what being what they were entailed, and were accepted unconditionally for it. Something I again lacked. The birds twittering in the distance, the squirrels racing up and down some of the trees, and even the wind all had peace with themselves and I didn't. What did it truly mean to be a Winged Ailuranthrope?

"Can I show you something?" Aldric asked, breaking the silence.

I nodded.

"Is it okay for me to hold your hand?"

I nodded again.

He had touched me before. Held me before. But this time as his fingers intertwined with mine, a surge of electricity that pulsed throughout me was exciting. So much so that I never wanted our hands to part—*our* hands. The thought made my very core purr and one very content purr escaped my lips. I covered my mouth, but it was too late; Aldric had already heard me. He chuckled a little before brushing his lips against the top of my hand. I blushed nonetheless; not just because of the purr, but because of how unsure I was. Unsure of why he had this effect on me. Yes, I had this strange feeling that he and I had known each other since we were in our mothers' wombs, but it was still just—weird. We didn't really know anything about one another. How could we feel so comfortable around each other? How could he ever like someone like me? A girl who has spent her life, up until recently, in a dingy basement, forced to fight for the profit of the King Cobras.

I continued to ponder these thoughts as I followed him deeper into the forest, up a steep hill, and over slightly treacherous large rocks. As physically exhausting as it was to fight in The Pit, it was nothing compared to the hike we were on, which though it felt like hours, was most likely only twenty minutes. So I was, to say the least, beyond relieved when Aldric said we had made it. I leaned against a nearby tree as I caught my breath. Then he let go of my hand and gestured for us to sit on a large rock.

I'll admit I had totally overlooked the view in front of us until I joined him on the rock because I was wondering why I had trusted him enough to bring me here—wherever here was. A decent amount of distance from the mansion for sure, but that was all I was sure about at the moment. Nor did I understand why it was so important to be sitting on such a jagged rock. I didn't feel comfortable enough to sit too close to Aldric and was pleased that there was enough room on the large rock for there to be a decent distance from him. There wasn't any shade by the large rock, so the sun was beaming right into my eyes. Was leading me here the real punishment for speaking so boldly to Aldric? I could certainly see why it would be, but my stomach felt like it was turning in anticipation.

However, when I lifted my hand to block the sun's rays, I was struck with awe at the canyon, or at least the closest thing I've ever been to one lying before us. The trees had been a wonder when we had stood below them, but that was nothing to how they looked from above; large and snowflake-shaped without the delicate nature of an actual snowflake. How small we were compared to what was before us. Although the only test of whether I was afraid of heights had been the night I had been rescued by Aldric's pack members, I was still surprised at how unafraid I was now, especially with the limited space between us and the edge.

And despite having never learned how to fly with my wings, I closed my eyes and imagined what it would be like to soar across the highs and lows. To feel the wind under my wings and against my face. It would be the epitome of true freedom and I let out a sigh of joy at the thought of it, however foolish it sounded, and the amount of practice it would take to learn how to use my wings—were I ever to be given a chance to do so. The likelihood of that happening seemed very unlikely. But what appeared to be more likely, I hoped, was to ask Aldric what he meant by us being "mates."

"Beautiful, isn't it?" Aldric remarked, breaking the silence.

"Yes," I responded and then quickly followed it with the question I wanted to ask before I lost the nerve to do so. "What did you mean by us being mates?" A slow smile spread across his face.

CHAPTER FIFTEEN

I turned my head to face him, still needing the shade provided by my hand on my forehead. He looked confused, or perhaps bewildered; either or both would be understandable given my sudden change in subject. There also seemed to be an inner battle waging within him as his lips thinned, his brows folded into themselves, and his eyes nervously went from left to right before returning to me.

"I don't want to overwhelm you more than I already have today," Aldric said slowly, shifting his weight and releasing a heavy sigh. "I dropped a big one by revealing that Agatha, Beatrix, and I are werewolves... I promise I will explain what I meant soon—when the time is right, okay?"

I nodded, hoping my disappointment wasn't visibly displayed in my slumped body language and on my face. As the quiet between us returned, so did my focus on the vast view before us. I tried to enjoy the peacefulness of it all. The rustling of the trees as the wind once again swept through. The chattering of the birds around us and the somewhat startling gallop of deer behind us.

"Look, I can't even begin to imagine what you went through," Aldric said, breaking the quiet. "And I know I will never truly understand... and I know I have already said this and you don't know exactly why I ardently say this, but... I will do everything in my power to protect you and prove to you that not everyone is like those horrid King Cobras."

"I just ne-need time," I stuttered.

"I know," Aldric said, releasing a heavy exhale through his nose. "To answer part of one of your other questions, I brought you up here to this mountainside because it's my favorite place to think and recharge after a bad day. But my reasoning for not answering your question comes purely from my fear of possibly scaring you away."

"You're worried about scaring me?" I asked in genuine surprise, for how could a man—a werewolf and a leader who knows many other werewolves—be worried about anything.

He chuckled and nodded.

"Why?" I pressed out of curiosity and to suppress how good it felt to hear him laugh—because hello!!!! Totally crazy! But more importantly, getting back to the subject at hand, and the main reason I was so confused, I continued, "I'm nothing. A pebble in most people's shoes, or at least I have been for the last six years, maybe longer. The people who I thought were my real parents, I don't think they truly cared about my feelings even before they discovered my true freakish form. And you, a successful businessman and an Alpha with all of your good looks and power, is worried about scaring me with an explanation of what you meant by us being mates? You grew up around what it meant to be a werewolf. Had others who accepted you for your true nature and I, and I—"

Aldric's hand rested softly on my thigh, cutting my ramblings short. My attention drifted downward to where his hand laid, so innocently—so compassionately that I realized it would take me an inordinate amount of time before I could ever be even slightly okay with this small gesture of true kindness. When I finally looked back up into his beautifully large hazel eyes, they held just as much compassion as his touch did, and I nearly lost the ability to breathe. Not literally, but I just didn't know what to make of his words or his reaction or anything. The only feelings I was able to make sense of were the gentle breeze upon my skin and how the humidity made the air feel a bit heavy as I breathed.

"So, you find me good looking?" Aldric asked, a smirk stretching the corner of his mouth.

I looked away, hoping he wouldn't see how red my face was quickly becoming. An awkward and uncomfortable day that wasn't going to get any better because he now knew that I found him good looking. I'd had only one other "crush" in my life and he was a part of the lustrous bunch who was most likely still dealing with what I did to him that fateful day in gym class. If memory serves correctly, he lost the use of his legs because of me. Rehashing this memory made me never want to have another crush again. I didn't want to hurt anyone... Well, anyone who wasn't Ross and Gregory anyways. If I had the strength and courage to inflict harm on either, outside of the ring in The Pit, that is. Although, having a crush—scratch that... a *possible* crush on a werewolf, may be a safe bet. But who am I kidding? I had more than a mere crush on Aldric. It still seemed very insane to admit this, even to just myself, because there was still so much I didn't know about him and vice versa.

Sensing this ever-expanding and unexplainable connection between us, there was a need to quickly reconcile the reality of being strangers with this connection. I wanted—no, *needed* to know everything there was to know about him so that I could feel whole again instead of half. A half of myself I hadn't known was missing until that moment he and I had shared in the library as he read to me. It sounds crazy, I know it does. It is also crazy to say that if I parted from him, even for one minute, it would fully break me. But how can that be? If it was even possible to break that final straw in my already broken spirit.

I mean, the night in the library was only last night, so how can I make such a declaration? How could I and why did I have such desires of being closer to him, not just physically but emotionally, when he and I had just met last night? Sure, I had been aware of his presence in The Pit, in Agatha's medical room, and in my room, but I still wouldn't call these occasions proper introductions. Just when I didn't think I could be more confused and uncomfortable in these new surroundings. It didn't help that Aldric allowed the silence to linger, granting my usual inner monologue to continue.

If I was going to survive here or be less awkward, I guess I had better put a lid on my rambling mind. The two had been okay with the King Cobras because I was nothing more than a live piece of property. But I wasn't with the King Cobras right now, and though I strangely believed Aldric intended to protect me regardless of the short time we'd known each other and perhaps my better judgement, I didn't know how long it would take Ross to find me. He was the most stubborn person I knew and therefore would go to great lengths to get me back, even if it meant killing me. Ross would kill me and justify it by claiming I had run away.

But I didn't want to think about Ross. Instead, I wanted to focus on my two new goals: surviving, being less awkward, not apologizing so much, and getting to know the mysterious werewolf that was Aldric. Okay, so there were four goals, but that didn't make any of them easier to achieve. First step in being less awkward was changing the subject from his question on whether I found him good looking—which I did, but that's beside the point—to something that would help me get to know him better. Or at least I think that is the next step... hopefully?

"I was just joshing you," Aldric finally said with a chuckle before clearing his throat and changing the subject, which I appreciated greatly. "This place is also important to me because my dad used to bring me up here a lot before he passed the title of Alpha and decided to travel to all the places he and my mom planned to go to prior to her passing. This is one of the places the other pack members aren't allowed to come to, so he could tell me all the secrets about what made a good Alpha, amongst other things, without worry of being within earshot of anyone else."

"I wish I had any memories of my parents..." I found my-self saying, seemingly out of the blue because of how rarely I spoke about anything personal, especially to someone I barely knew. And though I couldn't explain why I felt I could trust Aldric yet, it still felt okay to lower my guard a bit. "I recently discovered that the people I thought were my parents were actually my adoptive parents, so..."

I didn't know how to finish the sentence because I hadn't really planned on revealing as much as I did and immediately felt awkward about it. I almost expected Aldric to say, *"Well, that would explain why you don't know as much about your kind and the supernatural world..."* But instead, he took my hand into his again and gave it a little squeeze.

It really was beautiful out here and I was grateful to be allowed to be in a place that many were not. I could tell by the way he spoke of his parents that he loved them very deeply and that they were amazing parents. I couldn't help having a tinge of jealousy toward the relationship I imagined Aldric had with his parents. However, I tried to let that feeling go because I had given myself enough pity parties already and I didn't think it would help in achieving my goals; especially the ones about being less awkward and not apologizing so much. And letting my mind wander again, as well as apologizing to myself for the thing I felt I lacked, definitely qualified as being counterproductive to two of the four goals I set for myself.

"Can I ask you a question?" I asked, hoping I could redeem myself, though I couldn't help blushing at the forced small talk. Okay, to everyone else this may not have seemed forced, but to my very limited knowledge on 'how to act with people outside of the warehouse,' it did.

"Anything," Aldric answered.

"How long have werewolves and winged ail—whatever, existed?" I asked, already feeling myself automatically cringing in anticipation of being ridiculed or laughed at for even ask-ing such a question. This prompted me to follow with, "It's just, up until now, I thought any supernatural creatures only existed in fiction. I'm not saying I think vampires, witches, and fairies exist too—wait, *do* they exist? Oh God, I'm burying myself further in my own grave."

I didn't know I had voiced the last sentence until hearing Aldric's angelic and hardy laugh again, which he tried to hide with a couple of fake coughs. I averted my gaze because if I weren't blushing already, I'd be *super* blushing from embarrassment. My first instincts were to run back to the mansion and hide in the bedroom, but after a few deep breaths, I reminded myself that this thought would also be counterproductive to my goals. So, I bit my lip, made a few side glances, and waited for Aldric to answer—if he *would* answer.

"Sorry, I didn't mean to laugh. You're just so cute when you get nervous," Aldric started to say before clearing his throat again and momentarily turning his gaze away from me. I could swear I saw him blushing like he was embarrassed for admitting that he thought I was cute or that he had crossed the line a little because the amount of time we had known each other was small or maybe a little of both—maybe none of those things. Maybe I was projecting what I hoped was running through his mind. Either way, I waited for him to continue.

"I keep forgetting how little you know of the supernatural world... uh, I mean, Doc said you might not know a lot or anything at all. But to answer your question, werewolves and Ailuranthropes or werecats have been around for almost as long as humans have. The Greeks and Romans were a little more accepting of the supernatural world until a huge war forced us to go into hiding. I won't bore you with the details, but the war resulted, long term, in the truth of supernaturals to be nothing more than mythology or fiction."

"But they all still exist? Supernatural creatures... aside from werewolves and werecats, I mean," I interrupted.

"Yes... and no," Aldric started to say, but paused for a minute or so as though he was trying to choose his next words carefully. "Werewolves, vampires, fairies, witches, and other creatures written about in mythology still do. Most of them have found ways to live amongst humans, not in the open or 'out of the closet' but for some close to it. While others prefer to live in secret and not without reason... a few bad apples, closed-minded humans, and overdramatized films didn't paint a pretty picture of them. But then there were... umm..."

Aldric suddenly stood up, running his hands through his hair until they intertwined in the back of his head. He was nervous, but I didn't know why. What I did know was how brown his hair looked against the sun's rays and how his shirt was taut under the weight of his perfectly formed back. Stupid, I know. Here Aldric was trying to say something—something that he was finding it hard to communicate, and I was over here fawning over some of his physical attributes. But in truth, I didn't know what to do in this moment, how to feel about this bit of information, or most importantly, how to comfort him.

The latter was the strangest and newest thing for me because I never had to comfort anyone, not in a very long time at least. Also, and this is where the strangeness really came in because I couldn't find a rational explanation for it, I swear I felt his anxiety within my chest and stomach as if it were my own. But I knew it couldn't be my emotions because I wasn't nervous... awkward and overwhelmed with this new information about there actually being other supernatural creatures in the real world and not the fictional one... but nervous? Uh-uh. Normally, I would be telling you how this proved how crazy I was or sounded, but given what I've just learned today... within these past few hours—the notion that I was possibly feeling his emotions didn't seem so crazy. And usually, this would also be the not-so-perfect moment I'd blurt out a question on why this was, but if he was really this nervous about whatever he was nervous about, I was going to wait for him to speak. I just hoped that doing so would be comforting enough for him.

"The Winged Ailuranthropes, your species," Aldric said in a breathy manner, as though he was trying to replenish the air in his lungs, his attention still facing the open space of nature in front of us, "were the most revered creatures in the supernatural world. The Venus Council, originally formed to maintain all the different supernatural species' laws and the peace between our world and the natural world, was primarily composed of your ancestors. It is said that they lived in the clouds amongst the gods, but no one knows for certain if that is true. However, when the two heads of the Venus Council were murdered by a band of Minotaurs about eighteen years ago, the council dismembered until the prophecy came into fruition."

"How could a band of Minotaurs kill the heads of this council if they supposedly lived in the clouds?" I asked.

"I'll admit supernatural history was never my favorite subject growing up," Aldric said, turning to face me, though his gaze didn't meet mine like he was ashamed of this confession. "But if I remember correctly, this particular band of Minotaurs was outcasted by their species for some reason and had blackmailed a group of witches and warlocks into casting a spell to disguise them to look like Winged Ailuranthropes. See, this band of Minotaurs was infuriated with their species and yours. They believed all Minotaurs were the superior species, more so than those who made up the Venus Council because of their brute strength and skills on the battlefield, and were infuriated that most Minotaurs did not agree with their way of thinking. They also felt that your species was too soft and allowed the human world to have too much control over Earth and deplete the planet's natural resources. And so, the Minotaurs sort of 'Trojan Horsed' their way into the living quarters of the council heads and slit their throats. Since then, every supernatural species has abided by their own laws. But like I said, I wasn't the most attentive student in supernatural history, so..."

"And the prophecy?" I asked.

"That I really don't remember. Look, there are books in my library about it, if you're interested?" Aldric said, running his hand through his hair like a nervous tic. He paced back and forth for a bit before his eyes finally met mine. "This may seem totally out in left field and definitely—most awkwardly a subject-changing question, but um, would you be up for me showing you something?"

With a confused look on my face toward the question aside, I couldn't help thinking that my waiting for him to speak may not have been the best comforting action because he still seemed to be on edge, but agreeing to go wherever he want me to go did seem to satisfy something within him and so did my hand taking his, for a smile crept across his face. Although the smile didn't quite reach his eyes, I'll admit it was a selfish decision in both agreeing to follow him to wherever it was he wanted to take me and sliding my hand into his, because I desperately wanted an excuse to feel that amazing jolt of electricity I felt when my bare skin touched his. I still didn't know why I felt this deep connection; perhaps it had to do with this "mate" thing he was refusing to tell me about and following him was definitely foolish and scary in a way—and yet, every fiber of my being was agreeing with me when I told myself that I would go to ends of the world for him. Crazy, right?

CHAPTER SIXTEEN

As I scooted off of the large rock, I briefly looked down to ensure that my feet wouldn't lose my bearings and noticed Aldric's free hand open and close as it hovered by my waist. While it may seem silly that I was fearful of my bearings given the small drop from the rock to the ground, I didn't want to embarrass myself in front of him. Yet on the flip side, Aldric second-guessing whether it would be okay with me if he put his hand on my waist to help me down was possibly his own attempt to not embarrass himself in front of me. Or at least that was how I chose to interpret the semi-awkward situation.

If my assumption was correct, that meant I appreciated him more as a person, or rather a werewolf. As I followed beside him back into the thick of the forest and toward the house, I wasn't sure if it was still okay to say "person" in regard to him. Maybe because he was in his human form, I could say "person." I mean, I remembered hearing my old neighbors' dog being called a "boy," so... Oh geez, here I go again, getting lost in my own thoughts. Regardless of proper wording, I guess what I am trying to say is that it was nice that we were both embarrassed because it made me feel *less* embarrassed. Also, it appeared that he was making an effort to respect my boundaries. And apart from Ash, no one cared what my comfort levels were, or if I even had any, in a very long time.

This thought brought an ease to my breathing and made Aldric being a stranger to me less uncomfortable. Okay, okay, who was I fooling? I was still uncomfortable around him. I mean, why did he have to be so nice to me? He had no reason to be. Yes, I've already allowed my mind to ponder this, but I don't know if I'll get used to this. And the silence leading through the familiar small garden and into the kitchen was making me extremely antsy to say the least; antsy with anticipation of what he wanted to show me. I also couldn't help wondering when I would be able to go back to the library and learn about this mysterious prophecy.

"A penny for your thoughts?" Aldric asked so suddenly that I thought my claws might accidentally come out from how startled I was. They didn't, thank heavens, and I had never been in a situation where that had happened, but I felt with Aldric it might happen. How embarrassing that would have been.

"I... uh, was... um," I stuttered because I didn't know what else to say. The truth? That would be a disaster because my thoughts sounded crazy enough in my own mind let alone what he would think of them if I were to say them out loud.

He must have sensed my inner turmoil because he separated our hands, stepped in front of me, and lifted both hands in surrender before saying, "Hey, it is totally okay if you don't want to say anything. Judgement-free zone here."

I remained silent. It was as though my self-consciousness wasn't allowing me to speak a single word. Yet my self-consciousness didn't stop my face from falling flush as his gaze continued to bear upon me with incredible patience. Boy, this man—this werewolf was too good to be true. I averted my eyes from him a couple of times before noticing his hand innocently stretched out toward me. I found myself staring at his hand for what felt like twenty minutes as though it was one of those major crossroads in life. If I took his hand, I would be accepting or believing what he had just said about it being a "judgement-free zone" and I could tell him what I had been or would be thinking without worry or fear of any negative consequences from the moment my hand met his.

If I didn't take his hand, I would continue to revert to how I always felt when someone offered similar acts of kindness, which was that they had an ulterior motive. But both seemed completely silly—this whole thought of his hand representing a crossroad was just so very, very silly. It was just a hand. Nothing more, nothing less. And I had already held his hand, many times over—well, maybe not *that* many, but enough to know Aldric's intentions to be honorable and true. Yet, it didn't mean I had overcome or was letting go of the tools that had protected me and helped me survive my treatment with the King Cobras. I wished I would, someday. But for now, I decided it was perfectly safe to return the gesture and placed my hand in Aldric's once again. I followed him as we hiked back toward the large mansion in silence. The silence continued to linger as I followed him down into the basement and around one hallway and to another. My feet seemingly unafraid, unlike my racing heartbeat, as they walked side by side with my mate to wherever he was taking me.

I noticed a slightly familiar flight of stairs; the same one I had stumbled upon the other day. Once again, as we approached the bottom step, the very large and spotless gym presented itself. I was hyperaware of how uncharacteristically the fluorescent was blinding me, most likely due to the mixed emotions of confusion and curiosity coursing through me like the tingling sensation of nervous energy. I intently watched from where I stood on the bottom step as Aldric excused himself, disappearing into what looked to be a broom closet. Did this gym hold a similar significance as the place in the forest? I couldn't see why it would. Like the last time I was here, there was no discord, and there was not a single mark of white residue from sweat nor ingrained stain of dried blood.

The equipment was not held together with duct tape or the discolored blackened rainbow of over welded joints. This equipment looked brand new, which must have cost Aldric a fortune, if that was the case. Though with the overall luxuriousness of what I had seen of the house thus far, I shouldn't have been surprised by the newness of the equipment. Perhaps, it was almost and simply that Aldric cared. A vague statement, I know, but it was the best explanation I was able to come up with to make sense of what I was observing. And as much as I was trying not to think of Ross and the equipment in The Pit, a realization of Ross not caring how things looked as long as they got the job done and still turned a profit came to my mind.

And as I pondered this realization, a curious padded pole in the middle of mats with a painted yellow circle around its perimeter caught my attention. How I had failed to notice this contraption before was beyond me... Well, not *totally* unnoticed. I was in a state of panic because of how lost I had gotten and how angry I assumed both Agatha and Beatrix would be for keeping them waiting. Yet, as I continued to stare, I observed two long bars stretched perpendicular to the floor at opposite ends from the padded pole they were connected to and at different heights too; one just above someone's head and the other near where someone's ankles would be.

From top to bottom, I tried to figure out what its purpose was in this room. For some sort of exercise; yes, that was a given due to it being in a gym. The whole point of a gym was to exercise. I may have been naive and unworldly, but I wasn't completely stupid. At least I was fairly certain I wasn't. But what in the hell was this contraption used for?

The taped cord running along the mat to an outlet on the far wall hinted that this contraption moved electronically. Hearing sounds of Aldric rummaging in the broom closet, I cautiously walked over to it to have a better look at this strange contraption. Putting both of my hands on either side of the bar just above my brow and with some struggle, I pushed the bar until the other bar bumped against my ankle in front of me. I stopped pushing and turned my head to stare at the lower bar that had taken me by surprise. Now color me stupid because I still was perplexed at the purpose of this machine. I was so enthralled with the possible purpose of this machine that I failed to realize Aldric reappearing from the closet with two pairs of fingerless boxing gloves.

"It's used to test your balance and agility," he said, turning slightly to close the closet door.

"I-I'm sorry?" I stammered, jolting around to face him.

"The machine before you," Aldric said. "My Beta and I built it six years ago after watching *Spartacus*."

I was too embarrassed to tell him that I had never seen the movie, or at least I assumed it was a movie, nor was I about to ask who or what a "Beta" was, so I returned my gaze to the machine with a weak nod.

"You might want to step back," Aldric stated with an underlining excitement in his voice.

I did so, looking downward to ensure I wouldn't accidentally trip over anything, though I had no reason to believe I would, and then turned my attention to him; he was bending over to flip the button attached to the taped down cord. I jumped a little as the contraption began to whirl and hum. As I looked back to this machine inspired by "Spartacus," I saw that the two horizontal bars turned so much faster than they had when I tried to do it manually. Whereas eventually I would have piece together how it would test my balance and agility, I barely had time to react to Aldric's sudden jump and ducks out of the reaches of the horizontal bars. I thought I moved fast given the fact that I was a winged werecat or whatever that long "a" word was, but this—his quick dropping of the two pairs of boxing gloves into the claws of this machine in a matter of seconds—was unbelievable and strangely beautiful.

Why it was strange, I couldn't say, because my mind and eyes were just too mesmerized watching him to focus on anything else. I couldn't help comparing what Aldric was doing to the girls in elementary school playing Double Dutch during recess. You had to keep moving and pay close attention to where the rope was at any given time. Yet, as I watched Aldric duck and jump, both bars missing his head and legs by mere milliseconds, I couldn't help but stare and drool over how the muscles in his perfectly sculpted arms and legs contracted and released. They were large and powerful in such a magnificent manner. Even the beads of sweat somehow accentuated the grace in his movement; it would take Gregory several lifetimes of training to measure up to *half* of Aldric's agility. It would most likely take me nearly the same amount of training time if I were being honest. It should have frightened me that Aldric possessed the strength to overpower and harm me, but it intrigued me more than anything.

After some time, he jumped to the side to turn off the machine. The noises coming from the gears and mechanisms sounded as though they were being sucked by a vacuum and winded down until Aldric's heavy breathing was left in their stead. I waited for his shoulders to slump forward, his hands gripped to his knees like I had seen so many times with the fighters after a workout in The Pit, but this didn't happen. He didn't do it. Not for a second or in an effort to impress me. Aldric stood tall, his beautiful hazel eyes staring right back at me. Though his breathing and the sweat still dripping down from every inch of his body seemed to me to say otherwise, this god-like stance illustrated that mini demonstration of the "Spartacus" contraption was nothing more than a warmup.

However, I sensed that his stance was also communicating a playful challenge. Normally, had he been human and an opponent in The Pit, I would have reveled at the audacity of the non-verbal challenge. But as it was, I was a bit taken off guard. Never in my six years of live-or-die training back at the warehouse had I ever encountered such a machine, and I wasn't certain if I would come out as collected and cool as Aldric just was when he jumped away from the machine. Yet if six years of training mixed with the other many forms of abuse had taught me anything, it was that you didn't back down from a challenge. The main difference from the many challenges prior to this one was that I had a choice. Or at least that's what Aldric's eyes seemed to be conveying, which threw me off into a sort of confused hesitation about whether I should accept his challenge.

Freedom of choice? Could that be? Impossible as my mind wanted to believe it to be and for the life of me, my body or perhaps my freakish-feline part stepped past Aldric and crouched in acceptance of the challenge as I waited for him to turn the machine back on. It was also as though my freak- ish-animal side finally felt official unleashed—even... even... free? Free, the word still sounded foreign. Yet, the moment the "Spartacus" machine whirled back to life, I mimicked how Aldric had jumped right in. I didn't have time to be surprised with how easily I fell into rhythm, jumping and ducking like I'd seen Aldric do, despite how much quicker the bars seemed to move in comparison to how they had appeared when I was an observer. And as the word "free" became more and more tangible and without even realizing it, a smile crept across my face.

Another reason the word was becoming more tangible, though it almost made me lose my concentration, were the words of encouragement coming from Aldric. Words like "good," "re- member to exhale when you duck and inhale when you jump," and "trust your instincts." The only words of encouragement I'd received from Ross or Gregory were, 'Why do I even both- er?' 'I will beat you from an inch of my life if you don't get this right,' or 'Hurry up! More important real boxers need to use the equipment.'

I can't properly express how or why I felt both uncomfort- able and relieved at the same time that after fifteen minutes of still working out on the "Spartacus" contraption, Aldric not once appeared annoyed or impatient. I didn't dare look over at him because I would definitely lose my focus. But I felt his presence. His intoxicating aroma of the salty ocean air and campfire smoke fueled my adrenaline. And when I finally decided to jump aside and away from the machine, taking a moment to catch my breath before finally turning my attention to Aldric, he had the biggest grin across his face. His arms folded across his chest. It was almost as if he was proud of me. But how could that be? How could he be proud of someone he barely knew—someone who had been told several times that they were nothing, to the point of fully believing it to be true? How? The exhaustion of jumping and ducking for as long as I had must be playing tricks with my mind and imagination, I thought.

"Wh-why are you looking at me like that?" I managed to ask, suddenly becoming very self-conscious. I rubbed my arm, desperately trying not to resort to my normal reactions of running away or curling into myself as I wished the look to go away. I wanted to be steadfast in one of my new goals of trying to be less awkward, though I was pretty sure I was failing at following through with the goal at this moment.

"I'm sorry," Aldric finally said. "I didn't mean to make you feel uncomfortable, but—God! You were magnificent. Like you were one with the machine."

He said those last few seconds like he was exasperated or a Looney Tunes character swooning over a love interest. I reluctantly and quickly pushed away the latter idea because, while I had always been swift, especially during a fight in The Pit—hence the "need" for the serums—I was anything but "magnificent." Yet the reason behind my reluctance, to push aside again the notion of him saying what he had said out of romantic feelings, was a desire to be closer to him. To know he felt this unexplainable connection between us too. There were hints that he might, but not enough for me to be certain and secure about it. Regardless, I blushed so hard that I hoped the blood already rushing to my cheeks from the workout would hide how uncomfortable I was from being uncharacteristically complimented.

It wouldn't have mattered anyway because, when I stopped

fueling my inner pity party, I noticed Aldric's face was nearly as flushed as mine. Granted, he could have still been cooling down from his demonstration of the "Spartacus" machine earlier. Unlikely as the notion was with how long I had been on the machine, my knowledge of werewolves' physiology was very limited, so I didn't know how much time they would need to cool off in comparison to a normal human male. From the small amount of fantasy novels I've read with werewolves in them, I knew that their body temperature ran higher than humans. Now whether it was true or not, I wasn't sure. I know this was true for me, but that didn't mean it was for him as well.

"Ahem," Aldric uttered, breaking the awkward silence by clearing his throat. "I was going to have us spare a little, but given the time... I, uh—thought we would go up to the kitchen. You must be starving."

"Famished," I said as I bit my lower lip because I was still self-conscious from the awkward moment that had just trans-pired.

As I waited for him to put the boxing gloves away in the closet, I was still curious as to why he had wanted to show me this machine he and his "Beta" had built. I was also curious as to why we hadn't changed into more appropriate clothing to exercise in. I hoped neither Beatrix nor he would be upset that the clothes I was wearing were damp from my sweat. Beatrix in particular, since she was the one who had bought me these clothes. Yes, with Aldric's money. Regardless, the other more pressing worry with Beatrix, apart from the clothes, was how much time she had taken to thoroughly wash and style my hair, which I'm sure was in a terrible disarray. Noticing the many mirrors, I rushed over to see how much of a mess my hair truly was. Though it didn't look too bad, I found myself smoothing and fixing any hair that may have been out of place.

It was weird to be worrying about such a thing because it was something I had gotten out of the habit of doing or think-ing about during my time with the King Cobras. Ross didn't care about how I looked as long as I gave him a good show and made him money. Though the fear of Ross finding me and assuredly starting a war with Aldric and pack was still present, I was regaining my sense of freedom and I wasn't about to lose it; especially to a moron like Gregory. So when he emerged, I pushed away those horrid memories trying to dominate my thoughts and followed Aldric up the stairs toward the kitchen.

CHAPTER SEVENTEEN

As I followed Aldric toward the stairs and around the hallway, with each turn and all of the ups and downs of the steps, I decided that I would make mental notes so I would be less likely to get lost again if I should find myself in the gym again. Yet as we approached the kitchen, the waft of sizzling meat filled my nostrils, causing me to not only to forget all of my mental notes, but to drool like crazy. When I noticed Aldric turn his head in my direction, presumably to make sure I was still near his side, I quickly covered my mouth with my hand. The last thing I needed was for him to catch me drooling like some feral animal.

He chuckled a little before saying, "Smells like Beatrix is cooking lunch... and our mother's recipe for split pea soup with ham, no less. Don't worry, I'm just as hungry as you are. Hopefully, my sister sliced enough of Agatha's homemade sprouted multigrain bread to go along with it."

I said nothing as I slid my hand away from my face and followed him in, toward the chair I had occupied the last few times I had been in the kitchen. And for the life of me, I couldn't tell you why Aldric taking the seat next to me both made me a little uncomfortable and excited me all at the same time. Uncomfortable because the only other man who dared to sit somewhat close to me was Ash, and it was usually when he was either on guard duty outside my room or giving me some words of wisdom right before a fight. Maybe I felt uncomfortable because I wanted him to be sitting closer to me, to feel him touching me like he had done to calm me in the woods, and I felt weird to be having these sorts of feelings toward a man I barely knew.

I know I'm repeating myself by saying all of this, but it's not like these emotions were going to magically disappear with the snap of my fingers. Six years of abuse and learning that my parents were my adoptive parents, who couldn't even love someone like me, even before they found out I was a freak of nature, were also not going to dissipate in seconds either. I couldn't change the past as much as I wanted to, and I couldn't predict the future. All I knew was that it was going to be a process and a journey. And as much as I wanted to get the journey over with as soon as possible, I'm wasn't so naive to think that life works like that.

Idle conversations occurred after Agatha finally came into the kitchen and joined the three of us, with Beatrix placing a bowl of split pea soup in front of each of us. And just like Aldric had hoped, Beatrix placed three baskets of the homemade bread in the center of the table. The amount of bread seemed excessive, but with how hungry I was, I wasn't about to complain. Yet I waited for Aldric to grab the first slice, spreading what seemed like an inordinate amount of butter across the surface. My eyes unconsciously widened at the sight of butter— real butter! Not old leftover bacon and meat grease scraped from the pan and formed to look like some gross blackish-grey and awful-tasting butter. I knew that faux butter was not actual butter, although many of the King Cobras members tried to convince me to believe that it was. But this! Well, I wouldn't be surprised if the butter had also been homemade, though I hadn't seen or heard a single cow to prove it.

Another thing that surprised me was, though I hadn't been in this house for very long, how much I felt at home here. "Home" felt like a stranger word than "free," for it was a word I hadn't truly ever felt, even before that fateful day in gym class and the early years with my adoptive parents, who seemed to actually love me unconditionally because I had been blissfully unaware of how they truly felt about me. A pebble in their shoes, as I was.

Had they given me a room decorated with pink ballerina motifs and over-the-top girly furniture in hopes that I would become less of a thorn in their side and resemble something of a normal child to them? Maybe they had before they agreed to adopt me. Maybe they thought they were about to receive a graceful and girly child, but they got me instead. Someone who had always had always felt out of place and had none of the traits they had hoped for. Hence, being someone they were stuck with until the opportunity to sell me to that tyrant, Ross Templeton. The only grace I might have had pertained to the ring in The Pit, and even that took a lot of hard work to get to that point. Yet "free" was an unattainable concept beaten out of me within the first few weeks of my imprisonment with the King Cobras.

But "home" meant acceptance, safety, and the ability to breathe comfortably without judgement or consequences. But that was the biggest pipe dream—bigger than the word "free." And yet both words felt interconnected. Was this because of how kind and generous these three people had been to me thus far? Was it because they were werewolves and my feline side finally felt less on edge around them? Or did it have to do with Aldric and this weird connection between us? God, I wish he hadn't clammed up when I had asked about what he meant by us being "mates." I was fairly certain it wasn't the British slang for "close friends."

Regardless, I quietly cherished this moment and had a feeling, though there was still a part of me that didn't know if I should trust it or not, that this wouldn't be the last time I'd be thinking this. And so I delved into the soup, dipping the bread daintily into the creamy goodness with savory pieces of ham because, as extremely hungry as I was, I still didn't want to give any of them a reminder that my table manners had completely vanished during my time at the warehouse. And before I could protest, Beatrix refilled my bowl not once, but *three* times. A huge grin spread across Aldric's face. I noticed every time I had turned to refuse another helping from his sister—up to the third time—that I could no longer keep quiet about how creepy his smile was. I just couldn't understand why me eating brought a smile across his face—or if there were perhaps another reason. Did he get his kicks watching girls eating? Did he do this when he brought strange girls into his home for a meal? It was really irksome. I had never, prior to my stay here, had anyone watch me eat with such joy.

"What?" I asked, a bit of the split pea soup unconsciously dribbling down my chin.

"It's just so good to see you finally eat a full meal," he said with a tone that seemed to indicate a huge level of pride in me. By the sincerity within his large and beautiful hazel eyes, I knew he hadn't meant to be in jest. That still didn't mean I didn't find his choice of words to be even creepier than him grinning at me. I shifted, slightly uncomfortable in my seat, and went right back to eating.

It was then that both Agatha and Beatrix excused themselves from the table, making a point to tell us they would return to clean up later. Agatha's excuse was that she wanted to be home before her sons came back from school. I wanted to ask if werewolves went to school with humans or if there was a special "werewolf" school, but decided to keep quiet about it out of fear of sounding stupid. Now that I knew other supernatural creatures actually existed outside of the written page, other than myself, I knew I had *a lot* to learn. But with the small amount I had learned today being more than a little overwhelming, I wasn't in a hurry to know everything about this other world—not yet anyways. Even if I had been in a hurry to learn more and had the courage to ask about this other world—now my world, I guess—I was quickly distracted by Beatrix's excuse of having plans with her "boyfriend." I mean, she actually made air quotes with her fingers, which I found sort of odd, but then again, there were a lot of things I found odd about her and this was quickly becoming the one of the things I liked about her.

And then, it was just Aldric and me sitting side by side, alone. It was almost completely silent, our breathing and nature seeping through the closed doors to the garden and barely filling the room. I stared out into the garden ahead of me through the glass panes of the doors and I noticed a couple of bluebirds hopping along the soil. I had seen illustrations of these birds in one of my moldy nature books in my room back at the warehouse, but never in person. What a vibrant shade of cobalt blue the male had, and the reddest chest that seemed to magically glimmer from the sun's rays. I know that may seem not probable in comparison to the infamous iridescent feathers of the male peacock. But trust me, this male bluebird's coloring was a distant second in my eyes. He strutted his stuff and sung to the female bluebird, who was only a few feet away from him.

From my books, typically male bluebirds compete with one another in an attempt to woo and prove to the selected female that they would be the best mate and father of her offspring. I turned my attention toward the female and felt nothing but a kinship with her. I understood her dull, earthy colors were beneficial when it came time for sitting on her eggs as she waited for them to hatch because it protected both her and her eggs from any predators. The reason I felt this sort of kinship toward the female bluebird's outer color was that I internalized it as a reflection of what I felt inside and outside, unworthy of any suitor or mate—***mate!***

And then it hit me... There were many animals, not just bluebirds, who mated to another of their species for life from what I've read in many zoology books. Was it the same for werewolves and werecats? Is that what Aldric had meant earlier today? However, this confused me, for the animals who mated for life had a choice in who they were going to be with. The way Aldric had said that we were mates made it seem like there *wasn't* a choice...

As this stewed and festered in my head, the words "free" and "home" faded away and were replaced by "panic" and "fear." The idea that I had, when I had first become mentally aware I was no longer in the warehouse, that I had possibly left one hell and entered a new one, didn't seem so crazy anymore. So much so that I stood up very quickly, the chair slamming against the checkered tile floor. I knew I had startled Aldric in the process because his chair groaned to face me. But I couldn't look at him for long as I moved back a few steps, my arms wrapped tightly around my chest. In my mind were images of the females of every species who mate for life being nothing more than "housewives" being forced to live submissively and breed as many offspring as their male counterparts wanted.

I'm only eighteen, I'm only eighteen, I thought over and over again. During my six years at the warehouse, not once did I ponder whether I wanted to have children. Surviving the next day, yes. But never children. Now, if this is what Aldric had meant by us being mates, I wouldn't have a choice in the matter.

"Vivila, what's wrong?" Aldric asked out of concern.

However, with my whirling in chaos, I was having a hard time distinguishing whether he was being genuine or not. I walked backward away from him, in continual feelings of confusion and panic. And it wasn't until my back unknowingly slammed into a part of wall filled with hanging pots that I spoke. But for whatever reason, my words were only coming out in broken sentences.

"Mates... bluebirds in the garden... other animals mate for life, but they have a choice," I said with labored breathing, the blood draining from every part of my body except for my cheeks, heart thumping rapidly. Regardless, it was the last thing on my mind. I was too focused on trying to communicate the millions of thoughts swarming in my head about the whole mate thing. "Submissive females... housewives... forced to give as many offspring as their male counterparts want... no choice, no choice... I left one hell only to enter into another."

I knew I was making no sense, and it wasn't until I realized I had somehow fallen to the floor, my arms wrapped around my knees as I rocked back and forth, that I noticed Aldric standing up and slowly approaching me. When he squatted down in front of me, I felt an unexplainable wave of power behind his intoxicating scent, as though it was trying to calm me—like it had a mind of its own. And while it did, it didn't erase the thoughts pulsating within me.

"Don't touch me!" I screamed as his hand gradually started to reach out for my shoulder.

"Vivila, I would never hurt you," Aldric said calmly, retracting his hand. "Talk to me. I promise you haven't entered into a new kind of hell. This is about what I said about us being mates, right?"

I nodded, eyes staying averted from his.

He let out a heavy sigh like he was trying to piece together my scrambled and fragmented words in order to figure out how and what he was about to say next without scaring me more. I watched his darting and pensive eyes with an intensity that nearly distracted me from my chaotic psyche. I observed his mouth partially open and close, as if it were indecisive on whether it should vocalize one thought or the other. He ran his fingers through the longer strands of his black hair. When he stood up and started pacing around the kitchen, the suspense within the silence was killing me—not literally, of course, but it wasn't helping my anxiety. He stopped for a moment by the door that led to the garden, presumably seeing the same pair of bluebirds as I'd seen, and then gradually returned to sit in front of me. I watched as he crossed his legs together, placing both hands firmly on his knees before finally breaking the silence.

"I'm not going to pretend I understand exactly how you

are feeling," Aldric said slowly. "That being said, I think I understand where your confusion lies. You are correct that most animals mate for life and have a choice in who their mates will be. But my inner wolf balances your inner feline because we are destined to be with one another. Before you ask what I mean by that, let me answer with the fact that supernaturals like us live with a duality within them that coexists and works as a team to protect us when need be. I'm guessing because you never grew up with others of your own kind that you never learned to communicate with your inner feline or learned what her personality is like.

"But I digress. Yes, for birds in particular, the male is visually more colorful and/or has to prove his worth to a prospective female, showing he can provide a well-constructed nest and a level of protection from predators. I can see where you may think that the female is like a submissive housewife or feels enslaved; similar, I'm guessing, to your experience had to endure with the King Cobras. *An unwarranted situation where the male constantly chips away at the very core of the female until there is nothing left but a hollow shell and not a balanced appreciation of one another and partnership.*"

Aldric said the last sentence through huffed, gritted teeth, trying to keep a high level of anger at bay. His eyes kept shifting from yellow to hazel as his fists curled so tightly that his skin not only turned to a purplish color but was also beginning to sprout jet black fur. In what I presumed to be a way to regain his composure, he combed his fingers through his hair as he let out a heavy sigh before continuing, "However, the relationships between werewolves or werecats and their mates are completely different from the bluebirds in the garden and other animals. And while we both live harmoniously with our animal and human sides, I feel I must strongly reiterate we are different when it comes to our mates. For it is predestined by the Great Ones above. It is similar to two halves of one soul coming together. A yin and yang sort of thing. An unbreakable bond with neither dominating the other.

"I'm not sure if I'm explaining this properly, but I promise I'd never force you to do anything you don't want to do or aren't ready to do. I'll admit I wouldn't mind having children of our own, but it's not a set-in stone thing for me. Plus, there are other options, when the time comes, for an Alpha to name an heir for his pack that *aren't* biological."

I had a feeling there was more he wanted to say because he lightly bit his lip and shifted his eyes to either side of him. The information was overwhelming to say the least and while I would need time to process and make sense of what he had just explained, it was good to know that he and I being mates was not like what I had originally thought. That said, I had loads of questions, but where to begin was the main thing racing through my mind.

And I could almost swear I could hear his racing thoughts over my own; so much that, without rhyme or reason, I needed to touch his arm before I could even think to voice my questions. And the moment my hand did so, his tense muscles relaxed. I slowly lifted my gaze, observing the deep rise and fall of his chest as it fought against the taut fabric along his perfectly sculpted abdomen and then at last to his eyes, which had finally stopped shifting between his wolf and human colors.

"Promise me something?" I finally mustered to say despite my brain feeling so overwhelmed that I thought it might explode. I had never been so bold to ask anyone to promise me anything without fear of violent consequences. And yet, there was something within me that needed to take the risk of asking this in order to fully trust Aldric once and for all. If you gave me ten years, I still wouldn't be able to tell you why.

For the seconds of silence as I waited for Aldric to answer, I sure was regretting asking it. Maybe more than regret, it was fear of what his answer would be. Regardless, my gaze surprisingly didn't avert from his unreadable eyes. Had he been Ross or Gregory, I would never have dared to ask a question such as this. As simple and as innocent as it may seem, it wasn't if you ever experienced their wraths: individually *and* combined.

Yet here I was, staring Aldric dead in the eyes, waiting for his answer like my inner cat or whatever I was, not about to back down from the challenge she was mysteriously sensing; and not only that, because this train of thought wasn't weird enough and I had just claimed to have such a thing as an "inner cat" *and* that she had her own personality, she was taking pleasure in this alleged challenge. I never thought of myself as having this duality like Aldric seemed to be alluding to. Yet, when Aldric finally broke the silence with a shaky sigh and intense eye contact, "she" backed down in heartache to see him wrapped up in fear and nervousness.

~~A man. A werewolf.~~ An Alpha who appeared worried about giving the wrong answer. Perhaps what he said about mates being two halves of one soul, I don't know... I just don't know. We were more alike than I originally thought. But if that were true, then I had it all wrong about playing the role of the submissive wife thing and what I lacked, he made up for, and what he lacked, I... I... I... what? What did I make up for? A gorgeous man like him must have had at least a dozen girlfriends, while I, the hot mess that I was, had never had a boyfriend—hell, I'd never been on one date.

So, what do I have to offer as the yin to his yang; especially if I'm making him feel what he's feeling right now? Whatever it is, I don't like it right now. I just want him to be happy, which is weird too. How can I desire him to be happy and not feel the feelings I was perceiving to him have, as if they were my own, when I still barely knew him? Though I felt this connection, both unconsciously and consciously, of knowing him completely to my very core from my very first night in this large mansion, how can I expect him—Geez Louise, why was it so difficult to properly put into words as to what I mean? Maybe it was a mate thing. Regardless, I decided to shut my brain off because he was finally going to speak and answer my question about whether he could promise me something.

"Anything," Aldric said breathlessly in response to my bidding for his promise in what I had to say next.

"No more secrets," I said quickly, temporarily forgetting about the thousands of questions I had in relation to his explanation about us being mates, for I wasn't expecting the answer he had just given. So simple and almost perfect until a sudden realization interrupted, sending my nearly calm heartbeat to race once again and my face to flush in panic. "Wait! If we're mates, destined to be together—to complete each other—and you're Alpha to the Red Rose Pack... What does that make me?"

Aldric stood up from his squatting position so quickly that the feeling of dread and uneasiness filled not just the small space between us but the whole kitchen. I could feel my breath grow shallow as I watched his hands, which had been cupping his stubbled chin, move up and around to the back of his head, where they remained for some time. I watched as he released a deep and shaky exhale before pacing back and forth. His chest heaved in discomfort, as he contemplated once again how best to answer my question. As if my heart hadn't been breaking before, when I had asked him to promise me not to withhold any secrets from me. Is it totally crazy to say that I was starting to fall in love with him? Probably. But when I could swear I heard the pounding race of his heartbeat from where he stood only a few yards away from me and I watched as he slid his cupped hands forward again, through his already disheveled black hair, until the hands acted as a mask in front of his face... I wasn't so sure.

For how could someone who never knew the true meaning of love—because she had been rejected so many times, by her birth parents, her adoptive parents, and nearly everyone, aside from Ash—ever know what it is like to love and be loved?—To quote Eden Ahbez. Regardless, and without rhyme or reason, I wearily pushed myself up to stand, using the wall to momentarily aid my balance, and walked cautiously over to him. I was about to do something I had never done before, and I was very unsure of the reaction to come.

My anxiety chilled and tingled my cheeks, my shoulders to my legs, from this huge secret Aldric seemed reluctant to tell me. I wanted so badly to resort back to the coping methods that had served me so well in the past. But a need beyond my comfort level was telling me to keep going toward Aldric. I was literally and metaphorically walking into a lion's den—or rather a wolf's—but my feet didn't seem to care until I was standing mere inches from his face. This was the most courageous thing I had ever done, more than any fight in The Pit; I softly placed my hands on his and guided them away from his face. His eyes were closed and I waited for them to meet mine before I said anything.

"Tell me," I said warmly and calmly, though every fiber inside me was anything but calm.

"Luna," Aldric whispered. "You will be—*are* the Luna of this pack."

CHAPTER EIGHTEEN

My hands slid down to his chest, pushing away just a bit as I tried to process what he had just said. My eyes never left his. But Luna? I was not only destined to be with Aldric, but also to lead a pack of werewolves alongside him. Lead? Was he kidding me? I barely knew what it meant to be a Winged Ailuranthrope, who my real parents were or why they abandoned me, nor the rules and laws of werewolves. At least I assumed there were rules and laws.

Of course, my assumption was based on the many fantasy novels I'd read in my room and there was a distinct possibility that there weren't rules and laws because this is real life and not a work of fiction. Nor could I be certain of there being rules and laws in the werewolf community by the many nature books I'd read either. Aldric did mention that supernaturals such as us lived harmoniously with our animal side. Yet, I had only become truly aware of mine just minutes ago, when I saw how uncomfortable and unhappy Aldric was. I'd also just discovered that Aldric, Agatha, and Beatrix were werewolves— that the supernatural creatures I thought were mere fiction, aside from myself, could most definitely be real.

But... leading a pack of werewolves? Damn, I just don't know. I could barely stand up to Gregory, let alone Ross. Leading meant being able to not let people like Ross make you feel small and unable to make decisions for the good of those, in this instance the Red Rose Pack, you are responsible for. And there was no way I'd be able to do that with Ross's voice in the back of my head still chiseling away at my self-esteem. Despite him being miles away from here. Yet this awareness of not being able to stand up to Ross and the rest of the King Cobras, Ash again excluded, festered in my mind for some time. I know one of the goals I had made back on Aldric's and my walk in the woods earlier was not to keep having my mind wonder into lengthy inner monologues, but God Damn! I just couldn't help myself. I mean, this is huge and a lot of responsibility.

"You've got the wrong person," I blurted because my current inner monologue was adamant in voicing it. Try as I might, I just couldn't maintain eye contact with Aldric, nor could I control how my body began to shake or the racing of my heartbeat. I managed to continue, despite how uncomfortable I was about Aldric staying quiet. "I can't lead anybody. I couldn't stand up to Ross and most of the King Cobras during my six years with them! And now you're telling me I'm the Red Rose Pack's Luna?"

I really wanted to resist my natural instincts to run or curl into myself on the floor, especially with how kind and patient Aldric was being as I finally looked him dead in the eyes again. But geez, Louise. I said it once, and I was sure I would say this many times in the future, but this was all too overwhelming. I didn't know how transparent my emotions were or that the day's new information was showing on my face until Aldric pulled me into a hug. A hug I initially wanted to pull away from because very few people had every dared to give me one, including my ~~parents~~ adoptive parents (even before the gym incident when I was twelve), so it caught me by surprise and was a little uncomfortable, **but** there was something calming about it. It was as though all of the overwhelming feelings and thoughts just washed away. And not gradually either. It was immediate.

"Is this a mate thing?" I asked, somewhat muffled by my face being nearly nuzzled in Aldric's armpit, my thought escaping my lips without fully realizing that it had until I felt the low grumbly vibration of a chuckle radiating from Aldric's chest and through my resting ear.

"What do you mean?" Aldric asked in return. I swear I could almost hear the smile, or rather joy, in his voice in his question. I know that this most likely doesn't make any sense, but there is no other way I can describe it. Did he know what I meant and was he teasing me with this retort, or did he really not know what I was asking? How was I suppose to interpret the tone of his question?.

I'll admit, I was a little embarrassed to explain myself because the reality of there being a supernatural world was new to me, let alone what it meant to be mates. I realize that I may be repeating myself, but here I was, in the arms of someone who grew up knowing what it meant to be who he was, who was surrounded by others who were just like him and could guide him in the different rules and laws of his kind and of other supernaturals... and I, I, I didn't know a damn thing. A normal person or supernatural creature may not ponder this train of thought, but I have been completely in the dark in all of this and not just about my own species, but this realization of his upbringing. It was just too much to comprehend. At this point in time anyways.

I felt almost like an infant, super naïve, and embarrassed about how sheltered I truly was, not only these past six years, but for the last eighteen years of my life. I took comfort in Aldric not being able to see my face. Well, until he pulled away and placed his large, warm, and somewhat rough hands on either side of my face, lifting my head so that our eyes met. There was such compassion and love in his eyes, something I still didn't think I would see in a leader of a ~~gang~~ pack. I shouldn't have been surprised because Aldric wasn't like any other man I had ever met, including Ash.

"All of my worries seemed go away as soon as you pulled me into your embrace," I finally said, lifting my head just enough so that my voice didn't sound muffled as it would if

I continued to bury my face in his arm. I could hear the pulsating drum of his heart as I nuzzled back into his arms. Just when I thought his very presence, many yards away or two feet away, caused his special scent to invigorate me alone, this closeness—this hug made his scent seem like a drug to me. I never wanted to let him go and wanted to know everything about him. I felt a possessiveness rise from within me, which frightened me slightly because I had never felt like this toward another being. It was such a new feeling.

Don't get me wrong, my mind was certainly starting to nag me again on the huge responsibility of being a Luna. And regardless of the waves of calmness that had only short moments ago appeared to wash away, my mind and body fully pushed away from Aldric until he and I were standing a few feet apart. Oh, why was my mind ruining this perfectly wonderful and strange moment? I could almost feel my walls rising up again, my instincts irrationally telling me I needed to protect myself and reminding me that this was all going too fast.

I mean, I still barely knew this guy. When he took a step forward, confusion visibly conveyed across his face, I immediately took a step back. I suppose what I was now beginning to feel was trapped, and though this was vastly different from my entrapment—or rather slavery—with Ross and the King Cobras, I didn't like the feeling of, once again, not having a choice. Like my life didn't belong to me—my choices didn't belong to me. Whether it was being locked in a dingy room in the basement, only to be let out to fight men like a trained tiger to the sexual advances from Gregory to being "rescued" by a pack of werewolves to being told I was mated to the Alpha of this pack or being surprisingly bestowed the title of "Luna"— this was just too much! Too much! TOO MUCH!!!

Without realizing it, though I should have with searing agony rippling and spreading down my back, my wings and tail appeared. My claws shot out, and my fur undulated up my arms and down my legs. I ignored the nearly deafening pain of my ears elongating because of the anger radiating through-out my body. Dodging around Aldric's grasps to stop me and without care, I charged through the glass-paned doors that led to the small garden.

I ran. As fast as my legs would carry me. I couldn't tell you where I was going or why I thought it was the best course of action. All I knew is that I needed to run. Aldric, Agatha, and Beatrix had been nothing but nice to me, yet still I ran. And when I heard Aldric calling my name and his feet hitting the earth so hard that I thought the ground would quake un-derneath him, I stretched out my wings, unbearable as it was because I never really had the chance to do so in my whole life, and beat them with as much force as I could manage. Into the air I might have started, my only lesson in flying from watching the birds from the barred window in my room back at the warehouse, but I crashed almost immediately, my right shoulder and part of my face taking most of the fall. The warm liquid of blood trickled down my face and bits of grass and dirt blurred my vision. Nonetheless, my body screaming for me to give up, I struggled and stumbled as I pushed myself up and attempted to run and fly again. I could still hear Aldric as he bridged the gap between us, but he was slightly muffled by the searing agony coursing throughout me.

I do have a choice. I do have a choice, I thought as I ran, one of my legs beginning to drag behind me. *I can't lead anybody. Ross was right when he said that I am nobody and will never be nothing more than nothing. And that is why I had to ruin a perfectly good moment between Aldric and me. I am nobody... important... I am no... body...*

As my wings felt as though they were filled with lead from exhaustion, I crumbled to the ground and let out a grunt, and everything around me grew dark. I saw Aldric approach me and kneel before me. And as I sunk further into the darkness of unconsciousness, I floated upward on a cloud. A very serene and protective cloud. Like the many times before when I had passed out over the past few days (more times than I care to admit, including my first few fights in The Pit), I struggled to grasp the amount of time that had gone by.

However, unlike those times before and regardless of the overpowering anger that led to me overexerting myself, followed by an unknowing shift into my feline counterpart, I felt surprisingly safe... and if at all possible, loved. My usual desire to over-analyze why I was sensing this was too tired to care because it felt nice. I had ruined the moment of being caressed in Aldric's arms earlier, but I was determined not to ruin this. Yes, I had little choice because I was after all unconscious, but still—I was going to let this feeling of being protected and loved wash over me as I continued to float on this cloud with all the strangeness it encompassed because of my limited experience with either feeling.

I had expected as I slowly came to, my eyes fluttering open, that I would be in one of two places: Agatha's medical room or in the bed of the room that Doc had claimed was mine. My mind was foggy, so I couldn't be sure where I was. What I did know was I was lying on a couch, my elbow bumping against the back of it. A blanket stretched over me and a soft pillow under my head. And though I appreciated the kindness from whomever had placed both there for me, my whole body throbbed from my two falls, nonetheless. My back and tailbone in particular.

I must have shifted back into my human form, for I did not feel the cushion of my wings beneath me, nor my tail wrapped down and around the couch to the floor. As I tried to focus more on my surroundings with my eyes, gradually moving my head to get a better look, I realized that the circular stone room was most certainly not Agatha's medical room or "my bedroom."

A most unusual and yet extremely beautiful coffee table stood perpendicular to me. The top, while most definitely wood, was shaped like a thick sliver from a tree trunk... a very shiny sliver. And similar to the table that I had seen up in the living room, the legs sanded in such a way as to not erase where the small branches had been sawed off to create the legs of this table. There seemed a common theme of nature, wolves, and the moon within this very large house. Which I suppose made more sense now that I knew Aldric, Agatha, and Beatrix were werewolves.

However, a transparent bowl and two separate piles of cloth was what really caught my eye. The liquid in the bowl was most definitely water at one point, yet it had been diluted with a deep red liquid. I concluded that it was my blood that had caused the water to be red, for I could see no evidence to dispute it otherwise. From my unintentional shifting of my wings and tail to the two falls in my attempt to fly, there was again no other explanation. Then there were the two piles of cloth, one folded and pure, untainted, and the other a chaotic mess stained with blood. Without reason, I lifted my hand to my head. I'll admit, my arm felt extremely stiff and painful as it made the gesture, causing the movement to feel as though it was in slow motion. As my hand finally reached the injured area, I expected to find it to be bare and the wound open.

In the past, more specifically during my early years with the King Cobras, whenever I had been punished for fighting poorly with many punches to the head by Ross's heavily ringed fists, the wounds had been left unbandaged and the blood dried, matting parts of my hair and covering my clothes as I slept on my old dirty mattress. I remember quite vividly the uncontrollable tears that would form as I struggled, quite dizzily, to the door when I awoke, banging—screaming for medical attention. No one heard me, or if there had been anyone there, they chose to ignore my pleas.

I also remember screaming how I just wanted to go home, not that I had a home to go home to because it was the people I thought were my parents who sold me to this hell. It was in the middle of the night, my hand and head still pressed up against the steel door, my legs having crumbled beneath me, that I was awakened by the heavy clicks of the door being unlocked. I felt too weak and too tired to move away nor care who was on the other side of the door. For all I knew, it was Ross coming to finish me off, which would have been a blessing because I didn't know how much more of this hell I could take.

But instead, as my whole body fell backward on the plastic pallet-covered floor, a man, who I would soon recognize to be Ash, stepped through the threshold. I recalled whimpering and him soothing and hushing me. I must have blacked out soon after, but a bandage had most definitely been wrapped around my head when I came to in the morning. And I knew it had been Ash who had mended me because it was he who brought me my breakfast and confessed to tending my head wounds. It was in that moment of unprecedented kindness that I gained a tiny sliver of hope that I could survive this hell I had been shoved and enslaved into.

With that memory pushing through my slightly foggy mind, when my fingers finally and carefully touched my head, in this strange room, I was surprised to find a small bandage between the wound and my fingers. Surprised not so much that there was a bandage and not the expected open cut, but that the bandage was so tiny. I was fairly certain that when I had hit my head, the gash was a lot, a lot larger. Yes, I have always been a fast healer, but not **this** quickly. Was this part of what I had overheard of Agatha's and Aldric's conversation during my first conscious day in this mansion when I strangely couldn't open my eyes but heard every word they had been saying? That the serums Ross had made sure to have injected into me had not only caused me to partially shift and dull my senses but had also prohibited the bulk of my naturally quick healing abilities too? However, before I could contemplate this train of thought further, I could hear the heavy footsteps of boots behind my head followed by an all too familiar scent of campfire smoke and salty ocean air. I wanted to turn to face the direction of where Aldric was coming from or at least pull myself up to make room on the couch, but my body was too sore to move.

"Please do not get up," Aldric said calmly, his arm firmly yet gently guiding me to continue to lie down. "You need to rest."

"I'm sorry," I said almost in a strained whisper, and then pointed to the bloody rags on the table. I wasn't sure what exactly I was truly sorry for. Was I sorry for moving due to six years of being expected to apologize if I moved without permission in front of Ross? Or was I sorry that I bled so much to cause the bowl of water and the unfolded pile of cloth to be stained with my blood? Not to mention, and most likely, the couch.

I watched as Aldric came around the couch, carefully pushing the bowl aside and using some of the folded clean rags to scoop up the bloody pile of rags. He pushed them backwards as the formerly clean rags wiped away the blood on the table before sitting in front of me. His face was a mixture of concern and guilt. I could tell, though I wasn't sure why, he was struggling to keep his posture. However, when he let out a heavy sigh, running his hand through his gorgeous mane of black hair, his whole body appeared to crumble into a slouch.

"No," Aldric said breathlessly, "I should be the one to apologize. I know I promised not to withhold any secrets from you. But learning that werewolves existed, what it means for us to be mates, and that you are to be the Luna of my pack—our pack—is not how I saw the day going. With all that you've been through and in an ideal world, I wanted to ease you into this world that you hadn't known was real until now. Especially with how little we know each other. I mean, our animal sides do because of the whole mate thing, but...

"And before you say anything, some of the blood came from me. You scratched me a bit prior to passing out," Aldric said with a small chuckle and showing his arms. "And if you are worried about the couch, I went through a bit of destructive phase a few years back when my father thought I was ready to be Alpha before I was ready. He decided he needed to travel the world and believed it was time to step down. It wasn't until I saw you fight at The Pit and my wolf recognized you as my mate that I understood why my father left. In retrospect, I'm surprised he didn't immediately step down after my mom died.

"When a werewolf's mate dies, a part of them dies too. The idea of living without the other half of your soul becomes unbearable... from what I've heard. But I suppose my father knew it would be a dishonor to my mother's memory to abandon me and my sister at the ages of nine and seven.

"But that's neither here nor there. I had Agatha attend to the bulk of your injuries before I carried you here..." Aldric's tone quickly changing from nonchalant to sullen.

"Where is here?" I interrupted, not knowing how to respond to all that he had said. I wish I could say that the heartache I felt from being sold by my adoptive parents was equal to the heartache his father, his sister, and he felt from the loss of Aldric's mother, but I can't because it isn't—not by a long shot. I wish I could promise that nothing like one of us dying will happen to us, leaving one of us to cope with the empty hole in our psyche. Even with my less than limited knowledge of the outside world and the supernatural world, I know life is not predictable like that or as easy as making a promise or wish to make it be so.

While I took a little comfort in knowing that Aldric struggled with being given the title of "Alpha," as I currently was with being given the title of "Luna," the sadness I could feel emanating from him made my simple question seem inappropriate with what he had just opened up and revealed to me. How I could feel what he was feeling as if it were my own body was extremely unexplainable. Yet I waited patiently, just the same, for him to answer. How long I would have to wait, I didn't know. But six years with the King Cobras made me almost an expert in patience—whether I wanted to be or not.

CHAPTER NINETEEN

I watched tears beginning to form in Aldric's eyes, as he cleared his throat and lowered his head in an attempt to compose himself. I continued to wait for my answer as to where we exactly were. The more time passed, the more stupid I felt about asking my question—interrupting a subject that was clearly a very sensitive topic for him.

So, without rhyme or reason... well, maybe not totally—for it made me very uncomfortable to see him like this; especially as his sadness continued to course through me as if it were my own—I placed one hand on his wrist and the other on his shoulder, pulling him closer to me. His knees began sliding toward the floor until my arms were completely wrapped around him. I may not have known how to comfort him before, back in the forest, but as the shirt I was wearing became damp and his body shook, I knew that it was a start in the right direction. I had ruined the moment in the kitchen before I had decided to run and fly, but I wasn't going to ruin this one.

However, I would never had thought I would see the day a man of authority, or even one without, be so vulnerable like this and feel comfortable showing this side of themselves, which I would have thought would have been kept well hidden under lock and key. I suppose this came again from being treated as the weaker sex and as someone of no importance because of my freakish nature. Or perhaps I had been conditioned from my ~~parents~~ adoptive parents and the majority of the King Cobras members, Gregory and especially from Ross, that men were to be feared, respected, and could do whatever they wanted as long as they gave no sign to indicate they were as weak and vulnerable like women. They had no use for being comforted by anyone. Yet here I was, ignoring the physical pain I was in, holding Aldric as he cried. Did this mean he was less of a man or a weak leader?

With deep consideration, I decided not. I knew Ross was wrong about a lot of things despite how afraid I still was of him, and so I decided he was wrong about this too—he must be wrong about this too. I won't lie and say I didn't have some lingering doubts in my decision with Ross's voice still trying to push its way into my mind and the guilt of thinking against all the lessons Ross had forcefully instilled in me, but in this moment I desperately wanted to dismiss them, for I was enjoying being this close to Aldric.

It felt safe and like I was at home. Similar to how it was earlier, in the kitchen, as I listened to Aldric, Agatha, and Beatrix converse while we ate. And after a time, I couldn't say how long—ten minutes, thirty minutes, an hour—Aldric pulled away from our embrace until our eyes met. Regardless of how red and bloodshot his eyes looked, I found myself still seeing him as the most handsome man I had ever laid my eyes on.

"I'm sorry," he said in a raspy and broken tone. "I don't usually behave like this."

I shook my head, my eyes searching for a way to tell him he didn't need to apologize in a way that words simply wouldn't do—which is another thing I never thought I would do. I was the one, since before I had ever smelled and sensed his presence at The Pit, who always had to apologize. Maybe, and I'm paraphrasing Beatrix's words to me not too long ago, there are just some things you don't need to apologize for. I wanted to stop him from continuing, but I felt a bit wrong in doing so; especially if changing the subject would help him feel less vulnerable.

"This room," Aldric continued with a cough in an effort to

once again regain his composure, "was built under my grandfather's orders to be a safe haven for the Alpha of this pack without fear of being attacked by intruders, or if he just needed time to be alone. As you may imagine, being an Alpha has a lot of responsibilities. You're required to be the best fighter, to make decisions that are for the best for your pack as well as care for the individual needs of your pack members, and form and maintain alliances with neighboring packs. It can be overwhelming at times.

"So, the front door is three feet of solid steel, the walls around the room behind it are nearly indestructible, and the glass in the ceiling is bulletproof. There used to be three different types of keys to open the door; however, when my father was made Alpha and because he found the keys to be a little outdated, he installed not only a new door but also an electronic panel that required a passcode outside the door."

"Okay," I said, feeling the need to say something to communicate that I was listening to every word he was saying, so he could release the sadness surrounding his parents that he seemed to want to suppress with this subject change. This now made my question appear a little less stupid; especially because it was helping.

"The passcode is 1-9-5-8. It's important that you remember it, okay?" Aldric said very seriously.

I nodded before answering calmly with, "Yes, I can remember it... But why are you telling me this? Why did you bring me here and not into Agatha's medical room or into the bedroom across from yours?"

"To be completely honest," he said slowly, "I thought about what you said about how we don't really know each other, us being mates and all... I'm not saying I'll be perfect at it; especially because I've never been in a serious relationship or really into the whole romantic-love thing and... you've been through more than anyone should—ever... and I don't want to rush you into anything, aside from dumping a massive amount of information in one day—I thought we could take it slow and get to know one another by continuing where we left off in *The Lion, the Witch, and the Wardrobe*."

A huge grin spread across my face. A definite Lucy- and Mr. Tumnus-like moment for sure—but was Aldric like this with his pack, gentle and sensitive, or was it just with me? Surely, he couldn't be this compassionate and vulnerable with his pack; none of them would take him seriously or trust in him to make the tough decisions or strictly follow the laws of the pack. Regardless, I watched as he leaned back to reach behind the bowl of blood-soaked water and grabbed the book, tucked in the back waistband of his pants. And as I watched him flip through the pages to reach the dog-eared page and begin reading, the long part of his hair falling across his face and partially covering the shaved sides of his head, I basked in listening to his soothing, raspy, deep voice. Occasionally, I looked around the circular nearly all brick walls with built-in bookshelves filled with DVDs. But for the next few weeks and a few days after, I was healed enough. When he and I weren't training in the gym, the two of us came into this room and Aldric would continue to read to me. Though we had finished *The Lion, the Witch, and the Wardrobe*, I still felt like Lucy, in a way, entranced by Mr. Tumnus' flute that was Aldric's voice as he read anything from Charlotte Bronte to Charlaine Harris. Of course, there were still meals in the kitchen with Agatha and Beatrix, yet slowly but surely, I started to feel a little out of place in this huge mansion—though my worry of Ross finding me and possibly starting a war between the Red Rose Pack and the King Cobras still lingered like a gnat flying in front of my face, refusing to leave as its buddies joined in to annoy me. Yes, Aldric had made an offer to Ross in exchange for me—but because Ross was too much of a stubborn tyrant to take it or lay idly, Aldric, true to his word about rescuing me, sent his pack members to carry out this promise. For me? Because he and I are mates? And I'm sorry, but I still wasn't and am not comfortable enough yet to accept that I'm not only a part of a werewolf pack, but also its future Luna.

I was also still not comfortable enough to use the bathtub or wear the heels Beatrix had bought, when she had gone shopping during my first few days, but I got the hang of most of the hair care tips and I didn't need Beatrix's help anymore... well, almost. And I still wasn't completely comfortable with how revealing the clothes were, mostly because of the scars that didn't heal correctly. "Correctly" according to Agatha, who insisted on doing weekly wellness checks, especially after my two failed attempts to fly out of anger. The wellness checks were followed by, much to my dismay and under the supervision of Aldric, practice shifting into my feline form in an effort to build up endurance to the pain.

"Close your eyes," she would say each time, "and focus. Imagine your wings and tail emerging out of you like a gust of wind. Then look inside yourself for what your inner feline looks like and then picture yourself being her. Focus. It won't work until your inner feline and you learn to trust one another—be as one."

It sounded like a lot of nonsense, especially coming from a werewolf who didn't have wings. Maybe if I had the chance, however small, to have another Winged Ailuranthropes or rather winged werecat training me, perhaps the exercises wouldn't seem so impossible to achieve. I must have fainted fifteen times already. Plus, I didn't think my true form was anything more than what I had more or less shifted with the aid of Ross's second serum. Yet despite Agatha's limited knowledge on winged werecats, she was fervent that my true form was that of a very large cougar—with barn owl patterned wings, of course. She based the "cougar" theory on the colors in my wings. She was also optimistic that in a month, I could start practicing stretching my wings and flying. I couldn't help laughing a little at the last part, if my two failed attempts were any indication of how that would go.

Regardless, true to Aldric's word, he didn't force me to do anything that I wasn't ready for. He made sure that any mention of me being the *future* Luna of the pack was off limits, for now at least. I emphasize the word "future" because according to Aldric, he and I hadn't completed the mate bond, and he again didn't want me to rush me into a role I wasn't ready for. He said Beatrix was temporarily taking this role until I was ready. I also wasn't ready to meet some more of or the entire pack. I mean I'd just started trusting Aldric, Agatha, and Beatrix, so how could I be certain I could trust the pack? I mean, I could trust Ash, but I didn't trust any of the other King Cobras. But again, did I really needed to remind myself that Aldric was not Ross? No, I suppose not. If Aldric trusted the members of his pack, I could learn to trust them too... in time.

And as curious as I was to learn more about this alleged prophecy that may or may not have been about me from a few books Aldric was able to obtain from a local pride of werecats, I was enjoying the hand-holding during our hikes to the spot he had taken me the first time. Soon after Aldric finished reading the C.S. Lewis novel, we would sit on the couch together and he would tell me stories about the first werewolves, growing up around other werewolves, the rules and treaties between other packs, or about things he thought were trivial like his favorite movies on the shelves of the "Alpha Room." This was a title I came up with because it seemed appropriate. Somehow calling it "our room" still felt a little weird.

While I enjoyed listening to Aldric tell stories and talk, I appreciated him not asking me personal questions. Though there was an anxious part of me dreading the day that he would, despite how well he kept his promise to not push me into things I wasn't ready about. I felt guilty nonetheless because he was being an honest with me and I wasn't being as forthcoming about my horribly sheltered life. Well, not entirely, because anytime he talked about books, it seemed like I couldn't shut up about the one I'd read.

Initially, I was a little shy about it, for it was something no one, aside from maybe Ash, wanted to hear about from me—they, more specifically didn't want to hear anything from me at all. It would have been preferable if I were mute, with the exception of the times Ross or Gregory demanded me to answer their questions. Questions like the ones Ross had asked me assumably hours prior to Aldric's pack members had rescued me or ones that would somehow prove how macho and tough they thought they were in front of other King Cobras members. But it was different—immeasurably different with Aldric. There was so much sincerity and patience emanating from his eyes, not to mention his overall presence, that made the shyness I was feeling go away.

"I wish I had the freedom to find out who I am as a person... as a supernatural creature. To be accepted and loved," I unconsciously admitted to him after he had told one of his stories in the Alpha room.

He said without hesitation or judgement, "The past doesn't matter. Yes, it has made you who you are, but it only holds as much power over you as you allow it. Your past has made you strong regardless of all the hardships you had to endure. You can't change the past but there are people who are willing to help you along your journey if you let us—if you let me. Not out of pity but out of a desire to help you see what I see you to really be... What you can be—will be. I don't expect you to open up to about every aspect of your life prior to living here, I just needed you to know that. And when you are ready to talk about your past, I'll be there."

I don't know what compelled me to do this. It was bolder than any action I had done since I had been brought here, including my failed attempts to fly away from here and my pulling him into my embrace when he had been upset. I scooted closer to him and curled my whole body into his with my head resting over his heart. It was in this moment that I realized I loved him, a thing I didn't think was even possible for a broken freak such as myself, and after only knowing him for nearly a month. With each passing minute, hour, day, and week, I could feel our bond growing stronger. Had I heard myself think all of this during my first few days here, I would have been totally freaked out and done something more crazy than attempting to fly and run away—or maybe I would have caused physical harm to the three people who have been there and done more for me than any other humans have, just so that I could escape these strong romantic feelings that were so new and frightening to me. I may have even overlooked the sedatives Agatha had on hand. Well, maybe not that extreme, but it was still crazy how *not* crazy I felt about the growing mate bond Aldric and I were experiencing.

It was like I was living in a fantasy or dream where I slowly lowered my guard enough to not fear ulterior motives or consequences for my actions. And like Aldric had said, I would find myself apart from the damage done by my not at all "Parents of the Year" adoptive parents or the conditioning abuse I experienced from Ross. I learned that there were things I enjoyed doing apart from reading and training on the Spartacus machine. With the help of Aldric and Agatha, I learned how to garden; how to tell what was a weed and why it was important to pull them. Like myself, plants needed room to grow without being strangled by the "big bad, negativity" weeds. Then, after stumbling upon a room that resembled an art studio, I learned that I also loved art; in particular, working with clay. I probably wouldn't have found it if I hadn't been looking for the storage closet holding extra towels.

I then followed Beatrix, who was taking over my training on one particular day because Aldric had some meetings, and she vaguely pointed to one of the many identical doors in the basement. Why she thought to suddenly and casually point out this particular door was beyond me. It piqued my curiosity enough for me to stop following my mate's sister and really take it in. What made it stand out from the other doors was a golden plaque with a name engraved on it: "Karlen Dawn O'Connor." Whenever this plaque had been made, it was pristinely clean. Not a speck of tarnish. And when I reached to open the doorknob, I fully expected Beatrix to call out to me as a reminder that we still had training to do or to say that what lay behind the door was forbidden. Why it would be forbidden, I'm not sure, but still my fingers hovered over the knob for some time before I worked up enough courage to open it. I heard Beatrix's footsteps come up behind me.

Here it comes, I thought with bated breath as I waited for one of the two outcomes to pass.

I was surprised when neither came to pass and Beatrix simply reached around me to flick the light switch on, revealing what looked to be an art studio, with everything from a small kiln in the far corner of the room to paints, canvases, clay, clay tools, large tables, and open shelves with clay sculptures resting on them. I strained to remember art class at school. It was the only class where I felt free from the bullies and to be myself. And though I had spent many months, after my imprisonment at the warehouse, reading partially torn art books, nothing could prepare me for what was before me now. I still wasn't sure if I was any good at making art, but the fun possibilities of creating were still deep within my heart.

And when I finally pulled my attention away from the beauty as I continued to stand in the doorway, turning to ask Beatrix about the name engraved on the plaque, the funniest thing happened, making me feel really guilty about asking. Beatrix, who exudes such a high level of confidence and sassiness, was at a loss for words and nearly at the point of crying. After a while, she turned herself away before turning back around to face me again, her eyes and nose bright red and her usually perfect eye makeup a little smudged. She confessed that this studio used to belong to Aldric's and her mother. It had been locked since her death, and only Aldric still had the key.

"Then why is it unlocked?" I asked, backing away from the

doorway until I bumped into the stone wall on the other side of the hallway.

"Aldric thought you might like it," she said, her voice still wavering from the remaining tears attempting to make one final fall from her beautifully long lashes.

"Why?" I asked. This question had been one I'd been trying to stop asking whenever the three of them, specifically Aldric, had given me anything. Not just material things, but acts of kindness. This wanting to stop asking this question arose more or less when I learned their true natures were actually pure during my second, weird, conscious but non-conscious day here in this mansion.

"I suppose he thought you would like a relaxing way to express yourself. Outside of training, practicing shifting with Doc, gardening, and reading," Beatrix said with a shrug before giving me a tearful wink and a somewhat forced smile—forced because she was most likely thinking of her mother and how her mother would never be in this room again, regardless of how long it had been since her mother had passed.

And as I watched her walk away, I couldn't help feeling a tinge of jealousy. To have that level of love toward her mother—her mother must have been one hell of a woman. From Beatrix's reaction to the art studio to the way Aldric talked about how *The Lion, the Witch, and the Wardrobe* was a book their mother loved to read to them, his parents' relationship and how devastated his father was when his wife—his mate—died, I just couldn't fathom having parents who had a mutual and unconditional love for one another. Yeah, jealousy was definitely what I was feeling. But I didn't want to feel that because like Aldric said, I couldn't change my past though it shaped who I was... well, as much as I allowed it to—but I could change my present, my future.

I'd read somewhere that "love knows no bounds." And as I looked back and forth from the door to the corner that Beatrix disappeared around, it was clear that both sets of my parents—biological and adoptive—had boundaries... had conditions to the extent of their love, and none included me. And yet, for some reason, the more time I spent with Aldric—and of course Agatha and Beatrix—I was learning that perhaps what I had read was true. Not just with the love Aldric and Beatrix had for their parents, but with their kindness and acceptance of me. This lessened the bit of jealousy I had toward Beatrix as I returned my attention to the door with her mother's name on it before daring to enter through the threshold.

But yes, I soon discovered my love of art. I had remembered loving art class as a child and class projects that required visual elements until the popular kids would always find a way to destroy my dioramas. Then, after that, I forced myself to not enjoy art-making in hopes that the other kids would just leave me alone. It didn't stop, but at the time I thought it was worth the effort. Nonetheless, as more weeks passed and from time to time, Aldric would peer in to see how I was doing and if it would be okay for him to sit and watch my make art. He didn't say much, apart from telling me how good I was at sculpting and drawing. While I knew he was being sincere, not to mention his presence was a bit distracting because, let's face it, he was like an Irish god in the looks department. I still didn't think the art I was producing was *that* great.

But like I said earlier, these passing months were like living in a dream... a very wonderful dream. However, like all good dreams, you have to eventually wake up and return to reality. And in my case, the events that followed were a harsh and terrible awakening. I may have been working extremely hard training in the gym with both Aldric and Beatrix and practicing shifting with Agatha, but this is one awakening I wasn't prepared for. Not yet, anyway. And all my fears that had been withering away were now crashing in at an alarming rate.

All I could think was not yet, not—yet. Not now.

CHAPTER TWENTY

The crashing of the dreamlike world I was in during my stay in this mansion snuck up at a very unexpected moment—and around a moment I was determined not to ruin. I won't lie and say that there weren't many areas of the mansion I didn't have memorized, mostly because the mansion was huge but also because I didn't find the need to be curious about the unknown areas of the mansion; it would just take away from my time with Aldric. I was cherishing, most fervently, my time with Aldric when he wasn't busy with Alpha things or sleep. While I was fearful and hesitant about this fervent emotion because it was all so new to me, I still couldn't imagine how I managed to survive or live before I was rescued by his pack members.

That said, and on this particular memorable day in the early afternoon, Aldric and I were about to enter the Alpha Room to watch a movie, instead of our usual reading. Leading the way up the unpolished marble stairs leading to the door, I was stopped by a wave of emotion washing over me. An emotion that was not mine. It wasn't the first time that this had happened, but it was the first time it was this strong. A mixture of emotions yo-yoing between yearning and hesitation. I stopped on the landing, halfway between the hallway below and the door to the Alpha Room above, and turned to face Aldric. His facial expression wasn't sad. Although if I were someone else and not mysteriously able to feel and read his emotions, it may have appeared that he was.

"What's wrong?" I asked, curious to know why he was

feeling both a yearning for something and a hesitation.

"Nothing," Aldric said, unconvincingly.

"I don't know if this is a mate thing, but I can feel what you are feeling right now," I said, trying not to sound accusatory or angry, but in a calm and understanding tone.

He sighed, running his hand through his thick mane of hair before speaking. "You know I don't want to rush you into anything you're not ready for, but holy wolf—the way you walk, and though you may not see this about yourself, you are the most beautiful woman I've ever seen or will ever see... and I just—I just—really want to kiss you right now."

I stood, staring at him in awe. I didn't know what to say. He finds me beautiful? No one has ever said that to me. Not even my ~~parents~~ adoptive parents told me that in the twelve years I lived with them. And I'm not going to lie, I'd wanted to kiss him since the first time I dared to look into his eyes upon our first meeting in the circular library, but I had kept that feeling hidden because I'd never kissed a boy before nor was I sure if the feelings were mutual because it was before I had learned of he and I being mates. Now, I had seen what kissing was supposed to look like plenty of times during my years before the King Cobras, in movies, television, YouTube videos, and the older kids from the middle school that stood across the street from my school. I even observed the subtle facial and body movements that led to two people kissing. Yet, seeing it done was one thing; actually doing it yourself was another. I was certain Aldric had kissed his fair share of girls. I mean, he was like an Irish god. He probably had girls lining up outside his door just to have a chance at kissing him.

Okay, that's a bit of an exaggeration, but you get the picture. But nonetheless, he was most likely an excellent kisser. How could I compete with that? And yet, he'd just told me how beautiful I am... cross that... he'd told me that I was the most beautiful woman he had ever or would ever see AND he wants to kiss me. Woman? Yes, I'm eighteen and legally an adult...

gasp... Oh my God! I'm overthinking this. I could feel my heart racing so fast, so hard that I was certain Aldric could hear it. My breathing went so shallow and quick, I was also certain I was close to hyperventilating.

Yet, I found the courage—where it came from I couldn't tell you—to step down until there were mere inches between us, my gaze never leaving his as I did so. And though he was at least six inches taller than me, as he placed my hands on either side of his magnificently defined face to pull his face closer to mine, our heavy and warm breaths seemed to shakily be in unison.

"Are you sure?" Aldric asked before my eyes had a chance to close.

I nodded. Although in truth, there was a small sliver of doubt. Not just due to my lack of experience, but the unwelcomed memories of Gregory drunkenly trying to force himself on me while his lackeys watched and the mornings after, Ash coming into my shithole of a bedroom to care for me with a bundle of cleanish clothes that he had taken from his sister. No, no, no. I will not ruin this moment. I want this. I want to kiss Aldric, and he wants to kiss me. I'm closing my eyes, leaning in, and my lips begin to ever so lightly touch his...

Hard as I might try, and despite the deep desire to kiss him, to finally experience my first real kiss, I just couldn't push those unwanted memories and thoughts away from my head. My mind clearly had other plans, and it was so frustrating, frustrating—frustrating! An embarrassed warmth rushed to my face as my heart began to race as if it was trying to escape the embarrassment, since my legs were unable to. I tried to steady my breathing but found myself unable to. I didn't face him—I couldn't face him. And the more time passed in silence, the hotter my cheeks grew.

I stared at the light from the electric lanterns hanging on the ceiling in the hallway at the bottom of the stairs and how they seem to waver like a flame on a candle. Though I knew that wasn't possible given that they were—well, electric. Then I counted the light bulbs on either side of this curved ceiling tunnel that he and I were in, up to the step I was still standing on—until I felt two large warm hands on either side of my face guiding my head once more to face Aldric. It took a few more moments before I worked up enough courage to look him in the eye.

"If you aren't ready, you aren't ready," Aldric said. So simply. So warmly. And what he said next was the cherry on top of what I needed to hear. It was so perfect that it made my heart skip a beat. "I've waited seven years for you and a couple of months; I think I can wait. There's nothing wrong with feeling whatever you are feeling, okay?"

I nodded like some automatic reflex of a robot or a way to shake away the lingering embarrassment. There was a need to give him an explanation, regardless of his reassurance of it being okay, as to why I pulled away from our "almost kiss," but, for whatever reason, I couldn't find the words without seeming repetitive or years younger than I actually was because of how sheltered I'd been over the past six years.

In truth, I was tired of hearing the same old excuses and wondering if I truly was safe from Ross and the King Cobras, which again there was a small part of me that was unsure. Then again, a gang of humans carrying guns with non-silver bullets against who knows how many werewolves in the Red Rose Pack—maybe I shouldn't be. There was no maybe because Aldric had said I was beautiful and that he would never let anything bad happen to me. Perhaps I was in a seemingly perpetual state of wanting to believe him and not believing him because of being told how ugly and worthless I was so often by the King Cobras; I thought so insistently that it was true. But I didn't want to be, because when I was with Aldric, I felt like I mattered, and I enjoyed his company so much that I never wanted to be parted from his side.

In an effort to change the awkward situation and to turn

my thoughts into something more positive, I turned to walk up the rest of the flight of stairs to the door of the Alpha Room. I could hear Aldric's footsteps follow behind me. And though he chuckled almost every time I did this because he said it wasn't necessary, I covered the keypad with one hand as I typed in the code that would unlock the door: *1-9-5-8*. When the magical thunks slightly shook the wall surrounding the metal door, I turned the knob and pushed it open. I hadn't bothered to check if Aldric was behind me because one, I knew he would be, and two, he said I could choose whatever movie I wanted.

Turning an awkward moment into a not so awkward moment, I thought as I began to walk around the built-in bookshelves filled with DVDs and studied nearly each and every one of them. Okay, it was still awkward, so who was I kidding?

"*Young Frankenstein?*" I finally said, turning to face Aldric, whose arms were crossed together, with a smile creeping across his face. And while his body language was nonthreatening, I could feel my cheeks become flush and my body slouching in embarrassment, like I may or may not have chosen the right movie or something.

"It's one of my favorites," Aldric said before teasing me with, "Are you sure you've never seen it before?"

I shook my head. Regardless of recognizing when he was kidding and not, I again couldn't help having a mini flashback on how my ~~parents~~ adoptive parents raised me. There were very few movies I had been allowed to watch, but, as I quickly shooed away the memory before it had an opportunity to unravel itself further, Aldric didn't need to know that—not yet, anyways... I hoped.

We situated ourselves on the couch after Aldric plopped the movie in and pressed play, my body curled so close to his that I was practically lying on his lap. He didn't seem to mind. Correction, he *never* seemed to mind, which made me feel safer and more relaxed. All the worries I had during the moments leading up to our "almost kiss" washed away once more. I watched the black and white movie, laughing so hard I was almost afraid I was going to leave bruises on Aldric because of how much I tilted back and forth and from my body twitching. I did try not to accidentally knock the top of my head against his chin resting upon it, but it was difficult because the movie was just that funny.

When the movie ended and Aldric was about to get up, insisting it was his turn to choose the next movie, my hand unconsciously grabbed ahold of his shirt and I shifted just enough away from him so that we were face-to-face. Those big, mesmerizing hazel eyes looking back in surprise and his scent of ocean air and campfire smoke being more intoxicating than it had ever been before, I don't know... I just... I just... Oh God! I just needed his lips against mine, if only to know what they taste like—what they felt like. Damn his experience in kissing and my lack of experience. Damn whether I was ready or not. It was like my animal side was taking over and while there was still a small part of me that found it kind of scary, to a certain degree, it was kind of exhilarating at the same time.

But my lips upon his, the pressure of his touch was so fervent that I thought my whole body would burst from pure joy. Needing to be closer, I straddled Aldric's lap. I felt Aldric's hands slide and his fingers curl firmly into my hips like claws. I never knew what was meant by an "out of body" experience until now. It was dangerously a pure-animalistic desire (if there could ever be such a thing), but all around perfect. We hungered for each other—another experience I had never felt before. Our breathing in rhythmic shallow breaths with one another's. It felt like we were floating on a cloud as my arms moved like snakes, slithering up and around his neck.

I waited for his tongue to slip into my mouth, similar to what I had remembered seeing from the upper classmates and the few television shows I was allowed to watch in my childhood—but it never occurred. Not that I was complaining given that this was my first real kiss and all. I closed my eyes, fearing that any second I would learn this was all a dream. I appreciated how much of a gentleman Aldric was being, regardless of his feelings, which were pulsating through me so hungrily and a hell of a lot stronger than what I had felt on the stairs. I avoided the eye contact thing I had read about in books and went straight to resting my head on his chest, my arms pressed against either side of him. My fingers wrapped around the fabric of his shirt like I needed to in order to make the room stop spinning from how amazing the kiss was.

With my ear pressed against his pecs, his heartbeat, while racing at the same speed as mine, was strangely and rhythmically soothing, which made me want to hold on to the fabric of his shirt more. Yes, his intoxicating aroma may have played a part, and his hand slowly stroked my long white curly hair until his fingers were comfortably entangled around some of my ringlets, but it felt nice. More than nice. I felt loved. I felt accepted. It was truly peaceful.

However, the peacefulness of that moment was quickly interrupted when a startling ringing came from behind us, and I soon found myself at the edge of the opposite end of the couch like a cat in a tree. Aldric, while not as frightened by the noise as I was, held up a hand to me to communicate that it was nothing to be scared of and turned around for a moment to pick something up.

That something stopped that alarming ringing sound and was a something I hadn't seen in six years, maybe more... a receiver to a phone. Not a cellphone, but an actual phone. The kind of phone my ~~grandparents~~ so-called grandparents had with a curly cord attached from the receiver to the almost pyramid shaped box with numbered buttons. The kind of phone that, when it rang, you had no idea who was calling until you picked up the receiver to answer it. Well, unless you had a separate electric box attached to it with caller ID. Based on how Aldric answered, the phone didn't seem to be the kind that had the caller ID box.

"Hello," Aldric said in a non-aggressive but still authoritative tone. Yet, the tone quickly changed to agitation in response to whatever the person on the other end had just said. I could tell as he pierced his lips, ran his free hand through his hair, along with some heavy nasal exhales, that he was trying to remain calm for my sake, but his annoyance with the news he had just received still came through in his voice. What was annoying to me was that I strangely couldn't hear what was being said on the other end. Me! With my heightened sense of hearing. Nothing but the sound of Aldric's voice as he finally spoke again, "Where is he now?—Mm-hm. I'll be right there."

After hanging up the receiver, Aldric looked up at the paned-glass ceiling and muttered some curse words under his breath, both of his hands cupping the top of his head before slowly sliding down until his bottom lip was pulled to his chin. He held that position for some time as he looked not at me but passed me for what felt like a nerve-racking eternity. Now, I would usually say that I am a patient girl, especially with all the conditioning Ross had instilled in me, but after five, maybe ten minutes, I just couldn't take the anticipation game of waiting for Aldric to speak. Whatever the news was, it was clearly upsetting to him and I needed to know what was wrong in order to see if maybe I could help the situation. As doubtful as it probably was.

"What is it?" I said, trying to sound as calm as I could.

He didn't answer.

"What is it?" I said again, ignoring my attempt to be calm and going straight to annoyance.

Still no answer.

"Goddamn it, Aldric!" I raised my voice, not caring where this authoritative part of me was coming from. I just needed to know what was said on the other end of the phone conversation. Though I must say, the feeling was really empowering. And if he told me it was nothing for me to worry about, well shit, I was going to make it important enough for him to tell me anyways. I wasn't going to take no for an answer. "You better tell what was said now!"

"There's a human male that has stepped into our territory," Aldric finally said, understandably taken aback by the power I had packed behind my voice. "He claims to be a member of the King Cobras and to have come in peace with important information that may prove vital in keeping you safe."

"What does he look like?" I demanded.

Aldric turned back around to bring the receiver to his ear again. I could hear the clicks and beeps as he dialed a phone number.

"Brian?" Aldric said. "Describe him...'Soon-to-be Luna?' She *is* your Luna and why would you think I would immediately trust what he has to say? *Now, describe him or so help the Great Wolf, I will hang you by your tail for a week.*"

I know the last sentence wasn't geared toward me, but the manner of his voice made me want to cower and obey him immediately. My empowering moment and feeling safe around him vanished into the shadows. I could have run toward the metal door, but Aldric would have seen me for sure because, as he stood up, that was the direction he was facing. I looked around the room for a place to hide—any place to hide, until I saw a plain white door at the far opposite end from the metal one. It looked like it opened to a bathroom.

Turning my head back toward Aldric to make extra sure he wasn't watching—because this was a side I had never seen or heard from him before, and it was too much like Ross, so it terrified me—I jumped off of the edge of the couch and ran to the door before slamming it shut and locking myself in. I didn't like this side of him, not one bit. Here I thought I could trust and possibly fall for him, only to be reminded that everyone has a dark side. Some more prominent and proud of it than others, like Ross. Regardless and despite the fact that this hiding in the bathroom was probably not the smartest of ideas, I leaned my back against the door before crumbling to the floor. I stared into the darkness, my hyperventilating breathing matching the panic racing in my heart.

"Shit!" I heard Aldric say. "Brian, I'll be right there. Don't interrogate him any further until I get there."

After he hung up the phone, I could hear Aldric approach the bathroom door. I heard a few taps on the door, but I neither moved nor answered.

"Vivila, would you please answer the door?" Aldric asked calmly. "Look, I didn't mean to scare you with my 'Alpha' voice."

"Alpha voice?" I somehow mustered the energy to say, though it came out sounding like a pubescent squeak.

"It's a thing the Alpha of a pack can do to make sure their orders are followed or when they need their pack members to understand the importance of what they are saying," Aldric answered with a sigh. "I lost my temper when I was talking to Brian and the voice just slipped out. I really am sorry if it frightened you or caused any flashbacks from your inhuman time with the King Cobras, but—if this human is claiming to bring news that may be for the benefit of your safety, I need to know if it's a trap. Vivila? Please open the door."

I sat there, my back still leaning against the locked door, listening to the sincerity in his words. It did bring back flashbacks of my treatment with Ross and the rest of the King Cobras, yet not as many as it would have during my first week here at the mansion or rather "The Red Rose Pack House," a term I was still trying to remember to use.

As my breathing and heart slowly returned to normal about five minutes later, I rolled onto my knees and pushed myself up to unlock and open the door. I was surprised to see Aldric facing the door in a kneeling position with his head bowed low. It was very submissive. Leaders were never submissive, at least not in my limited experience. Nonetheless, here he was like someone's pet dog awaiting their human to let them know that they are still loved. A position I knew all too well and one I would never be forced to do. It was humiliating and over time, could make the strongest person's spirit feel completely broken.

Yes, I knew that feeling most ardently. And however shaken I had been moments earlier by the "Alpha voice," it shattered my heart into a million pieces into the pit of my stomach. Here was someone that, up until this point, had proven to be a man of honor and compassion. How could I trust, be "mated" to, and love even, someone who was seemingly just as much of a tyrant as Ross? Who could lose his temper at any moment? Would he lose his temper at me in the future? I couldn't predict that. I'd hope not. Then how could I not trust someone who positioned himself so submissively and apologized so sincerely? I crawled cautiously forward with these dueling questions circling so frantically around in my head that it almost made me dizzy, and lifted him up just enough to wrap my arms around his neck, like a mama cat comforting her young.

CHAPTER TWENTY-ONE

As Aldric continued to sit on the floor in this submissive position I greatly disliked, I walked away from the bathroom and moved closer to him. I kneeled in front of him, gently placing my hands on the sides of his head, and a soft kiss on top of his beautifully thick black hair before saying, "The 'Alpha voice' did scare me and made me a bit scared of you in that moment when it was used, *but* I still love you."

His head was still in the grasps of my hands as he lifted his head to look up and into my eyes. "You love me?"

"I do. I can't explain it—but I do," I replied, almost breathlessly, with a bit of a surprise for finally having the courage to say it aloud to him.

His face lit up as he pulled my arms from where they were wrapped around his neck and our lips touched once again. Our knees and toes were the only things keeping us balanced, though I was almost certain that at any moment we'd be floating. Sadly—or rather, unfortunately—werewolves and werecats don't possess magic. And as much as I wanted to ponder whether winged werecats possess some form of magic, it was not high on my list or anywhere near my list. The description of the gang members from the... the... Oh my God! Aldric is a phenomenal kisser! I couldn't care less about the lack of a kiss before, as I never wanted to kiss another person for as long as he and I both should live. Similar to the last kiss, a few seconds felt more like several hours. Unlike the last kiss, when our lips parted and my eyes reopened, my gaze was fixated on his. Our smiles mirrored one another's. Our faces red and our breathing rhythmical, almost panting.

"Not... to be... a mood killer," Aldric said as he gasped for more oxygen and rested his forehead against mine, "but I really need to meet with Brian at the detention cells."

I groaned in protest.

"I'm sorry, my love."

"My love?" I know I confessed my love for Aldric—but I hadn't realized that I had opened Pandora's box, so to speak; therefore, allowing endearing pet names. No one, that I could remember at least, had ever called me anything nice. Not my adoptive parents, Ross, any member of the King Cobras nor Ash. I mean, Ash called me "V" and "Viv," which at the time I thought were endearing because they weren't any of the cruel or degrading names I had become used to over the years. Yet this, "my love," was on a whole different level from what Ash had called me. I felt special and accepted. Both feelings were still absolutely new to me. But I was so distracted about the triggering fear caused by Aldric's "Alpha voice," the mind-blowing kiss, and the uncertainty of how I felt about this pet name, that I totally forgot about the King Cobras guy mentioned in Aldric's conversation with Brian. If it was Gregory, I hoped... well, not so nice things that I'd rather not mention, if that's okay with you.

I knew it couldn't be Ross because, unlike his son, he was smart enough to not get himself caught or dare to approach the pack house without backup. But what worried me the most was that it might be Ash because of how nice he'd always been to me, much to the dismay and disgust of the whole King Cobras' gang. I pleaded in my mind that it wasn't him. And yet I needed to know. My face scrunched together in curiosity at the thought. I could see Aldric's mouth about to form the word "what" but I was quick to interrupt him.

"What did Brian say about the description of the King Cobras guy?"

"Light-skinned, dreadlocks, athletic build, ears gauged," Aldric said, a bit confused as to why it was so important to ask what the guy looked like. I suppose with how poorly the majority of the gang treated me, he probably assumed I wouldn't care or want to know.

"His eyes?" I asked in a wavered whisper as I could take a pretty good guess as to whom it might be. For it would be the only person, other than the three werewolves who resided in the pack house, who would risk his life for me. "What color are they?"

"Why is that important?" Aldric asked, slightly suspicious.

"What color are his eyes?" I demanded. "Is one of them hazel and the other brown?"

"I didn't think to ask. Why?" Aldric asked, his eyes searching mine for a clue as to why it was so important to know.

"Because it might be Ash," I said, quickly standing up and making my way toward the metal door.

But before I could come close to reaching the door's only knob, Aldric had already blocked me by standing right in front of me. Goddamn, werewolves are fast! His hands hovered around my shoulders.

"How can you be so sure it's him?" Aldric asked quizzically. "And where do you think you're going?"

"Because he's my friend! And I'm coming with you because of this reason!" I yelled, the mysterious authoritative courage in my voice returning.

"But it could be someone else—someone else who will try to hurt you or kidnap you," Aldric said in concern.

"But Brian would have said that he didn't come alone, wouldn't he?" I asked as I attempted to find some way around him but failed. "Don't you have other pack members guarding him aside from Brian? Plus, you'll be there to make sure things don't get out of hand."

It was clear from his facial expression and somewhat more relaxed stance that he had momentarily forgotten about that point, which I tried to use to my advantage. I nearly succeeded, nearly had the tips of my fingers on the knob, but Aldric's arms grabbed ahold of my waist and pulled me back.

"The only pack members you've met have been Agatha and my sister," he said, after I stopped trying to squirm out of his grasp. "You told me on multiple occasions that you weren't ready yet and I've respected your wishes. But now you want to meet at least five pack members, including Brian? Plus, this man being Ash or not, we know the King Cobras have figured out where we are, which means a war is possibly about to ensue. Even more reason to have you stay here."

In truth, I wasn't thinking about these two facts. I wasn't ready to meet more pack members, but this was Ash we were talking about. I just needed to know for myself. Which led to the next truth—if it were Ash, it would mean Ross had finally discovered my whereabouts. It would mean an excruciating torture because, though I had no control over being rescued, Ross would still see it as an elaborate ploy of escape. I would also be punished in front of my Aldric as an example of what it means to steal a valued piece of his property. It would, regardless, as my Aldric put it, bring "war" upon the pack and I didn't want any of them to get hurt or worse on my account.

And if it wasn't Ash, then I could rest easy that he wasn't hurt. Regardless, I spent weeks training. Learning the correct skills I thought I had mastered with Ross's "learn or die" methods. You may think I meant "trial and error," but let's be honest—this is *Ross* we're talking about. Nonetheless, I worked really hard to pay attention to each lesson with Aldric and Beatrix, I needed to at least try to learn how to overcome my fears like meeting more pack members and Ross wanting to start a war because of me.

Human or not, the first fear seemed more surmountable at the moment, but I wasn't going to give Aldric the satisfaction of being right about the two truths he had just mentioned. I was going with him, and that was final.

"But isn't this all of what my training was in preparation for? I may still not be able to fully shift comfortably yet, but I've been mentally preparing myself for the day Ross would find and repossess me. I have a good and bad feeling that it is Ash. And knowing Ross, he wouldn't have let Ash leave without having him roughed up by some of the King Cobras as a message of what's to come of me—of this entire pack. Ross may be human, but he's ruthless. So if it is Ash, he will need medical attention..." I paused at the brink of crying at the thought of Ash possibly dealing with broken bones in different areas of his body.

"I understand, regardless of who it is, that Ross knows where I am now and that scares me. I know he will do to anything to anyone who is affiliated with the pack to get to me. I can't have that on my conscience. I *won't* have that on my conscience. But if you think I'm going to stay here like a scaredy-cat without seeing for myself whether or not it's Ash, you've got another think coming."

Frustration and worry began pumping through my whole body as I stood ready to fight my mate, both physically and mentally, if I had to—because I was ready for Aldric to stand his ground and not let me go with him to the detention cells. Regardless of him being a werewolf with super strength and agility, confident, both taller and bigger than me, I was still ready to take him on. I wouldn't want to do any real damage—I wouldn't be able to live with myself if I did, but damn it, I was going with him... whether he liked it or not. I just really needed to be sure it wasn't Ash they had captured. Goddamn it! Aldric's face was unreadable for quite some time as we continued to stare at each other. I almost felt like a bull seeing a red fabric flashing in front of his face because of Aldric's lack of response to what I had just said and his stone-faced stance.

But then, just when I didn't think he couldn't surprise me—though let's be honest, his actions and words will probably always surprise given how much we still didn't know about each other and my upbringing up until my arrival here at the pack house—Aldric closed whatever distance there was between us, placed his hands on either side of my face, gave my forehead a light kiss, and pulled away with the biggest grin on his face as his eyes returned to looking into mine.

"Okay," Aldric said matter-of-factly and with seeming sense of pride in his voice, which made my face scrunch up in confusion.

"Okay?" I asked, bewildered.

"Okay," he repeated with a shoulder shrug and taking a few steps back to extend an offer of his hand.

I stared at his hand for a bit, trying to understand the change an attitude. I placed my hand in his, almost instinctually, but it didn't lessen my need to know why he was now okay with me going all of a sudden.

"Let's go, my Luna," Aldric said, guiding us toward the door.

When we crossed through the doorway and made our way down the stairway in the direction toward where I assumed led to the cells, I couldn't help but wonder if Aldric could read my emotions just like I had read his earlier. Was that why he used the word "Luna"? I was now well aware, however unprepared or unworthy I still felt about the title, that being mated to an Alpha meant I automatically was given the title of Luna, and Aldric had been very understanding about my feelings and hesitations about it. Yet, was it because of what I had said moments ago and my confusion in his sudden mood change that led him to address me by my reluctant title? I just didn't know. Before I knew it, we were standing in front of a thick metal door that reminded me of the door to my bedroom back at the warehouse. But instead of having four sliding windows in it, this door only had one.

"Are you sure you want to go in?" Aldric asked, turning to face me. "There are surveillance cameras in both the cells and interrogation rooms. You can, if you would feel more comfortable, go back to the Alpha Room and watch everything from there. I know how adamant you were about coming, but it's perfectly okay if you've changed your mind..."

"Yes, I still want to go in," I said, feeling my heart beating in the back of my throat in anticipation.

He nodded, his hand giving mine a little reassuring squeeze before looking up at a camera above the door with another nod. I could hear the locks thinking and clicking as the door suddenly creaked opened, which, while I knew was most likely going to happen, still startled me. My cheeks were flushed with how stupid I felt for being so alarmed by the noise. More especially so when I saw a blonde, doe-eyed, somewhat curvy woman who couldn't have been much older than twenty-five and was dressed in all black standing on the other side of the metal door.

Some Luna I am, being startled by a door being opened and a ~~woman~~ *female werewolf there on the other side with no real expression on her face,* I thought as I began to be worried about this strange woman's first impression of me. Also, I was still unsure what the proper terminology was when werewolves were in human form. Was it okay to say "this man" or "woman"? Or was I supposed to call them "this werewolf" or "were"? I'd get it right, eventually. Maybe if I would just listen to Aldric in conversation or his sister and Agatha, I'd discover the proper terminology. I know, I know, I could just ask Aldric, the next time he and I are alone... when I could work up the courage to ask. He's been so understanding that I shouldn't feel too embarrassed because I've gone eighteen years in the dark about the true existence of the supernatural world.

All of this didn't seem to matter to her, because she lifted her head and appeared to purposefully expose her neck to the two of us before saying, "Alpha. Luna."

There was that word again: Luna. I again knew that was my title now, though Aldric and I hadn't completed our "mate bond"—whatever that entailed—and I was slightly okay with

Aldric calling me the word. But hearing it from a pack member I'd just met made feel without a doubt incredibly uncomfortable. I may have felt more and more comfortable around Aldric, Beatrix, and Agatha without feeling out of place in their world, being called "Luna" by this ~~woman~~ werewolf gave me that sense once more of not feeling worthy—worthy of being considered not only part of this pack, but one of the leaders. Regardless, I tried to keep this to myself and hoped Aldric didn't pick up on my emotions through our bond. I wanted to start having my thoughts, vocal or not, be my own and to feel comfortable in my own skin without the bearing influence of another. Then and only then, I hoped, I would truly be worthy of the title of "Luna" and Aldric's mate.

Without knowing why, I half-expected—because I was aware enough to know we were still in the basement—that it would be like the extremely rundown version of the warehouse's hallway leading to the King Cobras' detention cells. Or as Ross called it, "The Dungeon." How did I know what The Dungeon looked like? Well, each time I broke through the door of my room, before they finally installed the thick metal door, I was forced to spend the night in one of the cells while the King Cobras replaced the door.

Regardless, just beyond the open door and the female pack member was a long hallway, its walls made with plastered cement just like the warehouse's, but the main difference was that this hallway was significantly cleaner and well lit. No humming and blinking fluorescent lights either. One side held no window, which I half expected because the warehouse's detention cells didn't either; the other had four periodic breaks by each cell's crisscrossing bars. Yet, with how pristinely white everything was, the hallway was still very daunting, which was most likely the point.

And when the woman, whose hair was a beautiful shade of lavender, lifted her head to bare her neck to both Aldric and me, I wasn't sure if I was meant to return the gesture. I briefly looked over at my mate to see how he was going to respond. But when he didn't bare his neck, the situation and space felt more daunting.

"Vivila, this is Angela," Aldric said, breaking the silence.

"Nice to meet you, Angela," I said politely, trying to resist the urge to cower behind Aldric and instead standing as confidently as I could beside my mate, so that perhaps I would appear worthy of the title announced to me by this woman female werewolf. Damn it! I really need to ask Aldric about the proper terminology.

However, when I extended my hand so that I could shake hers, Angela stared at my hand with wide eyes like she wasn't worthy to shake mine or it wasn't protocol to return the gesture of her new Luna. Immediately embarrassed because I was still learning about the ins and outs of werewolf customs, I retreated my hand into my pocket.

As we made our way down the hallway, I noticed that the first three cells were unoccupied and far nicer than my bedroom in the warehouse. The cots were elevated, the small mattresses weren't moldy nor were any springs exposed, and the toilets and sinks were sparkling clean. There may not have been any windows in this part of the mansion, but still. A clean, hole-less blanket would be more important than the lack of a window any day, in my opinion.

As we approached the fourth cell, we were met by a male pack member standing stoically and statuesque by the windowless side of the hallway. Though he was not as tall as Aldric, his large build and narrow brown eyes still made him intimidating. Like Angela, he too bared his neck to both Aldric and me. And I found that I was beginning to regret insisting on coming with Aldric, if not more so than I had to begin with.

No! I mentally shouted to myself. *I must be strong for Ash. I must know if he is okay. And... well, who knows how much time the whole pack had before the King Cobras descended.*

"Jeremy," Aldric said very seriously, which I found odd because it wasn't the same tone he had used with Angela. Was it because the introduction between Angela and me didn't go as I thought it would? No, that didn't seem right, but I did my best to not overanalyze it, which I hadn't done with Angela's lack of reciprocating my extended hand.

"Alpha. Luna," Jeremy responded in the same tone as Aldric. However, it didn't have an undertone of annoyance, but of high respect.

Though I still wasn't comfortable with being bestowed the honored title of "Luna," I wanted to return the level of respect being given by a large built werewolf because, unlike what I had seen too many times in the presence of Ross towards his gang members and myself especially, I felt a true leader should show their gratitude towards those under them. Respect out of love and not out of fear and tyranny. However, I was too distracted by my desire to see the prisoner that was my friend Ash.

When I spun to face Ash, I barely recognized him. His right eye was nearly swollen shut in an array of purple, yellow, and red. I spotted a small, torn slit in the center of the drying blood in and around his lips. But the worst part about what I was seeing regarding the man in front of me was how firmly he clutched his side as he tried to stand up straight. I could almost hear his broken ribs rub up against the muscles and tendons while he was attempting to breathe normally.

"Who did this to you?" I blurted the question in an exasperated whisper as my hands held two of the cell's bars. I knew the answer, but the shock of the state Ash was in was just so horrifying and heartbreaking.

"Ross gave Gregory and his lackeys permission to do as he liked after I said I wanted out of the King Cobras," Ash said with a slurping noise, almost to prevent any uncontrollable saliva and remaining blood from dribbling down his chin. "Vivila, he knows where you are and is preparing to start a war. When you left, Ross made claims that he wanted to find you so that he could chain you and inject the serums in you, then take you to The Pit's ring and allow anyone off the street to fight you for fifty bucks. Gregory wanted to bind you to his bed, so he could have you as many times as he wanted, and you wouldn't be able to put up much of a fight. But that's not the worst of it..."

Ash paused to wrap his arm further around his ribs, which caused him to almost lose his balance. My knees buckled from under me until I inevitably fell to the floor. My hands stung a bit from the friction of them sliding down the metal bars, but I didn't care. I reached out to Ash, though with the amount of distance between us, it didn't seem to matter. It didn't matter because I couldn't take away the damage done to my friend.

I suddenly felt Aldric struggling to control himself with what he was hearing and his body tightened, as if my body and mind were reacting similarly. Was I feeling his reactions because his hand was unintentionally squeezing tightly on my shoulder or due to the mate bond or a mixture of both? And regardless of the low growl from deep within Aldric's chest and the heartbreaking pain I saw in Ash's eyes, I needed to know how much worse the situation was that we were finding ourselves in regarding the war Ross wanted to start.

"What's the worst part?" I asked, and when Ash didn't answer, I asked again with more urgency alongside another pertinent question, "Ash! What's the worst part? How much time do we have before the King Cobras attack?"

"They're Minotaurs!" Ash screamed. "And they plan to attack within the next forty-eight hours!"

CHAPTER TWENTY-TWO

Although my ears heard exactly what Ash had said, my mind was failing to fully register the first sentence he uttered. Minotaurs? All of the King Cobras or just Ross and Gregory? I had read Greek mythology books and knew what the mythical creatures were, but there was no way what Ash had just said was true—right? Plus, from what I'd read about Minotaurs, nowhere did it hint or mention that these creatures could shift into looking fully human.

You would have thought that in the last five years, I would have gotten some kind of inkling that Ross, Gregory, and who knows how many King Cobras members were more than human. In fairness, I didn't know there were supernatural creatures living in the real world until Aldric confessed he was a werewolf. Regardless, the biggest question that was coming to my mind was how were the King Cobras able to pass as human? Was there a witch or a wizard in the gang? And though I shouldn't have been surprised at this point that witches and wizards most likely exist outside of the fictional world of Harry Potter—I was.

"How can you be so sure?" I finally blurted out without a thought as to how it sounded.

"What do you mean how can I be so sure?" Ash said angrily under gritted teeth, which caused the broken bones in his chest to be in more pain than he already was because he seemed to be trying to keep his annoyance toward my naïve question in check. "Were you not listening to what I just said?"

I could feel the burning and rising anger emanating from Aldric from the tone Ash was using toward me. I moved my body, so that I could look up into Aldric's eyes, and placed my hand gently on his stomach to communicate that it was okay and that I could handle the hostility coming from Ash. I could feel Aldric calm down a bit, though not completely, but enough for me to return my gaze toward Ash and try to process what he had just said. In truth, it wasn't just Aldric who needed to calm down. It felt like a snake had wrapped itself around my insides, causing my heart to rapidly beat up to my throat and my breathing to go shallow. I closed my eyes for a brief moment in an effort to fight against this snakelike hold and answer Ash.

"Ash, of course I heard what you said," I said as calmly as I could, trying to suppress the shock I was still in from the information Ash had just dropped before everyone in this detention cell area. "I knew he would start a war—maybe not this soon, but I knew..." I said this with some difficulty due to the guilt behind why this war was coming, then continued, "But my question was more in regard to how are you sure the King Cobras know of my location?"

"I was part of one of the groups to discover your location," Ash said as he collapsed upon the cot, his breathing becoming more and more labored. "Honest to God, I hoped we'd never find you—that I would never find you. One night, Ross called for me to come into his office before I was to go home for the evening. As I got off of the elevator and before I approached his office, I could hear only his voice yelling, so I knew not only that he was on the phone because I saw no sign of anyone through the opaque glass panes, but also that he was in a foul mood. What made it strange was how monstrously nasal and booming his yelling was. I swear, the whole second floor shook like I was caught in an earthquake and I fell to my knees.

"His conversation wasn't in English either. Ross may be

smart enough to lead one of the most feared gangs in Pennsylvania and his various businesses, but he's never had the patience or the wits to learn another language. I'm not going to lie and say I wasn't freaked out because I was. My racing heart and every fiber of my being was telling me to just get back on the elevator, but knowing what Ross would do to me if I did... Well, I'd be in worse shape than I am now—" He broke into a wheezing coughing fit before he continued, his eyes never leaving the ceiling.

"I managed to get up and knock on his office door. As I waited for his permission to enter, I could hear some kind of strange noise resembling a mixture of high adhesive being torn off a way and boots trudging through thick wet mud. Then Ross's normal voice said I could come in. When I looked into his eyes as I entered, they glowed. It was only for a second, so I tried to brush it aside as being a trick my own eyes were playing on me. I said nothing as he immediately told me that he had reason to believe that you were in Ambler. He must have sensed that I wanted to ask why because he bizarrely waved his hand dismissively like I had asked and said he would bend the prophecy to his favor, no matter what the costs would be. It was more than a little suspicious. Plus, it made absolutely no sense. What prophecy was he talking about? It was like straight out of some dark young adult fantasy novel.

"Not as suspicious as the group of men he assigned me to go with—Gregory and his lackeys. At that moment in his office, I couldn't tell you exactly why I found it to be suspicious, nor during the car ride down to the street that led to where this house was. A quarter of a mile away, Gregory parked the car on the side of the road and commanded all eight of us to split up and search every house until we found clues indicating which one you'd be in. If we saw you alone, we were to stun you with a stun gun and drag you back to the vehicle. He showed us pictures of Aldric and his sister..."

Upon hearing about his sister being used to find me, Aldric's anger, which was already super high, skyrocketed. I blindly reached behind me until I found my mate's hand, interlocked it with mine, and closed my eyes for a moment so that I could concentrate on sending calming energy to him. I wasn't sure if it would work because I was still learning the limits and the possible boundlessness of our bond. Regardless of how silly I felt by trying to send this calming energy, it slowly appeared to work because his pulsating anger became less suffocating. It was like, through the connection of our bond, a few heavy layers of winter clothing had been pulled off.

"I was paired with Frank," Ash continued, briefly looking over at me before returning his gaze to the ceiling again. "As you know, Viv, he may be the strongest and somewhat most ingenious in getting people to confess through torture, but Frank is still not the sharpest tool in the shed. I guess you could say that about all of Gregory's lackeys, but that's beside the point. As all eight of us split off in different directions, Frank and I walked parallel to what I assume is an edge of this house's property, because I couldn't see a single house for quite some time until we approached the driveway.

"I managed to convince Frank to stay at the top of the driveway while I went to investigate. Stupid as he is, I still praised the sheer luck of him believing that he should keep an eye for any cars that may have possibly slowed down to turn and go down the driveway. I told him that if any driver coming down the road asked what he was doing, to tell them that he was a cop surveying the area and that there had been reports of suspicious activity. And being that he is a lot bigger than I, it would make the story more believable. Lastly, I told him, before making my way down the driveway to this house, if Aldric or his sister were one of those drivers or in the car, to wait ten minutes before coming down the driveway, so that way I know to hide and wait until the right moment arose to proceed. I didn't want to proceed... God! You have to believe me. But I couldn't arouse suspicion. Thank goodness Gregory and his lackeys are dumb as rocks or it would have been someone else and not me snooping.

"To move the story along, I saw you. How? With all the people that you must have guarding the perimeter..." Ash said as he turned his head just enough to lock eyes with Aldric before once again looking up at the ceiling. "But I did, Viv. And when I saw how happy you looked... so unbelievably happy. I wasn't going to ruin that for you—I didn't want Ross or Gregory to ruin that for you. So, I decided as I carefully made my way back up the driveway where I saw Frank still scanning for cars, that I would say that I found nothing. I swear, I kept my mouth shut. I could only hope my amateur acting skills would keep me alive long enough to distract Ross to lose hope in finding you.

"Yet, three days later, I was once again called into Ross's office. Once again, I knocked on his door and was beckoned to come in. When I did, Ross gestured for me to sit down. By the scowl on his face and how stiff his body was, I had a bad feeling he knew that I knew where you were. As I waited for him to speak, I kept thinking 'Please let it just be in my head. He doesn't know where Vivila is.' He first broke the silence by slamming both of his clenched fists on his desk, which made me nearly fall out of the chair."

As I continued to listen to Ash's story, it felt like an eternity of silence until he finally spoke again, which made me feel as though I were being sucked into some sort of vortex, transporting me back to the damp and suffocating shoebox of a bedroom. And though I could feel Aldric's gentle grip on my shoulders, trying to support me in every way, I could also feel my mate's steaming anger radiating within me, which wasn't helping me feel better or think that we had any chance against Ross. I had really hoped I was wrong about the latter. From my peripherals, I could see the other pack members stand closer than they had been before, entranced like I was at hearing about the events Ash had to endure before ending up in this detention cell. We all waited for what happened next to Ash in Ross's office.

"'Gregory said you didn't find her,' Ross had said, followed by an angry snort," Ash continued. "I told him I hadn't as calmly as I could. He started to pace around the room, then said, 'Somehow, I don't believe you.' 'Well, it's true,' I replied to him. I heard his footsteps stop right behind me, his hands gripping my shoulders so hard that I was sure the bones were going to snap at any second, and his hotter than the sun breath by my ears. It was difficult to keep my own breathing and heartbeat on an even keel. 'I know you saw her,' he finally said, rage building up behind his tone after a long stretch of silence. 'I promise I won't be mad. Now, I'll ask you a question and you better tell me the truth. Did you or did you not see Vivila in the kitchen of that Alpha mongrel's house?'

"I could feel the blood draining from my face. I mean, it was so oddly specific. There was no way he could have seen what I had seen unless he was psychic or there was a witch in the gang that I never knew about. Both seemed very unlikely because I didn't believe in either, not unless I was in some fantasy novel or something. I mean, this is real life, right? So, I said, 'No, I didn't see her.' No surprise, it was the wrong answer, because Ross yanked the chair from under me with such force that I nearly hit my head on the edge of his desk. I fell to my knees and released a painful grunt. I didn't have a chance to react before he took a good chunk of my locks and jerked my head to look up at him.

"But what I saw was more alarming than any of his intimidation tactics in all the years I've worked for him. Baffled and unable to find the words to name what I was seeing, but I knew it was him regardless. For one thing, Ross and I were the only two in the room, which wasn't too unusual. Although he did have a tendency of having other King Cobras members standing guard depending on the situation or his mood on any given day. Regardless, a very large half bull-half man stood glaring above me. His eyes seemed to glow red and the temperature in the room was hotter than hell; however, that could have been my imagination."

I would have too, I thought. I imagined my eyes were playing tricks on me when Aldric had first shifted into his wolf form. Looking around towards the pack members and then back at my mate, I noticed what seemed to be a conflicting mixture of surprise, but not at the same time. It was followed by stern and pensive facial expressions, as though they were already mentally preparing and strategizing battle techniques. The latter confused me a bit because I wasn't sure if I should feel impressed and safe or foolish for them due to the fact that there was only one story about a Minotaur. We didn't have a labyrinth to lure the King Cobras into and I'm pretty sure if Theseus, who defeated the Minotaur, actually existed outside of the mythology story, he'd be long dead at this point. So, how in the world did the Red Rose pack plan or even *think* they could plan to defeat a whole horde of Minotaurs?

"Then he spoke again, in the same booming and monstrous voice I had heard three days prior, 'Now whether or not you saw her, and I know you did, I want you to go to the inbred pack house and give them a message that we are going to attack in forty-eight hours and I will be the last thing Vivila sees before she dies.' I let out some shallow exhales before grasping what little courage I had to ask, 'What do you mean by "Alpha mongrel" and "pack house?"' A stupid question to ask, I know, given I had no clue as to what Ross was capable of in this form, but I had no idea werewolves and Minotaurs existed. Yeah, I know about your true form, Viv, but I don't know—I never gave it much thought that there might be other supernatural creatures in the real world.

"Yet, as I naively waited for an answer, a wide maniacal grin spreading across Ross's bull face, a knock came on the office door followed by five other Minotaurs entering the room. I recognized Gregory right away because he looked more human than bull and his usual oafish expression was hard to ignore. Pardon the expression, but Gregory and his lackeys all of a sudden descended upon me like a pack of wolves. Gregory took over his father's hold on my hair and dragged me toward the elevator with such ease, you could have sworn I weighed no more than a pillow..."

"Did you know Ross was a Minotaur? And I thought Agatha removed the tracking device from my neck when I was first brought here?" I interrupted Ash, quickly turning my head to look up at Aldric. I know Ash wasn't finished and felt bad for it; especially as it seemed he was beginning to lose consciousness given the long blinks and slurring of some of his words. I really did feel bad interrupting, given Ash's poor physical condition, but I needed to know if he knew of Ross's true nature before his invitation to my fight with Gregory all those months ago. Don't ask me why I need to know, because I wasn't sure myself.

Was I fearful that if he did know and had deliberately kept it from me, then who knows what else he was keeping for me? No, that wasn't it at all. Maybe it was easier to have hope of overcoming my incrementally huge fear of Ross, regardless of the war that was going to take place in less than two days. This was all when I thought he was human and now I knew this shattering news of who he really was—and who knows how many other members of the King Cobras were Minotaurs! This was beginning to make me lose hope in overcoming this hurdle.

Then there was the whole tracking device Ross had surgical implanted into my neck to let me know he would always find me. I know you may think it was a scare tactic, but let me tell you, it wasn't. It may have been over four years ago; however, just the memory of being shot with a small dose of a tranquilizer, strapped to a grimy table, and the searing pain of the doctor carving it into my neck while being ordered by Ross to show him the device before shoving into the opening—I could still feel the phantom pain of it. That being said, what if Agatha hadn't destroyed it, however unlikely? Yet, how else did Ross know where to send Gregory, his lackeys, and Ash? I continued to stare into Aldric's eyes, searching for reassurance that Aldric was possibly prepared for Ross to try such an action as to start a war on The Red Rose Pack—oh, to hell with it—*our* pack.

"Not at first," Aldric said with a heavy exhale. "There were rumors of Minotaurs being in Philadelphia. But to be honest, no one had seen a single Minotaur in the whole state of Pennsylvania in eighty years or so. I accepted Ross's invitation to your fight with Gregory because it's illegal in the supernatural world to exploit a supernatural creature, in particular to the human world. If humans knew some of us existed in the real world, we wouldn't be able to live in peace. It wasn't until I showed up that the night of the fight and shook his hand that I had a feeling he was more than human; especially with that amulet poking through his shirt buttons. But it wasn't until now that I was able to put my finger on what he actually was."

My brow furrowed as it tried to process what Aldric said. An amulet was the next clue after his instincts to make Aldric suspect Ross was more than human? But before I could ask Aldric what was so important about a piece of jewelry, Ash proceeded to continue his story, like Aldric and I hadn't just interrupted him.

"On the way down to The Pit, that's when Gregory and his lackeys started kicking and punching me... man t-those ho-hooves hurt more than any tattoo I've ever g-got-ten...ten. Then, I somehow found my way here."

When Ash's eyes closed and his head turned to the side facing the wall, indicating he had lost consciousness, the overall emotion uniformly felt by everyone in the detention cell area alongside the heaviness of the lingering silence was enough to make anyone feel paranoid and want to run as far as away as they could to hide. Using the cell's bars, I pulled myself back up so that I could stand and turn to face Aldric. I could see the gears turning in his mind through his eyes as he stared at the cement floor, trying to decide what would be the next course of action. I briefly looked back at Ash, then back at Aldric, and knew what the immediate course of action should be—getting Agatha over here to tend to Ash.

"We need to have Agatha to tend to Ash," I said, swaying my head back and forth until Aldric really looked at me instead of continuing to stare at nothing. Blinking a few times to snap himself out of his own thoughts, Aldric turned his attention over to Jeremy, who seemed to be transfixed at Ash's unconscious body. My mate snapped his fingers in Jeremy's direction until the pack member faced his Alpha. With a quick jerk of Aldric's head toward the direction of the door that led to the hallway, Jeremy nodded and exited the detention cell area.

My back leaning against the cold metal of the bars, I focused intently on the doorframe that Jeremy had just passed through until my vision went out of focus. I barely heard Aldric tell Angela to call every member of the pack to a pack meeting in an hour. Ash's unconscious body behind me and all the information that had just been revealed was continuing to sink further and further in. *What hope do we have against a gang of Minotaurs?* and *It's all my fault that this war is coming*, kept running through my mind like a broken record.

The weight of these thoughts pressed upon my chest, causing my breathing to become more and more shallow. But as much as my body wanted to crumble into a similar darkness as Ash was in, I also knew it wouldn't help the situation regardless of how frightened I was. Like what Aldric, Angela, and Jeremy had called me, I was the Luna of this pack. I may not have felt worthy of such a title, but I was the yin to Aldric's yang because he and I were mates. And I wouldn't be Aldric's soulmate if I didn't have the power within me to be a leader, right?

Oh God, I hope so, I thought. *No, no, no! Vivila, you are going to stop wallowing in self-pity. You are going to either let what happened to you these past six plus years hold you down until you are nothing more than a hallow shell or you're going to let it fuel you into doing something greater than yourself and make sure no one has to feel the wrath and imprisonment of ~~people~~ creatures like Ross.*

That was as good of as self-pep talk as I was capable of; especially with Aldric's hands on my shoulders and calling my name to get my attention. Although the big question remained...

How on earth does one prepare for a fight against Minotaurs?

CHAPTER TWENTY-THREE

I tried to remember the myth of the Minotaur. Made to live in the center of a labyrinth and feasting on maidens. Then there was a young man named Theseus, I think, using a ball of thread to help find his way out and killing the beast with a sword. But that was a myth and who knows how close it was to the truth as far as killing a real Minotaur. My doubt in how helpful the myth would be toward defeating the King Cobras was based on Aldric's explanation of the werewolves in fiction versus how werewolves actually existed in the real world. And I had been able to defend myself against Gregory, when he was drunk and tried to get a little handsy, which resulted in permanent scars on his manhood and face from my claws. I'd also defeated him in every match at The Pit; I hardly thought it would help in the war to come though, because Gregory was only half-Minotaur and not full. Would a full-blooded Minotaur have twice the strength?

As I pondered this, I couldn't stop my thoughts also drifting back to Ash's unconscious body in the cell behind me. I didn't think I would be able to leave him until Agatha arrived, any minute now, and let me know the seriousness of Ash's injuries. My mind also started to contemplate how it was possible for him to see me in the kitchen in the first place.

"Vivila?" I finally registered Aldric saying, his hands resting on both of my shoulders and his tone sounding as if he had been trying to get my attention for some time.

I blinked a few times, looking to either side of me before

realizing that, aside from Ash, Aldric and I were alone. Well, close to being alone. I could just make out someone standing by the entrance, out in the hallway.

"Sorry," I said without explanation and hoping Aldric wouldn't ask about the inner monologue I was just having. However, given that the two of us could feel each other's emotions and were mates, there was little to no chance of him not asking and going straight to talking about the pack meeting.

The latter made my stomach go into knots. For weeks, I had been able to avoid meeting the other members of the pack. Mostly because my social skills were poor and because I had trust issues that I needed to overcome. Plus, I felt out of place. Here, initially, were three werewolves who had known who they were—supernaturally speaking—and grew up with others of their kind. They were aware that other supernatural creatures existed outside of the many different forms of fiction. And lastly, they hadn't been made to experience six years of abuse, rejection, and punishment for their true nature like I had. I didn't resent Aldric, Agatha, and Beatrix for not having gone through it. No, I was still embarrassed. Feeling like a bigger outcast than I had when I was still in the ownership of Ross. Although my self-confidence had grown and I had worked up the courage to meet Angela and Jeremy, was self-pep talk to start acting like the Luna I am destined to be in my mind going to be good enough to stand next to Aldric in front the whole pack without still thinking about my embarrassing past? It was going to have to be.

"A penny for your thoughts?" Aldric asked.

I shook my head to bring myself back to the present before saying, "I was trying to remember the myth of the Minotaur and whether it would help us any in defeating Ross. Or how Ash was able to see me in the kitchen when you've told me that you have some of the pack patrolling the territory all the time. And... and how Ross discovered where I was... It just doesn't make any sense, and this is all my fault that the war is coming upon the pack. Maybe I should just leave. That way, Ross will follow me and leave the pack alone—and maybe…"

Aldric's finger rested softly on my quivering lips, interrupting my downward spiral of self-pity and guilt. I could feel the tears falling down my face. My pep talk melting like ice cream on a hot summer day—still strong—still but creating a mess that constantly needed to be licked up to prevent further mess. This feeling of not being in control and returning to who I was when I first came to the pack house wasn't what I wanted at all. I wanted all of the goals I'd been setting, not long after I initially woke up in the pack house, to stick. I welcomed the kiss my mate planted on my forehead, then on the tip of my nose, and lastly, upon my lips. Those three kisses were just what I needed without knowing I needed them to calm my whole being.

"Those are all valid points," Aldric said calmly. "But it is not your fault that this war is coming. Ross wants to reclaim something that wasn't his to claim in the first place. You are mine just as much as I am yours, and you belong to the pack. Now and forever. Okay?"

Why isn't he freaking out? How could he be so calm about all this? I appreciated the sentiment and I believed every word he said. Was it due to years of growing up in the supernatural world, being trained to one day be Alpha and knowing how an Alpha should act in situations such as these, was it a werewolf thing? Or was it all of these things that were helping in maintaining this controlled and calm demeanor? I wasn't sure. My trust in him came from more than just our mate bond. I trusted him more than I trusted Ash. And that… that had to be enough to calm my own nerves about these particular questions right now. And yet, there were still two questions that were bothering me more.

"But what if they don't like me? What if they think I'm not worthy of being their Luna?" I asked in not much more than a whisper. I felt foolish asking these questions because it was a little off topic and it was going against my goal to exude all that there was to be a worthy leader alongside Aldric. These questions went against my goal of feeling less pity for myself and most importantly, not letting my past define and hold me back. I wish I could have taken those questions back, but it was too late. I hoped Aldric could feel the overall emotions surrounding these thoughts, and in a way, he did. He kissed me, moving his hands from my shoulders to cup my jawline, before pulling away to smile at me. A smile that spread from the corners of his lips and up into the twinkle in his eyes.

"Come on," Aldric said lovingly. "Let's go for a walk."

I nodded, lifting my hands and placing them over his until our fingers intertwined.

We waited until both my breathing and heartbeat returned back to relative normalcy to leave. I looked back at Ash with my heart hurting at the thought of how much pain he must be in, before leaving the detention cell area and making our way through different rounded bends in the basement's hallway, and past Agatha's medical room, until a large set of stairs presented itself.

We walked past the very large living room, which I presumed would be the place where the pack meeting would be held, through the kitchen where Agatha, Beatrix, and two unknown people were, and finally into the fresh air. I don't know if it was the speed—though not as quickly as I made it sound—or hearing Ash's story in such confined area, but as soon as we entered the small garden—oh my, was it heavenly. I felt like I could breathe easily again, so I let go of Aldric's hand, unclear about when we'd started holding hands, and then I dropped to my knees. I didn't care how startled Aldric was by my action or if I got my clothes dirty on the few unswept areas of the flag-stone path. I soaked up as much sunlight as I could, savoring Aldric's intoxicating scent and the plants' beauty within the small garden.

"You okay, my love?" Aldric asked.

This wasn't the first time my handsome mate had used the word love with me, yet every time he said it, it made my heart skip a beat. God I love this ~~man~~ werewolf with all my heart. How could he be so calm and considerate in this moment? I don't think I'll ever get use to or grow tired of him genuinely caring about my wellbeing.

"Yes," I finally said with a heavy exhale, slowly standing up again as I brushed the dry earth from my legs. "I just didn't realize how stuffy the detention cell area was until now."

"You're going to do fine tonight, and you don't have to say anything if you don't want to," Aldric said reassuringly. To an outsider, him saying this may have seemed totally random, but to me it made perfect sense.

I nodded before saying, "I knew this day would come when I would meet the rest of the pack. I just didn't think it would be this soon."

"I know," he said lovingly as he slowly nodded his head. "But we have some time before the pack meeting, so let's try to think about something else for a while."

I nodded again and placed my hand in his, feeling him giving me some of his strength through our bond. I took off my shoes, needing to feel the warmth of the flagstones and the foliage brushing my bare feet as we continued to walk. Down a different path than usual. I took notice of the wood carved signs, the ones I had been told many times that Aldric had put up for my benefit, indicating where each of the paths led to. And in true Aldric fashion, he started talking about books, movies, and memories from childhood. It was nice. It truly was, but there were questions I wanted to ask my mate earlier that I just couldn't ignore.

"Aldric?" I asked, not wanting to awkwardly bombard him with a totally different topic than the ones we were talking about. Although, because it was me and I was still learning about social cues and how to interact with people normally, this transition was probably awkward anyway.

"Hmm?" Aldric replied, stopping so that his full attention was on me.

Apart from the rhythmic pounding of my heart in my ears, I could hear the wind sweeping through the trees, squirrels' crow-sounding territorial warnings, and birds communicating with one another—which made my nerves more hyperaware. I couldn't explain why I was so nervous about such simple questions. Perhaps it was because, these last few months, I had been able to think about Ross less and less. With Ash's horrible condition alongside his story, I was reverting to thinking about how Ross would react to the questions I was about to ask Aldric. Pretty silly, right?

Just ask, Vivila, I thought to myself as though my mind and me were two separate entities. *Just ask! Aldric is not Ross! We've been through this many, many times before.*

"How are you so calm about all of this?" I finally asked with a bit of a stutter. "A war is coming—and you're not scared or freaking out?"

"This isn't my or the pack's first war. We train every day in preparation for whatever obstacle we may face next," Aldric said, his calmness slowly turning to worry. "That said, it does bother me a lot that Ash was able to see you in the kitchen undetected and how Ross was able to discover where you are. And I am scared that Ross will somehow take you away from me despite how much I've watched you grow, and not just in your training either. I know he scares you, but he only has power if you let him. To quote a book, 'Your past doesn't have to define your present. Or your future. It's just your choices now that matter.' However, being scared or freaking out isn't going to help us prepare or defeat the enemy we're about to face. Staying focused, being willing to adapt, and strategizing for every possible outcome, to the best of our abilities, will."

It made sense because his quoting a verse from Mike Chen's novel *We Could Be Heroes* did put a smile on my face; it was exactly what I needed to hear. They were words that I strived to make my mantra; I tried so many times but continued to not believe it could be so. Hearing his reasons for being so calm and that he was scared about what I had been afraid of my whole time in the pack house did make feel a little better; however, I couldn't shake this panic coiling around my insides like a cobra suffocating its prey. It was way different from the nervousness I had surrounding the questions I had just asked or anticipation of meeting the whole pack, the latter of which was still very much present within my mind.

No, this was a totally different nightmare of a feeling. It brought back a memory I didn't think much of at the time I had experienced it, but it suddenly seemed very relevant to the war about to come. It was a fight against my old self and this new self that I was trying to maintain and nourish, a struggle causing breathing easily that much more difficult. And the more the quote from Mike Chen's novel and the hope of making it out of this war alive and victorious seemed like a foolish pipe dream.

"You know what gives me immense pleasure? It's giving my enemy a false sense of hope and total advantage over me," I unconsciously began to say. "I let them bask in it for a few hours and think they have plenty of time to prepare... the fools. Then, like a horde of wasps, I swarm in unannounced and crush them—Trojan horse style."

"What are you talking about?" Aldric asked, bewildered.

"It's what I overheard Ross say outside his office door one night when he called me to let me know about the start of using the mysterious serums," I mustered out from how suffocating this nightmare realization had washed over me.

"Okay?" Aldric said, still not understanding why I was suddenly bringing this up.

"I think what Ross said and did to Ash before dropping Ash off here is—a decoy," I said breathlessly.

"What are you trying to say?" Aldric pressed. Although it may have appeared that he still wasn't getting it from his question, I could hear the undertones of him actually needing to hear me say it aloud to be certain of what I was trying to say.

"Ross and the King Cobras are going to strike tonight," I said. Then I added, to avoid what I assumed was going to be Aldric's unspoken next question, "I'm certain of it."

I stared into the forest, the sun shining through just enough for me to squint my eyes, while it started to make its slow descent into the horizon as if it would magically shield me from the realization I had come to. When I finally pulled my gaze away from it, I looked over to Aldric, who stood nearly motionless apart from the weird facial expressions on his face. I could only conclude that he was communicating what I had told him through "mind-linking" to Beta Cillian or perhaps the whole pack.

Aldric had told me, during our many discussions about werewolf history and abilities, about what "mind-linking" was, and I had seen him do it a couple of times—but I was still getting used to identifying when he was mind-linking and when he was simply deep in thought. As I waited for him to be done, I decided I would try one of the meditative breathing exercises Agatha had taught me to center and calm myself.

"I moved up the pack meeting and communicated to our Beta to try and contact neighboring packs and covens for backup," Aldric said authoritatively, his face looking like it was made up with nothing but straight, serious lines. "Now I'm not sure if either of the three covens will consider helping us given they aren't huge fans of werewolves, but with you possibly being the one from the prophecy, they—"

But before he could take my hand or finish his sentence, something else occurred to me. I stepped away from him, needing to make sense of it all.

"What?" Aldric said, his brow knitting together in puzzlement.

"Trojan horse style," I said, lifting my finger in the air as if it would help to piece together my train of thought. "The prophecy. You said the Minotaurs that murdered the two heads of the Venus council were able to carry out this heinous crime because they had 'Trojan horse styled' their way in... right? And now I recall a memory of Ross using the same words. Isn't that a bit odd? What if... now I'm not totally positive, but what if Ross and the others in the King Cobras who are Minotaurs are the reason my kind went into hiding?"

Aldric stared at me for a few seconds before his eyes went wide with recognition and he snatched my hand as we bolted back toward the pack house. Due to the sweat forming on my forehead, some strands of my unnaturally white curls adhered to my face, causing some difficulty in seeing what was in front of me. I almost tripped over a couple of tree roots. Man, I wasn't used to running this fast. If this were under different circumstances, I might say that it would be exhilarating. But as it was, trying to keep up with Aldric, regardless of his hand firmly holding mine, was a little terrifying. Because even with the pack meeting moved up, how much time would we have before the King Cobras attacked? An hour? Three hours? I know Aldric said that he and the rest of the pack members had been training every day to prepare for a moment similar to this war about to descend upon us. However, the question still remained... Was the pack prepared to battle against a horde of Minotaurs? Especially if what Aldric had said was true about there not being a single sighting of this particular group of supernatural creatures in the whole state of Pennsylvania in roughly eighty years...

The pack property didn't have a large labyrinth to entrap them in. At least, I didn't think it did. Would it be worth digging randomly placed ditches and covering them with twigs and debris? There were so many ideas running through my head that each one seemed more ridiculous than the previous ideas. *Please let Aldric's and the pack's experience in matters as the one approaching be better than my lack of experience. Please! Please! Please! Trust—trust in Aldric, his leadership skill, and his unconditional love for me. And trust that the pack accepts me as being a part of them and not some outsider because I'm not a werewolf.*

I barely registered having gone through the small garden, passed the kitchen, and into the threshold opening up to the large living room with forest and moon themed décor, until I saw what appeared to be over a hundred ~~people~~ werewolves. It was like I had been hit with a ton of bricks... pardon the cliché. The pack members in the room—some sitting on the large couches, some sitting on the floor, and the rest standing—were of various ages. From my age to those old enough to be my grandparents. And while in truth, as they all turned their attention to both Aldric and me, there wasn't a single sign of judgement to me in particular—I still felt very intimidated.

I was about to back away and run, as rude and silly as the course of action would have been perceived, when Aldric's hand let go of mine, and he placed his hand around my lower back. I felt a surge of calmness being passed from him to me, which helped greatly. Then suddenly, and it was so quick that I wasn't sure if it had really happened, I swore I heard Aldric's voice in my head saying, *You got this!*

CHAPTER TWENTY-FOUR

Words of encouragement from my mate, both through thought and the transference of calmness, were what I needed to get through the meeting, but I was still very overwhelmed because again I wasn't aware of how large the Red Rose Pack was. With a few calming breaths and trying to focus on Aldric's support through our bond, I reminded myself that my latest goal was to be the Luna this pack deserved. It would take time to be worthy of such an accolade but with Aldric, Agatha, and Beatrix by my side, I was hopeful I would achieve it soon enough. Until then, all I could do was breathe as Aldric and I started to move to the center of the pack.

I couldn't help being hyperaware that similar to the two werewolves down in the detention cells, everybody lifted their heads and bared their necks. I realized it was meant to be a sign of respect toward both Aldric and me, but like I hinted before, it was a respect I didn't feel I had earned yet. Especially because this was the first time I'd met the majority of the pack.

Even with the calming vibes Aldric was sending my way through our bond and his assurance that I didn't have to speak, my racing heartbeat was forming a knot in the back of my throat. It also didn't help that it had gotten so quiet the moment the two of us came into view of the pack. I searched for Agatha and Beatrix; the younger pack member happened to be sitting up front for extra strength. And though I only saw Beatrix's face looking back at me because Agatha was tending to Ash, it still put ease to my discomfort.

"I would first like to properly introduce your new Luna, Vivila," Aldric said while turning to look in my direction. "And though she is a Winged Ailuranthropes and not a werewolf..." Murmurs erupted at the mention of my supernatural species. I caught words such as "No way," "I thought they didn't exist anymore," and "Aren't they hiding?" They continued to murmur phrases like, "Is she the one from the prophecy?" and "She does have pure white color hair..." all of which made me feel extremely uncomfortable... Well, more uncomfortable than I already was.

"Regardless," Aldric continued, clearing his throat to return the pack's attention back toward reason why this meeting had been called in the first place, "Vivila is a member of this pack, even though she hasn't performed the ritual for new pack members and the two of us haven't completed the mate bond. Both of which will not be forced upon her until she is ready. Is that clear?"

"*Yes, Alpha,*" the pack said in unison.

"With that said, we are about to go into battle with a horde of Minotaurs," Aldric said, scanning the room almost as though he wanted to make sure everyone one was listening, understanding the seriousness of the situation, or something. "I know the state of Pennsylvania hasn't seen or heard of a Minotaur residing here, but I have every reason to believe that this horde has a witch working with them who has created amulets to disguise their true nature and allow them to pass as humans. Nonetheless, we are at war with them because we have Vivila, and they want her back. I also have reason to believe that they plan to strike tonight."

"How?" I heard a male voice ask, but with the amount of werewolves in the room, I couldn't tell exactly who had spoken.

"Because it's how he operates," I found myself saying, though where the courage came from I could not say. Maybe it was tied to my goal of trying to become the Luna worthy of this pack. Maybe it was not that at all. But wherever the drive was coming from, I was going to run with it. For one of the first times in my life, I was going to run with it.

I continued, "Ross, the leader of the King Cobras gang, or rather the horde of Minotaurs, likes to send decoys or false promises to make his enemy feel somewhat at ease or that they could still have time to get the upper hand on him. But whether it's an hour or several hours, Ross attacks before the time has allotted his enemy any leeway. I've experienced his wrath firsthand, more times than I care to admit—and it isn't pretty. He takes pleasure in toying with and torturing his victims."

I had to pause for a moment, the wave of courage seemingly diminishing like steam escaping a small hole in a tire. I stared at the chandelier depicting the phases of the moon. I'd just never spoken about the topic surrounding my six-year experience in Ross's hold so openly or so nonchalantly. Well, with the exception of maybe to Aldric. The lingering silence in the room and every pair of eyes fixated on me wasn't helping the squeezing panic in my chest. I tried to remember the Mike Chen quote, which Aldric had used earlier: "Your past doesn't have to define your present. Or your future. It's just your choices now that matter."

My *choices now that matter*, I repeated in my mind as I took five calming breaths and tried to focus the calming energy Aldric was still sending me through our bond.

"Would it be worth reaching out to the neighboring packs?" a woman said, who looked to be Agatha's age with striking blue eyes.

"I've mind-linked Cillian prior to letting you all know the change in when the meeting was being held," Aldric answered, "which is why he isn't present at the moment. The three local covens are also being contacted. Now, with uncertainty of whether we will have aid from the other packs or covens and the uncertainty about whether the Minotaurs will play fair or dirty as far as firearms are concerned given the time constraint, we need to make sure the manholes throughout the property that we use during our 'capture the flag' nights are fully covered. I need ten volunteers to go right now and check them.

"I need another ten to check the trees with the hidden compartments to make sure our firearms are fully loaded and have enough ammunition. And aside from the usual thirty I have stay to protect the house, I want the rest of you to scatter to the four directions of the property, usual teams apply, to get ready for the attack just in case the neighboring pack isn't able to get here in time. Lastly, armor up, regardless of what form you choose to fight in. Red Rose Pack, work together..."

"Never alone!" the pack shouted in unison as the majority of them exited the pack house in various directions.

After the noise of the exiting pack members repeating what I assumed was the pack's motto, I stood there confused. Why hadn't Aldric mentioned how Ross knew where I was or how Ash had been able to get onto the property in the first place? Or that Ross and his horde of Minotaurs could possibly be the ones who killed the two leaders of the Venus Council, which caused my kind to go into hiding and disrupt the natural balance in the supernatural world? Was it just assumed that because Ross's wife is most likely the witch that it negates relaying the facts of my first question? Or maybe I should stop over-analyze and just trust that Aldric had his reasons for not mentioning any of it. What's important is the fact that we will be under attack very soon.

I looked over to Beatrix, but my mind was racing with so many thoughts that they might as well have been invisible. I started to think how unprepared I was for the approaching battle. Despite the amount of fighting I had done in The Pit and the training I had done during my stay here thus far, I still couldn't will myself to fully shift unless my emotions were super high, nor had I ever been in battle. I could mess this up. I could die today, or worse—Aldric could die.

With our mate bond growing stronger with each passing day, even though we hadn't completed the bonding ritual, I wasn't sure I would be able to go on without him. I remembered what Aldric had said about what happened to his father after his mother died. His father felt like half his being had been ripped apart, leaving a gaping hole... a hole his father has been trying to fill by traveling around the world aimlessly. It sounded awful and unbearable.

"Vivila?" I heard Aldric say calmly, but it took a few moments before I snapped out of the self-induced trance I was in and turned my head to look up at him. "I want you and Beatrix to go to the Alpha Room until I come and get you."

"What!?" I almost screamed in disbelief as the blood drained from my face. "No! No, no, no! I'm fighting alongside you! What if you get shot or stabbed with a silver bullet or weapon? There's no way I'm just going to idly sit still behind a heavy metal door! Ross has taken away so much from me. I'm not going to let him take you too! I... I love you too much for..."

I said the last sentence unintentionally like a goodbye, with tears streaming down my cheeks. Yet all the while anger, anxiety, dread, and a million emotions were swarming me like a tornado that I didn't know how to pull myself out of. For Christ's sake, I finally felt like I belonged somewhere, accepted by others unconditionally, and had found the sort of love I had thought for too many years only existed in the trashy romance novels Gregory and his lackeys would throw down at me in my crappy room at the warehouse through the grated window in the ceiling. And Aldric, my predestined mate, was seriously asking me to sit out of a battle that I was the cause for? Yes, I had just been worrying about my lack of experience on any battlefield and Ross still frightened me, but still.

"I love you too," Aldric said compassionately. "You complete me, body and soul. Although it is true that you're what Ross wants and the reason behind this war, if you think I'm also going to sit idly by for him to take the one person I've been waiting for my whole life—there's just no way. It's as though I've been training for my entire life for this—for you." Aldric let out a heavy sigh, one hand softly rubbing my arm and the other running through his magnificent black hair before continuing, "I'm not trying to impugn your intelligence or fighting skills by telling you to go in the Alpha Room with Beatrix. I'm telling you to do this for my own peace of mind. Please, my love, please."

What bind we were in? I don't think I'll ever get used to the amount of genuine love he has for me. I wrapped my arms around him and buried my face in his chest, deeply taking in his intoxicating scent, holding him so firmly as though I were afraid he and our love would float away into nothing. While I didn't like the idea... like really, really didn't like the idea, I had to admit he was right. He did have way more experience in training and on the battlefield. He survived them all, however many "all" were, so I had to have faith he would survive this one too.

"Okay," I said, though it was slightly muffled because my face was still somewhat buried in my mate's chest.

Aldric leaned backward, causing my face to part from his warm, comforting chest as he waited for me to look up at him again. He said, "Thank you," and kissed the top of my forehead.

"Viv, we need to go now," Beatrix said just suddenly enough to startle me.

I had forgotten she and thirty other members of the pack were present in the living room until Beatrix had spoken. I wiped the tears with the back of my hand, looking over briefly at my mate's sister, and nodded. Then, turning my attention back to Aldric and closing the height difference by standing on my toes, I pressed my lips onto his. I wanted the memory of our kiss and the taste of his lips to be burned into my psyche. His hands moved to the small of my back, sealing the remaining distance until it was nonexistent.

I could feel his hunger and desire as our lips continued

to lock together, as I'm sure he felt mine. The world was spinning, not just from our kiss, but also from the unknown outcome of events that were about to unfold. His scent of the ocean's salty air and campfire smoke seemed to be intensified as I once again forgot that the two of us were not alone. But I didn't care.

For once, and I hoped not the last time, I wasn't obsessively worried about what others thought of me or the consequences that may or may not come. All I cared about was how Aldric made me feel—but not just in this passionate embrace of our lips, our two bodies melding together into one complete being and how I could be my own individual self with my own interests and opinions when I was with him. And though I probably have a long way to go, in comparison to others of my own age who were lucky enough not to have to deal with abuse on top of the struggles of being a normal teenager and entering into adulthood, right now was enough for me. To start feeling nearly and completely free of the bindings of my perpetrators. And as Aldric and I pulled our lips apart from one another and his sister stepped forward to guide me to the Alpha Room, a small smile crept onto my face with the realization of this freedom. The smile didn't last long as reality set back into my mind and this distance between my mate and myself grew; I still cherished it, even as the tears returned with a vengeance.

Please come back to me, I thought, focusing ardently on sending the words to Aldric, just as his words of encouragement had been mentally sent to me during the pack meeting. I wasn't sure if he was receiving my thoughts, but I had to try, even if only to comfort myself—to affirm the hope I desperately wanted to have in my mate surviving this war.

As my eyes refused to leave his, while Beatrix's hands rested softly on my elbow and continued to pull me away, I swear he nodded in response to the thought I was sending. Perhaps I imagined it. But as Beatrix and I rounded the corner, Aldric disappearing from view, I knew that only time was in control and not my hopes and wishes. Beatrix, who I had grown to love for her outspokenness even when others wished she would keep her opinions to herself, remained quiet during the journey to the Alpha Room. She said nothing as she turned her head away so that I could punch in the access code to unlock the think metal door and we both entered, shutting and locking the behind us.

What I found even more curious than her silence was her walk over toward the large flatscreen television. I watched in fascination, while I once again attempted to stop the flow of tears from my face with the back of my hands, as she reached for the remote lying on the coffee table and turned the television on. I may have been kept in a horrible basement for the majority of the last six years, but I knew how some electronic devices worked: desktop computers, kitchen appliances, my adoptive parents' landline phone, and very old television sets. My adoptive parents weren't big on keeping up to date on modern technology. I was at a complete loss about the buttons Beatrix started pressing on the remote before placing it back down on the coffee table, then sitting down on the couch. As she made herself comfortable with her legs curled up on the cushion, I just stood almost frozen by the door we had just entered from, watching her press yellow, green, and blue buttons in calculated orders before placing the remote back on the coffee table that stood in between the couch and television.

"We can watch the battle from here through the surveillance cameras," she finally said calmly, as she beckoned me over to the couch, to which I obliged.

However, the heavy exhale through her nose seemed to be anything but calm. It wasn't in annoyance exactly—but it was close to it. Was she upset that she practically had to "babysit" me or sit this one out instead of participating in the fight that could occur sometime soon? Or was it something else? Or was it just one more thing I was imagining and she was letting out a snort just to let out a snort? I didn't know, but had to ask. Partly because I wanted to know, but mostly to keep me distracted from thinking about Aldric.

"I'm sorry you're stuck in here instead of being out where the action is going to be," I said with my own heavy exhale as I finally and slowly made my way to sit next to her on the couch.

"What did I tell you about apologizing so much?" Beatrix asked lightheartedly, looking over at me with a small smile. "I mean, yes, I would love to have a chance to kick some Minotaur ass, but this isn't the first battle our pack has been in, and I'm sure it won't be the last. So, there will be plenty of opportunities to kick other supernatural creatures' asses in the future."

"Then why did you let out a snort like you were annoyed or something?" I asked.

"Huh? Oh, that," she said, letting out a hearty chuckle. "Well, this is the first time I've been in this room and I wasn't sure if the buttons Aldric mind-linked me to punch in so that we could watch the battle would be correct. I'm not very tech-savvy and therefore, not very good at remembering the exact sequence of making things work. If that makes sense."

I nodded before turning my attention toward the television. The footages from four different cameras were displayed on the screen. They all, for the most part, seemed to be high up in the trees or in bushes based on the foliage swaying every once in a while in front of the camera view. And apart from pack members, some in wolf form and some in human, getting in position or checking the hidden compartments for the artillery like Aldric had told some of them to do, all seemed to be quiet... a little *too* quiet.

And as a half hour turned into a few hours, I began to wonder if maybe I had been incorrect about Ross's "Trojan horse style" attack as Beatrix pressed different buttons on the television remote to see what was going on through the multitude of the other surveillance cameras scattered throughout the property. Especially after the startling phone call from the Alpha Room's telephone, which Beatrix answered, from Aldric confirming that the neighboring packs had arrived as well as two of the three covens. Not that I expected a call saying "Oh, hey, Ross and his horde of Minotaurs have descended" or anything, because Beatrix and I would have seen it.

I was so nervous in anticipation that my claws started to protrude. I tried to hide them from Beatrix by placing my hands under my legs because I didn't want to show the physical manifestation of my anxiety through my claws. "I wanted"—being the key words here—to appear strong and calm. I know I didn't need to be either in front of Beatrix; she would be supportive and nonjudgmental, given the situation. Perhaps, however, it wasn't Beatrix I wanted to hide my claws from—perhaps I was trying to hide them from myself. If I hid them from myself, it would, in some strange and nonsensical way, give me hope that Aldric would be okay when the war started and I would be keeping my goal of being the Luna this pack deserved.

Lunas, not that I had any idea what that exactly entailed, aside from it being a leadership position, kept their cool under pressure for the sake of the pack. Or at least that's what I kept telling myself—and not well, I might add. Because as the day started to turn to night, I became more and more sure how wrong I was about Ross lying about not giving us all forty-eight hours before he attacked until all of a sudden... an enormous BOOM erupted from the northwest side of the property and caused the pack house to shake.

Through the audio emanating through the four-camera footages Beatrix had settled on for the last ten minutes, collective sounds of yells and snarls could be heard, which made my heart stop in paralyzing, panicked fear.

CHAPTER TWENTY-FIVE

With whatever had caused the loud "boom" sound—whether it be an explosive, perhaps a magic spell or something else entirely, the war had finally commenced. I looked up at the see-through bulletproof ceiling and into the nearing night sky and to the stars beginning their twinkle as if it would calm my nerves. But it didn't. Not that I didn't take notice of the moon being full. I suddenly remembered what Aldric had said about the full moon enhancing their strength and agility. I prayed with all that I had in me, to the heavens, that the full moon's powers would give us the advantage over Ross and his horde. But the one and only thing that was going to calm my nerves was Aldric.

I turned my attention back to the camera footage displayed on the flatscreen in front of Beatrix and me. Minotaurs, witches, warlocks, and werewolves swarmed from all angles and it quickly became a blur of who was fighting whom. Okay, that wasn't entirely true because the last three species I just mentioned were charging solely on the Minotaurs, who by the glint of moonlight and what light was still struggling to pour through the woods from the sun's light had tipped their horns in silver. Great—just great. But it was my high adrenaline that was causing my inability to focus clearly on who was fighting whom, making the cameras' footages to appear to be one big, mangled blur. And from what I could see as Beatrix clicked to other surveillance cameras and apart from whatever had caused the large BOOM earlier, there didn't seem to be a single firearm or knife in sight, not yet anyway.

Frantically, I searched for Aldric to show up on one of the cameras as five werewolves took down a Minotaur and weird shooting lights from a couple of witches' hands shot off in every direction. I squeezed my eyes shut for a few seconds as I saw a Minotaur swoop its head downward and dig its silver-tipped horns into the belly of two werewolves. So many bodies lying dead or injured started building up, so quickly too—it was... just... a heartbreaking and horrible scene to sit still and watch. Every fiber in me desperately wanted to intervene in.

And as much as I wanted to obey Aldric's plea for me to remain in the Alpha Room with Beatrix and remember his words of this war not being my fault, I still couldn't help but keep believing—that it was my fault. Ross and his horde were here because of me. I could feel my ears elongating, my fur growing on both my face and legs, and my tail and wings scratching to come out. Then there was the fact that I was the pack's Luna, officially or unofficially. What kind of an example am I setting by sitting on the sidelines? My lack of experience in warfare be damned. I mean, the whole battle was total chaos, and it had only just begun.

"Viv, you need to calm down," I heard Beatrix say, which only fueled the anger rising within me.

Had this been any other time, me shifting would be unbearable; especially with both my wings and tail breaking free. But with how angry I was and how much I felt like a wild, caged animal, the pain didn't even register. I leapt off of the couch and began to pace around the room, **really** not liking the idea of what was happening outside of this circular room, let alone the pack house itself.

Then, after an hour or so of total bloodshed, I saw something that momentarily halted my rage and angst. I saw a black werewolf and a Minotaur come onto one of the screens. They were both the largest and most muscular of any of the other species I had seen... and without reason or hard evidence, I knew it was Aldric and Ross. And so did everyone on the battlefield it seemed, because all, and I mean *all* matter of fighting stopped to watch. I leapt over the couch and coffee table until my face was mere inches from the screen.

"Make this camera view bigger!" I screamed like I was a freaking caveman.

"Maybe I should get the tranquilizer that Agatha gave me, babe, because you really need to calm down," Beatrix said, a little bit of fear underlining her voice. "Plus, Aldric can totally..."

"Make this bigger *now*!" I turned to glare at her.

"A please would be nice," she retorted.

"Please!" I yelled, returning my attention to the fight that was about to occur between my mate and the misogynistic prick who thought he owned me for the last six years.

When the camera footage filming Aldric and Ross filled the large flatscreen, I watched intently like a cat spotting a bird outside the window. The two opponents circled one another as they both waited for the other to make the first move. Ross, in all his egotism let out a growling moan and a donkey-like sound, making it seem as though he was mocking Aldric or that my mate was unworthy of fighting him. He turned his head toward what was left of his horde of other Minotaurs for support, to which the horde replied with a growling moan in approval.

Big mistake, Ross, I thought amusingly as I watched my mate lunge toward Ross's enormous bull neck.

Aldric's teeth sunk square into the meat of Ross's neck, which wrenched Ross's attention away from his horde as he whined in agony. Ross quickly lifted his hands to grip firmly onto either side of my mate's snout to pry his jaw apart before flinging Aldric thirty feet sideways through the air like my mate was an annoying insect. When Aldric's body slammed to the ground, temporarily stunned, Ross took the opportunity to charge, his silver-tipped horns leading the way. My heart raced with every step, closing the distance between the two of them as I watched my mate struggling to shake himself out of his daze. At this point, my claws were dangerously close to puncturing the flatscreen. Luckily, Aldric dodged out of the way, causing Ross's horns to get stuck in the earth. I sighed in relief.

I watched as Aldric rounded Ross, who was writhing to get his horns unstuck. Aldric was aiming to sink his teeth into Ross's stomach. So closely I was watching Aldric's moves that I failed to notice the gun Ross was reaching for behind his back. How in the world the disgusting, conniving tyrant was able to hide a gun behind his back given he was wearing nothing but a loincloth, I didn't know. But I should have. I should have known Ross wouldn't play fair. I should have known that Ross would know how to make a clean shot from his peripherals, regardless of whether his horns were still lodged in the earth. And when Ross managed to shoot my handsome mate in the chest before Aldric fully had the chance to carry out his move, I felt like the most idiotic being ever. My heart stopped and my breathing went shallow as I felt the gunshot wound as if it had happened to me. I instantly fell backward, clutching my chest.

"Viv! Viv!" I could barely hear Beatrix say as she rushed over to my side.

Uncontrollable tears and returning yet avenging anger flooded me. It was as though my heart was made of glass and Ross had smashed it on a hard surface, into a million pieces flying all over the circular room that was the Alpha Room. I didn't know what to feel but emptiness. But I knew and could only focus on two things in that moment. One, the front door was not an option to get to my mate because it would take too long. And two, Ross was going to die by my hands.

Pushing myself up and off of the floor, I spread my wings and looked up at the bulletproof glass ceiling. I didn't care about the impossibility of breaking through the ceiling or this being the second time I had ever used my wings. My mate was dead. My newfound reason to live. So what did I have to lose?

Nothing. Bending my knees in preparation to take flight, I felt Beatrix's hand on my arm trying to stop me from attempting this idiotic impossibility. With the help of the wing closest to her and not realizing how strong I was right or where this strength was coming from, I flung her across the room. Her body slammed into the wall and she fell unconscious.

I looked over at her, knowing I should feel sorry for doing that to her, but all I saw was red. Returning my gaze to the ceiling and without a second thought, I launched myself upward with all my might and for some miraculous reason, the ceiling ruptured. I flapped my wings, trying to mimic what I had seen of how birds used their wings until I reached a height where I could spot the crowd of supernatural creatures still standing in a circle around Aldric's dead body. And though the muscles in both my shoulders and wings ached like fire from having only done this once before, there wasn't time to dwell on the agonizing pain I was in. All I knew and needed to focus on was killing Ross, and I wanted to hold my mate's lifeless body in my arms. The latter may have seemed pointless—I wanted to hold on to the pipe dream that perhaps he was still alive, if only to say our farewells.

When Ross was finally able to get his horns out of the ground, having to drop the gun to use both of his hands to do so, I took the opportunity to swoop downward, beating my wings as fast as they would allow me, despite the pain I was in due this being just the second time I had ever tried to use them. I needed to gain enough momentum before Ross knew I was coming. I might as well have been flying at the speed of light because no one on the battlefield seemed to have taken notice of me until I was straddled behind Ross and had both of my hands on his horns. And with the same strength I had displayed not long before on Beatrix, I tore off Ross's horns and jammed both of them straight into his back.

The hornless bastard bucked me off of him before screaming at such a high pitch that everyone fell to their knees and covered their ears. And while I wanted to do the same, I also wanted to see Ross fall. After all that he had done to me these past six years, and on top of that killing my mate, I **needed** to see him fall.

He fell with one huge thud that shook the earth and made his remaining horde of Minotaurs and the other supernatural creatures on Ross's side cower back. And with that there was a small sense of relief, like I regained back all that he had stolen from me: a normal childhood, a family and freedom. Well, almost... though I could hear the cheering from the surviving members of the Red Rose Pack and the packs that had come to help us, there was still Aldric's limp body, which had returned back to his human form, lying next to Ross's. Not bothering to stand up, I crawled to Aldric, realizing that I had some shards of the glass ceiling embedded in me. Mostly in my wings and arms, but they still stung with each movement.

When I finally reached my mate, the painful shards of glass didn't matter anymore. Neither did my victory over Ross, how much of a mess I must have looked, nor the audience on the battlefield. My already broken heart seemed to break once again, if that were even possible, as I ripped what I could off of Ross's loincloth to cover Aldric's naked body before pulling him into my arms; one arm over his chest and a hand resting on his forehead so that his head rested on my shoulder. My fingers gently brushed over the open wound where the bullet had gone through. Although I thought I had run out of tears to cry, my grieving and broken heart told me otherwise as my tears continued to pour down my cheeks and over Aldric's magnificent black hair to his bullet wound.

I couldn't tell you how much time had passed or if there were still onlookers, as everything but Aldric and myself was a completely soundless blur. His words on his experience on the battlefield and how he'd survived every battle replayed over and over to the point that I was almost angry with him. Angry that he hadn't survived this war. Had he not heard my thought that I had so desperately tried to send his way before this war had even begun? But mostly, I was angry with myself because it should have been me that was killed by Ross's gun. It was me Ross wanted, not Aldric.

"You can't do this to me, Aldric," I hissed into his ear as if he could hear me. "You were supposed to come back to me. Come back, come back—come...back."

I shook his body with those last foolish words. Foolish because there was no way he would be able to come back. Just no... But before I could finish that sentence, a blinding light emanated from both his chest and from above. It startled me so much that I nearly loosened my hold on Aldric. I buried my face behind Aldric's head to shield my eyes from the source of this warm but very bright light until after what seemed like forever, the light vanished.

Cautiously, I lifted my head to find ghostly figures standing before Aldric and me. At first, I thought that they may have been angels because of their wings, and to be honest, after learning werewolves existed months ago, nothing seemed impossible. However, when I noticed an all too familiar barn owl pattern to their wings and similar feline attributes to mine, I gasped at the realization that I was face-to-face with my own kind for the first time since that fateful day in gym class. Dead-winged werecats, but winged werecats nonetheless. I stared in awe and bewilderment at the translucent golden glow surrounding them.

Should I speak or should I wait for them to speak? I thought, clutching onto Aldric as though the ghostly creatures were here to take him away from me.

"Jordan, look how grown up our baby girl is," the female ghost said, covering her face like she was about to cry.

Can ghosts cry? I asked in my mind, remaining quiet.

"I know apologizing for all that you have been put through is probably futile," the male ghost said, putting a supportive arm around the female's waist, "but trust us when we said had we known the humans would sell you to a horde of Minotaurs, especially to the ones who murdered us, we would have asked the Venus Council to place you elsewhere, and better hidden from our enemies. And it pains us that we couldn't be there during your formative years, that you were left in the dark about what and who you are up 'til now."

"I'm sorry," I finally mustered to say, "but who are you? And why have you decided to come now?"

"Valid questions," the male ghost started to say before being interrupted by the sobbing female ghost.

"We're your parents. And you, my sweet angel, are the chosen one from the prophecy!"

"Teresa!" the male ghost said sternly, briefly turning his head toward the female before returning his attention back to me. "We're not trying to frighten our daughter; especially during our first meeting with her. She just took on a Minotaur for the first time and defeated it and that's no easy task, so give her some time."

So these are my birth parents, I thought, a little suspiciously, as it was difficult for me to call these entities anything other than "male ghost" and "female ghost." There were so many things I had angrily practiced saying over the last eighteen years if I were to ever meet my birth parents, but now that they were right in front of me—dead, no less, I was at a loss for words or anger.

"But to answer your other question," the male ghost continued, "we weren't allowed to reveal ourselves to you until you finally came into your abilities and had taken a huge step in fulfilling your destiny in returning the balance in the supernatural world. We couldn't have been more proud of you, baby girl."

For whatever reason, that last part riled me up. Call it being part of the anger stage of my grief about my mate having been just killed or the shock of meeting my parents for the first time in eighteen years. And I might have been in awe before my so called "birth father" answered my second question, but I suddenly wasn't anymore.

"You're sorry for leaving me with such awful adoptive parents!" I yelled. "You arriving now, prophecy or no prophecy, isn't going to change the fact that my mate is dead. It isn't going to change the fact that a lot of members of my pack have lost their lives tonight."

Neither of them spoke for some time. I watched in seething anger as they looked at each other. Were they mind-linking? Is that something winged werecats do alongside werewolves? Ugh, I could care less. I wanted them to again explain themselves beyond being my parents and the stupid prophecy.

"Well?" I hissed, unable to withstand the silence any longer.

They nodded to one another before turning their gaze back to me.

"You already have," my "mother" said.

"What?" I asked, very confused about what she was referring to.

"Your tears have healed and revived your mate," she answered almost cheerfully, which was sort of weird.

"My tears can heal?" I asked, unable to bring myself to look down at Aldric to see if it were true.

"Yes and no," my "father" said. "It isn't just your tears. Now that you've come into your abilities, you can heal others with your hands. It may take a while to get the hang of it. However, you can only bring someone back to life when another life has been taken."

"Please do not abuse this aspect of your abilities," my "mother" said. "You are the Restorer of Balance now. You have a lot of responsibilities to carry in the future."

"*Restorer of Balance?*" I thought. *No pressure or anything.*

"I'm sure you're filled with more questions than we are allowed to answer," my "father" said. "Unfortunately, we were only allotted a short amount of time to speak with you."

"But know we are always watching and we love you so

much, baby girl," my "mother" said.

Then, before I could even say goodbye, the blinding light returned, and I hid my face once again behind Aldric's head to shield my eyes. And when the light dissipated, I looked up to the area where my parents had stood. I didn't know what to feel or think. Just as I was trying to process what had just occurred, I heard coughing followed by a low groan that almost startled me into quickly backing away. What stopped me were two masculine hands reaching up to keep me right where I was. I nervously looked down and found Aldric looking back up at me. The ghostly figures were telling the truth? Aldric was alive again? No way! This sort of thing only happened in fairy tales, right?

"Great wolf, it feels like I was shot or something," Aldric said with a husky chuckle as he rubbed his hand over his chest. Miraculously, the wound was no longer there. I didn't know whether to laugh or cry. I had to touch the area for myself. My fingers, ensuring I truly hadn't gone insane and wasn't imagining things, moved his wet black hair away from his face.

"You were—but I healed you," I said in a whisper, fearing if I spoke any louder that this moment would vanish into the crisp night air.

"Well, aren't you something, but I've always known that," Aldric said endearingly, if not a little cheekily too. "Plus," he pulled away until our foreheads rested against one another, "I had a promise to abide by."

"What was that?" I asked, still in disbelief at him really being alive.

"To come back to you, my love," he said nonchalantly.

I let out a laugh. Tears of joy trickled down my face. And as I leaned forward to kiss him, I could feel my broken heart mending itself again, my soul feeling whole once more. In my short lifetime, I have had to learn how to endure feeling completely unloved and unwanted, physical abuse, and feeling broken. I have also learned you can have a family who may not necessarily be blood related. And whatever responsibilities my parents were vaguely talking about, I knew I wasn't alone any longer... Not now. Not ever again.

Love truly has no bounds.

ABOUT ATMOSPHERE PRESS

Founded in 2015, Atmosphere Press was built on the principles of Honesty, Transparency, Professionalism, Kindness, and Making Your Book Awesome. As an ethical and author-friendly hybrid press, we stay true to that founding mission today.

If you're a reader, enter our giveaway for a free book here:

SCAN TO ENTER
BOOK GIVEAWAY

If you're a writer, submit your manuscript for consideration here:

SCAN TO SUBMIT
MANUSCRIPT

And always feel free to visit Atmosphere Press and our authors online at atmospherepress.com. See you there soon!

ABOUT THE AUTHOR

Storytelling, especially in the world of fantasy, has been a constant companion for Torie, even through four years at Moore College of Art and Design and the challenges brought on by her vision disorder. However, thanks to technology and Malory Wood of The Missing Ink LLC, Torie was able to manage her visual limitations to finally pursue her love of writing. She is an avid film enthusiast, which is hopefully evident in her writing. Torie currently lives in Philadelphia, Pennsylvania, with her two cats.